D1131878

SOMEONE
KNOWS
SOMETHING

CHRISTA WEISMAN

Copyright © 2019 by Christa Weisman
ISBN 978-1-7338403-0-9

No part of this book may be used or reproduced in any form or by any means, electronic or mechanical, including photocopying, recording, or by any information storage and retrieval system without prior written consent of the author except where permitted by law.

Disclaimer; This book is a work of fiction. All names, places, and incidents are the product of the author's imagination. Any resemblance to an actual person, living or dead, businesses, companies, events or locales is entirely coincidental.

Warning: This book contains adult content and sensitive topics

Editing & Cover Design by Murphy Rae,
Indie Solutions by Murphy Rae, www.murphyrae.net
Formatting by Elaine York, Allusion Graphics, LLC
www.allusiongraphics.com

SOMEONE
KNOWS
SOMETHING

This book is dedicated
to my husband, Dustin and my dad, George.
Two extraordinary men.
Even better fathers.

CHAPTER 1

First day gone

The shrill ring from the phone on his nightstand disrupted his restless slumber. His eyesight blurred, red and watery as he watched the shadows dance across the ceiling. How long had he been staring above him? Minutes? Hours? Had he even slept at all?

He closed his eyes when he heard it again, and for a moment he feigned being out of the house so he wouldn't have to answer. But then...

Lila.

His limbs were numb; it took more strength than he could muster to reach for the cordless phone. Still, he managed, knowing he couldn't ignore it much longer. He cleared his throat.

"Hello?"

"Chief?" Her voice was thick with distress. He knew who the caller was before she announced it. He knew everyone in this small town and more about them than he should.

"It's Anna Hudson."

He straightened up in bed, looking at his bedside clock. It was nearing noon. He was sweating, his shirt stuck to his torso. He tossed the blanket from his body and sat up to rest his feet on the cold hardwood floor. The coolness jolted him awake. He pressed two fingers against the bridge of his nose; his head was killing him. "How can I help you, Mrs. Hudson?"

"It's the boys, Chief." As if no names were needed, and in this town, they weren't. He knew immediately whom she was referring to. The only boys this town seemed to care about, coveting them like their own damn trophies.

"J.R. didn't come home last night." The panic was back, only she kept her voice low, as though she was keeping her words from being heard around her.

"I called over to the Young's," she continued. "And they said the same about Ethan. They figured he was here with us. I tried Kate but there was no answer."

Kate he knew would most likely be asleep after working her night shift at the hospital. "Maybe they're sleeping and didn't hear the phone?"

"No, J.R. never stays at Caleb's. And besides, he knows better than to stay out..." A sound came from the front of the house that caused her to pause. "Just a moment, Chief." He heard the clanking of the phone being dropped onto a table and rustling he couldn't make out. He ran a hand down the back of his neck, feeling the dampness of sweat stain his palm. "Never mind," she said back into the phone. "As I was saying, J.R. knows not to stay out without talking to us first. Or at the very least, leaving a message on the machine for us to hear in the morning."

He stood, feeling the strain in his back as he straightened. "Well, what about Grace? She's bound to know something. Weren't they together last night?"

She gave an irritable sigh. "Of course I called Grace. She hasn't spoken to him since Friday night's game."

He lifted a finger to his bedroom curtain to see the rain coming down in his backyard. The puddles were piling up like stepping stones in the grass. It had been over a week since Washington had seen rain.

An oddity for late November. Now, as he watched it come down, he felt the somber embrace of it. "That seems strange, wouldn't you say?"

"Nothing more than a lover's quarrel," she brushed off. "You do remember those, don't you, Chief?"

The remark stung and she knew it. She drew a shaky breath. "I'm sorry, Rex. I'm not myself this morning."

He ignored her apology. "What does your husband say about all of this?"

"Oh, you know Jameson. He says I'm overreacting, that I worry too much." Her tone turned mocking. "He says that boys will be boys and that they're probably passed out somewhere."

A memory flashed in his mind about the time, not so long ago, he had picked the boys up from drinking and taken them home in his patrol car rather than to the station. Jameson had given him the same runaround about boys and their behavior.

"But you don't believe that." He doesn't wait for her to answer. He closed the curtain and ran a hand through his cropped sandy blond hair. "It's a bit early for a missing person's report, Anna. What is it that you would like me to do?"

He heard her sharp intake of breath. "If you could just drive around, see if you see them out or even J.R.'s car anywhere." She paused. "And Rex, I hope you understand that I want this to be as discreet as possible."

His blood boiled at the mention of discretion. "Give me an hour," he said through clenched teeth.

"Thank you, Chief."

He hung up the phone and stood there a moment, staring off into space. His head was pounding and his heart was pumping so loud he could hear it in his ears. He opened the drawer on his nightstand table and pulled out the dark liquid bottle he kept hidden below a sports magazine. He unscrewed the top and allowed himself one long swig before tossing it back into its place. He dressed silently, careful to steady his fingers on each button. He didn't dare look at himself in the mirror. He couldn't stand the sight of himself. When his shoes were tied and his gun was in place, he took a deep breath, contemplated one more drink, and headed out down the hall.

Her bedroom was on the other end of the house. He'd hated it when she was just a baby, and often had her crib and then a small mattress in his room, but when the pre-teens hit followed by the full force of teenager syndrome, he was grateful for the distance. It was helpful for the nights he came in late from work and she was already asleep or the mornings he got called out early while she still slept. But at times, he felt that living far apart in the same house built an invisible wall between them. Her wing, and his, where neither dared to enter.

He stood at her door a moment. His hand trembled when he knocked. When she didn't answer, he slowly turned the knob. She was fully dressed but lay on her bed with her eyes closed as though she were sleeping. Her Discman sat atop her belly, her toes tapping in beat to the music streaming in her ears. She didn't notice him at first, but when she did her moss green eyes twinkled with annoyance. Maura's eyes.

It's in this position he had found her every day for the last week. She'd left him a note saying she was ill and taking a day from school. A day had become two, which had then turned into a week. Even though she was grounded from after-school activities, he expected her to go to school. Day after day that passed, he became worried, watching the weight and color drain from her as she refused food and only wanted to sleep. He offered to take her to Dr. Parker, but she adamantly refused, telling him it was a girl thing and to leave her alone.

He often wondered how different life would be for his daughter if she had a mother around. Not left with a fuck-up old man like himself who didn't know how to talk to teenage girls.

"You been up long?" he asked her when she took the headphones from her ears.

"About an hour, I guess." She looked him up and down, aware that he was in uniform and not his traditional Sunday jeans. "You slept late." She raised a brow. "Or are you just getting home?"

"No, I've been home." He paused, feeling like he should add more to the conversation. "But it was a late night. There was a party out at the Hoffmans' place I had to deal with."

Her eyes darkened. "I heard about that." She tilted her head, giving him a funny glance. "You okay?"

He swallowed hard. How many times had he asked her the same question? "Of course."

"Your eyes are bloodshot. You look like hell."

Normally, he would scold her for talking to him like this. But things had changed between them. "Just tired. Late night, as I said."

She shrugged, her eyes falling away from him —her way of asking for privacy.

"So, I'm heading in for a bit. I have some business to take care of. Should I bring us back some donuts from Lee's?"

She grinned slightly at him, and it was just enough to make him implode with emotion. He damned near cracked a smile. It told him she knew that he was trying. The color was starting to come back to her skin, the grey shadows clearing from under her eyes.

"Sure, Dad."

"Okay, I'll be back in a couple hours. Call down at the station if you need anything; they know how to get ahold of me."

"I know the drill, Dad." The sarcasm was back, but it wasn't enough to upset him. He watched as she slid the headphones back over her ears and closed her eyes. The length of her body took up nearly the whole bed, but he could still remember the first night she slept in it when she was five and swallowed up by stuffed animals. Ten years later and he had a hard time not seeing her as that little girl. Gone were the dolls and framed pictures of horses, replaced by posters of bands she liked that he didn't understand. But her fragility was still there. And damn if that didn't terrify him more than anything.

He locked the front of the house behind him and settled into his patrol car. He rolled down the driveway, not sure of where he was heading, or what he would find.

CHAPTER 2

Nine weeks earlier

They came in like a powerhouse, one right after the other. J.R. Hudson took the lead, followed by Caleb Weston, with Ethan Young just a step behind. They dominated the courtyard of Timber Falls High and walked with confidence, knowing all eyes were upon them, even though they looked straight ahead, seeing no one. They had waited their whole lives for this moment. The first day of senior year. Top dogs.

They proudly wore their blue and white football jerseys, the word Falcons stretched over their broad chests. There was never any question as to if they would wear the uniform; they've known their path since they were kids. Especially J.R., whose father, the Mayor Jameson Robert Hudson, had also been a quarterback for the Timber Falls Falcons. Ethan, having been best friends with J.R. since Kindergarten, knew no other life than the one that J.R. had laid out for them. Not that he minded; J.R. always had the best ideas— that was until Caleb had come into the picture in seventh grade and shaken up the way J.R. thought.

There were claps on their backs as they strode toward the gym, and cheers of good wishes for Friday night's game that no student or townsfolk would miss. The boys couldn't help but crack a small smile at the adoration that was passed their way. After winning last year's 1995 state championship trophy, they deserved the praise. This year's scorecard would be no different.

The students scrambled into the bustling gym. The excitement of the first day of school combined with the first pep assembly left no room for calm and control. The teachers and staff were abuzz themselves as they chatted among each other over the booming sound of the marching band. The football team took their places in the front row just behind the cheerleading squad that was already flying high in the air and practicing their new routine. The boys lost all sense of composure and engulfed themselves in the energy of the room, tackling each other playfully. Finally, Principal Dan Harris came to the center of the basketball court, a mic in his hand, and hushed the crowd. The students only got louder, stomping their feet on the bleachers until they even drowned out the band. Principal Harris threw his head back in laughter, making the kids go wild, jumping from their seats chanting "Falcons" to the beat of their stomps. He loved this moment as much as they did. He remembered being a student here twenty-five years ago, and the principal at the time, Mr. Jenkins, had rarely cracked a smile, let alone shown up at the pep assemblies. He'd sworn to himself that one day he would be in charge and they would love him. And they did.

J.R. met head cheerleader Gracelynn Morgan's eye and winked. She blew him a kiss back. Avery Quinn, who stood beside her and watched the whole exchange, turned to look at Caleb with the same adoration, but his eyes were on the crowd, his face twisted into a smug grin.

"Okay, okay," Principal Harris chimed in, his voice thick with laughter. "I know you don't want to hear from me. But I first want to start by welcoming our freshman class..." He was interrupted by an onset of booing, a tradition at Timber Falls High even when he had been a student there. The freshman looked stricken, even those who had been warned by older siblings. Principal Harris let the razzing go on long enough before taking command of the crowd again.

"And a big shout-out to the senior graduating class..." Cheers erupted through the gym as he continued, "Or to those of you who *will* be graduating this year. Not so sure about all of you. I've seen your transcripts." He cocked a smile. "I'm talking to you, Caleb Weston."

The guys jabbed at Caleb as he took what he thought to be a joke in stride. Hell if he knew if he'd pass senior year; hell if he cared. He was one of the boys, and if a college football coach came knocking on his door, he knew he'd convince Principal Harris to make some changes to his papers.

"Before we get this party started," the principal continued, "I'd like to pass the mic to a man you all know and trust, a man I got down and dirty with on the same field his son is now the captain of. Please welcome Mayor Hudson!"

The crowd applauded as J.R.'s father walked forward, the only man in the building wearing a suit. He was strikingly handsome, like his son with the same charismatic cinnamon brown eyes and naturally tanned skin, a rarity in the Pacific Northwest. He took the mic from Principal Harris, whispered something in his ear that made the principal laugh.

He straightened his navy blue tie at the neck and undid the button on his pinstriped coat. His version of getting comfortable. He looked ageless, even younger than Principal Harris, as though being Mayor of a small logging town in Washington state had caused no stress on his body. His pride in his good looks increased when his son was born and bore his resemblance. He never had a problem drawing the women's attention, not in high school, and not now. And just like back when he was a student, he continued to flourish in it.

"Welcome new and returning students of Timber Falls High!" he bellowed. "You know it wasn't that long ago that I was a student here with Principal Dan Harris." The students chuckled and he raised his hand in surrender. "Okay, you got me. But it feels like yesterday. I remember walking these halls for the first time as a freshman and for the last time as a graduating student, not knowing where my future would take me. Fearful of the path ahead. I loved these walls, the ease with which it becomes a second home to you." He smiled toward J.R., who was looking up at his father in admiration. "I can still taste Ms. McCarthy's chicken pot pie, and smell the sweat in the locker room after a tough practice or winning game." The crowd was silent, hanging on to his every word. "These four years of high school are the very best, no doubt about it. And I am trusting you all to be leaders in our community, to continue to keep Timber Falls safe and respected, and to make sure you put as much time into volunteering in the community as you do in your school studies and after-school activities. It is important that we stay united as a town and that begins with you." He paused, making sure everyone was listening. "You are adults in my eyes, and I will treat and respect you as such."

The crowd clapped loudly and high-pitched whistles echoed through the gym.

"And one last thing," he said seriously, though the gleam in his eye gave him away. "Can I count on all of you to be there cheering loudly this Friday night as we take on and *beat* the South Haven Panthers?"

Everyone was up, stomping their feet on the bleachers. Mayor Hudson walked toward his son and pulled him in for a bear hug. Just this year, J.R. exceeded his father's height, a fact that at first bruised Jameson's ego. But just like in every other area that J.R. excelled in, Jameson realized it benefited him as well. The more the town idolized his son, the more they admired him for raising a perfect specimen. And that made Jameson only love his son more. Maybe more than he loved anyone.

J.R. took the mic from his father and settled in at center court. "Hey, everyone," he said, his voice deep and raspy. "I'm quarterback J.R. Hudson." With those words, the students erupted in a cry that was so deafening, the other football players covered their ears. Mayor Hudson laughed and slapped his son's back before he stepped to stand next to principal Harris, allowing his son to take center stage. J.R.'s grin widened, landing on Grace who giggled and shook her head at him.

"I just wanted to say…" He tried to speak but couldn't be heard. He dropped his hand with the mic to his thigh and laughed to himself with a toss of his head. He had always wanted this. This exact moment he had dreamed of. But, he never knew it could feel this damn good.

"I just wanted to say thank you to all who have supported us, all of you who have been out for every practice cheering us on." Slowly, the crowd quieted to a low hum to listen. "And I personally want to see every single one of you out there Friday night, shouting as loud as you have been today as we kick some serious Panther ass! Go Falcons!" He dropped the mic and chest bumped with Caleb and Ethan as the crowd dispersed into a frenzy.

The cheerleaders took over the court, breaking into a dance routine. Their shimmery silver pom-poms glittered in the air. Caleb whistled between two fingers at Avery as she shook her hips for him. Her auburn hair was pulled up into a high ponytail, showing off the length of her neck that Caleb liked to bury his face in. J.R. turned his attention from Ethan to watch the way Grace flipped her dark, wavy hair over her shoulder to smile at him. He loved the way she moved and she knew it well, always teasing him with sideways glances and a lift of her lashes. Ethan was the only one not interested in the cheer team, never had been. He liked a girl with more grit than glamour.

He wasn't the only one not paying attention to the cheerleaders in the middle of the basketball court. Chief Rex Tourney, who'd never missed the first day of school pep assembly, took this time to scan the crowd for his daughter Lila, a sophomore this year. He spotted her sitting near the top of the stands, engrossed in conversation with her best friends, Hannah and Olivia. Her golden hair, the color of her mother's, covered her cheek, and he could only make her face out when her head tilted back in laughter. He smiled at her youthful happiness. She didn't notice him, nor would he expect her to. At age fifteen, friends trumped Dad. But that didn't mean it didn't sting sometimes.

He patted Principal Harris on the back and shook hands with Mayor Hudson before he excused himself to go back to the station. As he walked the courtyard, passing students who had trickled out of the gym, not one of them gave him a second glance as he would assume other students who saw police officers would. He was not a man of intimidation when he knew every one of these kids by name and had grown up with their parents. Still, he smiled in their direction on the off chance they looked up.

The day was warm, as it was still technically summer. Most kids wore cut-off jeans or dresses he thought were a little too short and banned on Lila, to her dismay. The sun shimmered off the gold Falcon statue that boldly took over the center courtyard, making it a focal hangout spot for students. Every year there were calls to the station in the middle of the night when one kid got stuck on top, often drunk, and needed help getting down.

As he walked to his patrol car, he couldn't help but feel a sense of pride for his alma mater. Like the other men, he too had played football for the Falcons, but had not been a star like Jameson or Dan. He was also several years younger than the two men and had looked up to them as upperclassmen. Now adults, he had a hard time shaking that adolescent admiration when he was in their presence. He wondered at times if they still saw him as the young underclassman rather than Chief of Timber Falls Police Department.

And though he loved his hometown, he often felt as though something was missing in his life. Pointless it seemed to be a chief in a place where nothing ever happened. Maybe he should have taken that job up north years ago when Lila was young, sold his land and started over. Now it was too late, he could never uproot his daughter when she only had a few years left of high school. But, after she graduated, maybe a change would do him good.

CHAPTER 3

First day gone

The Hudson home reeked of prestige in a way that made others envious. But tonight, no one would wish to be Anna or Jameson Hudson. It was after ten in the evening, hours after Anna had made the call to the chief, and no word had been heard from the three boys. Nick Young huddled in the Hudsons' lounge beside his oldest friends. His wife, Nora, refused to leave the house in case Ethan called or showed up. But Nick couldn't sit still; he needed to know that the police were on top of things.

The first thing that Nick noticed when Chief Tourney entered the room was that he looked like hell. That gave Nick some encouragement that he had been out busting his ass to find Nick's son. He'd never had a lot of faith in the chief, but then he never had to. Timber Falls was a safe place, extremely low in crime. He wasn't sure if he'd ever seen Rex pull anyone over for a speeding ticket much less solve a missing person case.

Nick's eyes wandered from the chief to Anna. She looked broken and fragile, as though if she stood on her two feet she would shatter. He wished he could comfort her, but he also knew that feeling that way just may have been what had gotten them into this situation.

Anna sat on the edge of the velvet cranberry couch, a cup of now lukewarm tea in her hand that she couldn't drink. She realized that she wasn't able to recall the last time she had eaten. Her tummy rumbled, but she felt a gnawing sickness in her belly that she couldn't shake. Food would only make that worse. Besides, there was no time to stop and eat. Her day had been slammed with endless calls to J.R.'s teammates and friends. She must have dialed every number in the phone book. It left her with more questions than answers.

He was not a five-year-old boy who had just walked away from her at a store or disappeared from his bedroom in the middle of the night. He was an eighteen-year-old young man, but that didn't make her worry any less. She had already been filled with anxiety when it came to her eldest son. She had seen the changes in him lately, feeling him pull away from her and into a dark space she didn't know how to get him out of.

She lifted her head to see Nick watching her. When their eyes met, they held the glance a moment longer before turning their attention to the Chief. He was standing between them, rubbing the back of his neck as he peered down at the notes he had written on a small pad of paper. He swayed a little in his stance, enough that Anna had the fleeting thought he may be drunk. But that was absurd, of course. He was stressed, as they all were, about finding the boys.

She offered to make him a pot of coffee, but for the second time that evening, he declined. He didn't want offerings from the Hudsons; he was there to work and needed to stay on the task at hand.

"So to clarify," he said. "Not one of you has heard from or seen the boys since nine last night."

Anna nodded. "J.R. was in a rush, but I saw him get into his car." Her fingers trembled, making a clicking sound with her teacup on the saucer.

"And what time did he leave the house?" the chief asked.

"It was some time after eight thirty," she answered softly.

He jotted notes on his pad of paper. "Did you ask where he was going? What his plans were for the night?"

She looked taken aback. "Well, no."

"Mayor?" the chief pressed. He hadn't meant to sound accusatory. God knows he didn't know every plan Lila made.

Jameson stood at the mahogany liquor hutch with his back to the room. He poured himself a glass of bourbon, neat, without offering a drink to anyone else.

"No, Rex," he answered hotly. "I did not ask my eighteen-year-old son what his plans for the evening were. Is that a crime?"

Anna closed her eyes. If she allowed herself to feel anything but distress for her son, it would be hatred for her husband.

Rex let the mayor's hostility roll off of him. There was a time, not long ago, when Jameson's cutting words would have made the Chief feel less confident about his job, but that time had passed. The Chief continued, "Nick, you recalled seeing J.R., correct?"

"Yes." Nick cleared his throat and repositioned himself on the chair across from Anna. "J.R. came to the door. I'd say it was close to a quarter to nine. Ethan was in his room, so I told J.R. to go ahead on up."

"And did they tell you where they were going?" the chief asked steadily.

"Only that they were going to get Caleb and then something about a party that night." Nick looked guilty that he couldn't give the chief more to go off of. He and his son hadn't been on the greatest of speaking terms, and if he hadn't overhead J.R. talking, he wouldn't have known anything at all.

"The Hoffman place," the chief answered.

Nick raised a brow. "You know about the party?"

Rex knew everything that went on in this town. The mayor may have claimed ownership of Timber Falls, but it was the chief who ran it. "I was called in to break up a fight. By the time I arrived, the party had died down from the looks of it. I didn't see the boys there."

"Had anyone seen them that night?" Anna asked desperately, leaning forward in her seat. "Were they there earlier?"

"I don't know, Anna," the chief answered. "I didn't ask."

Rex watched the way she trembled and he tried to put himself in her position, as if it were Lila who was missing. He scratched at the back of his head.

"I remember a handful of the kids there that night. It's a possibility that the boys were there earlier and someone knew where they had taken off to. I've got a list going of students to ask."

Anna's eyes widened. She was grateful for any lead. Of course, someone at the party would know something. "Thank you."

He nodded. "I also spoke with Grace and Avery, who stayed together at Grace's house Saturday night and were not at the Hoffman party. Her parents can confirm that. Neither had seen nor spoken to the boys since Friday night's game."

Mayor Hudson snorted as he took a sip of his bourbon. The mention of Friday night's football game left a sour taste in his mouth. His golden boy had become the butt of many jokes in the locker room after that game, and everyone in this room knew it.

"Do any of you think this has anything to do with Friday night's game?" Anna dared to ask. She was just as baffled as everyone else in this town by the embarrassing display the boys gave during the game. And to think that the coach from the Huskies was there that night, watching them ruin their reputation out there on the field. Anna had felt grief watching her son destroy everything he had worked so hard for. Jameson, on the other hand, felt betrayed.

"Of course it does!" Jameson said all too loudly. "Those boys just needed to blow off some steam. They got caught up in it and will be walking through this door anytime now with their tails between their legs. Wouldn't you?" he asked no one in particular.

Nick and Anna exchanged a look that said they weren't so sure. Yes, the boys were upset, but to leave without a word? It was Nick who said it. "I don't know, James, that's not like our boy to do that. He wouldn't scare us by not calling."

Jameson huffed. "They are grown boys who know how to take care of themselves. They're humiliated by what the town witnessed. Hell, I'da bolted for a day too, to clear my head." He pointed a finger at this friend. "And Nick, you would have been right there with me. Luckily, we never had to."

Nick leaned forward in his seat. He was doing his best to keep his cool with his friend. "We aren't talking about grown men here, Jameson. Yes, they're no longer minors, but they're still in high school. They live under our roofs. It's not normal behavior to just take off."

The tension was growing between the men, and everyone in the room felt it. Rex knew he had to rein them in if they were going to achieve anything tonight. He cleared his throat. "Let me ask if any of you noticed strange behavior among the boys recently?"

Jameson's nostrils flared. He didn't like anyone assailing his son's character. "Just what is it you're accusing them of, Chief?"

Nick sighed, clearly agitated by the way Jameson was handling this. The Chief was here to help them. Anyone who knew Ethan, and even J.R. and Caleb for that matter, knew they were harmless. "Please calm down, James."

Jameson shot back a drink in response to his friend's request. How could he remain calm when his son's actions were being called under attack?

"Mayor, no one is making accusations," the chief answered. "But anything out of the ordinary, behavior changes particularly, can lead us to answers."

"Of course there were behavior changes, they lost the game Friday night!" the mayor yelled.

Anna sighed at her husband's outcry. She knew Jameson well enough to know his anger was based out of fear, whether he would admit it or not.

"Anything other than the football game?" the chief added patiently. He refused to feel threatened by the mayor.

They all looked at each other, afraid of what the answer would be. The had their suspicions, of course. But saying it out loud, that could be detrimental to their own and their son's reputations.

"Okay, let's take another tactic," the chief tried, scratching under his jaw. He hadn't shaved in several days and wasn't used to the prickling shadow that had crept up on his face. "Has there been any sort of trouble lately with the boys?" He looked at Jameson when he spoke. Had Jameson told Anna or the Youngs about the night he'd brought the boys to the mayor's doorstep?

Jameson huffed as he took a drink. "You all are overreacting. We're talking about three strong, capable men. What harm could come to them that they couldn't get themselves out of?"

Silence again as they all contemplated this. Anna wanted to believe Jameson, but his words didn't calm the gnawing in her belly that said her son was in danger.

The chief cleared his throat. "I made calls to all the hospitals in a fifty-mile radius, and no one by their description has been checked in, but they know to contact me if they do."

He noticed as he spoke the way that Nick looked to Anna, stricken by the idea that their boys could be in a hospital somewhere without their knowledge. But was that any worse than not knowing where they were at all?

He continued, "I also put a plug out to officers in the surrounding towns to keep an eye out for a black '95 BMW 325i..."

"Oh, great!" the mayor bellowed. He couldn't believe they were taking this so seriously. "So now they are a target like some hardened criminals?"

"This isn't only about your kid, James," Nick snapped. He had been best friends with the mayor since they were in grammar school and one of the only people who could speak to Jameson that way and get away with it. Even Anna was envious of that. Attacking the chief of police for trying to help them was unacceptable, and Nick had had enough.

Jameson glared at his friend but didn't say a word. He nursed his drink as Nick continued. "Thank you, Chief, for your diligence. I know I'll feel better if I get out there and continue to search myself. I can't just sit at home."

Just then, the phone rang in the entryway. Everyone held their breath, frozen in place as though they had forgotten how to move.

Then like a switch had gone off, Anna jumped up and raced to the phone, picking it up on the third ring.

"Hello?" she answered frantically.

And then a sigh of disappointment that they all felt. "No, Mom. No word. Please, I have to go and keep the line open. I'll call you when we know more."

Anna returned, her shoulders slouched and her brow furrowed. It appeared she had aged in the two minutes she was gone.

"Mom?" They all turned to see the Hudsons' middle child, Emma, standing in the doorway. "Was that J.R.?" She was her mother's replica in every way but height. Emma at fourteen was all legs and limbs, not quite a woman yet, but she already towered over her mom.

Anna could only shake her head. Her voice was lost to her at that moment. She was filled with dread, guilt, and anger. Could J.R. have just up and left? Would he do that to her?

"Back to bed, Emma," Jameson said as calmly as he could, though it was clear he was fuming under his words. When she left the room, he turned to the crowd in his living room.

"Okay, that's enough." He set down his drink. "I want everyone out. This is clearly causing unnecessary stress, and we'll all see that this was a big misunderstanding."

Chief Tourney closed his pad and shoved it into his back pocket. He wanted out of that house faster than Jameson could push him. But he also knew it was his job to tackle all sides of this case. Jameson may not have cared where his boy was, but there was something in Anna that was about to crack, and Rex wanted to get to the bottom of it.

"I hope you know that my team and I are here to help," Rex said to Anna. She nodded at him, grateful that he was taking this seriously. "But in order to do that, we need full cooperation. Is there anything you can think of that would make them want to run?"

Anna fidgeted in her seat. Saturday morning replayed in her head the way it had since she first realized that J.R. was gone. She hadn't said anything to anyone yet, but now felt it was necessary. She lifted her lids to her husband and saw that he was glaring down at her as though he could read her thoughts.

"Jameson..." she started.

He shook his head wildly. "No, Anna." He practically growled. "Please, Rex, Nick, see yourselves out."

Nick stood on command, storming out of the house with the door slamming behind him. He wouldn't let Jameson deter him from what he felt in his bones to be true. His boy was in trouble and he would spend all night searching the streets for him if he had to.

The chief eyed Anna, willing her to confess what she was hiding from him. But when she turned her head and closed her eyes, he knew he had lost her. Whatever pull Jameson had on her was strong enough to keep her silent. He gathered his coat off the back of the chair and headed for the door. When he passed, he caught the mayor's eye. Before Jameson could look away, Rex saw something undeniable. Guilt. Rex knew enough about liars to know the mayor was hiding something.

CHAPTER 4

Eight weeks earlier

They rode in tandem, with Caleb and Avery taking the lead in his white convertible Jeep and J.R.'s BMW on his tail. Ethan rode in the back seat and Grace in shotgun. Avery learned from her father, a successful realtor in town, about an abandoned piece of property just on the outskirts of Timber Falls. It had fallen into foreclosure and was taken over by the bank a month ago. They turned down the long gravel driveway that led them into oblivion and away from any prying eyes.

"Nice find, Aves," Caleb said as he cut the engine but let the music still play over his speakers. His hand slid to her thigh and gave it a light squeeze. No one, especially Avery, knew when she and Caleb were on and when they were off. But from the way he was looking at her now, she decided that at least for tonight they were together. She gave him a flirtatious smile as she hopped out of the Jeep, her cheerleading skirt replaced with jeans.

It was easy to see the two-story farmhouse once was filled with life and love but now looked fallow and dark. It was surrounded by acreage, as many of the homes in Timber Falls were. They were tucked away from the road, hidden among the trees where no one would see the lights of their cars or the hear the sounds of their voices.

Grace laid out blankets from J.R.'s trunk while the boys gathered branches and wood to start a fire.

It was after ten, and the night was getting away from them. Friday nights always began with a football game, and tonight the win had been against the Wolverines in a way that was just pitiful to watch. J.R. ran his team like a well-oiled machine, systematic and powerful. His arm was the engine, hitting his target without strain. Ethan's hypersonic wheels ran that ball to the end zone while Caleb blocked the opposing team like a steel wall. They were unbeatable, and no team wanted to go up against them. Grace and Avery screamed from the sidelines, keeping the crowd chanting and entertained.

But now, as students gathered at parties where the stars were expected to attend, they chose to hide away from it all and congregated around the fire with a case of beer. Caleb's mom, Kate, always kept a twelve-pack in the fridge, though she never drank. It was understood among Caleb and her that the beer was for him, though she never said it outright. It took the guilt off of her for officially supplying it.

Caleb passed the cheap cans around, and the sounds of tabs breaking intermixed with the crackling of the fire. The night was cooler than the night before as fall was creeping around the corner. It wasn't as easy for them to pretend on these weekends that it was still summer, though they held on to it for as long as they could. The air was becoming crisper, the smell poignant with burning fireplaces and dying youth. This was their last year together. At least until they all made their way back after college, if they chose to do so. It was present among them, they could feel the ticking of the clock as if it matched the pace of their heartbeats. There was a craving for this part of their life to be over and another aching for it to never end. It's all they had ever known.

Grace settled between J.R.'s legs, nursing her beer, and laughed along as they discussed tonight's game in all its dignified glory. She may not have always understood the way the game was played, but she did know she was with the king of the team. The king of the town.

She had staked her claim on him in third grade, but he hadn't noticed her until middle school. Even then, it wasn't until freshman year that he officially became hers. Their name went together as though it were one. No one remembered what it was like before Grace and J.R. were a couple. Avery had never been good about hiding her jealousy over Grace and J.R.'s relationship. Not that she wanted J.R. for herself—no, he had always been too pretty for her taste. She just wished that Caleb doted on her the way that J.R. did for Grace. Grace told her the key was to keep the power in the relationship. She knew what J.R. wanted above all else, and as long as she held on to that, it would keep him on his knees. Avery's problem was she gave it up to Caleb at every opportunity she had.

"Where's that cute piece of ass you were playing with this summer, Ethan?" Caleb asked with a coy smile on his face. He knew Ethan wasn't the type to just mess around. That's what was fun about teasing him.

"Her name was Brittany, Caleb," Avery said, giving him a jab to the ribs.

"Brianna," Ethan clarified, taking a drink of beer. They all laughed at Avery's mistake.

"Whatever," Avery said with a roll of her eye. "How can we keep track when you don't bring the girls you date around us?"

"Can you blame him?" J.R. teased. He ran his free hand through Grace's hair, the way she liked him to. "You two treat any girl Ethan dates like an outcast."

"What?" Grace gasped. "We are just being protective of Ethan."

"Exactly," Avery added. She flipped her hair over her shoulder and smiled at Ethan. "No one has been good enough for him."

Ethan laughed, his face flushed from the attention. "Thanks, girls."

Ethan was used to being the third—or like tonight, fifth—wheel. It wasn't that he didn't have a list of girls begging to be next, but he kept his love life under wraps, unlike his friends. He had been seeing a girl over the summer from another school that he kept low key when talking about her to his friends. What he didn't share were the many late nights that had turned into many first for both of them. He thought they could survive the school year being apart, but football always took first place in his life, whether he wanted it to or not. And she did not have the patience for it.

Caleb finished his first beer, letting out a loud belch as he crushed the can in his hand and tossed it aside.

"You are so gross," Avery moaned, moving away from him. He slid an arm around her and brought her to his lap. She pretended to fight him off as though she didn't love the attention.

"Didn't your mom teach you manners?" Grace never understood Avery's attraction to Caleb. Ethan was a much better catch and a lot hotter, too, with his wavy golden hair and hazel eyes. Why couldn't she go for him? Grace always thought Caleb looked a little scary with his shaved head and narrow eyes.

"Nope." Caleb grinned. "I've had to learn them all on my own, and not from my maid."

Grace glared at him. J.R. felt her tighten in his arms and laughed to calm her down. "Okay, Weston, lay off."

Caleb feigned innocence with a lift of his hand as to say, "What did I do?"

"Grace loves me." Caleb smiled. Grace rolled her eyes but couldn't deny it. For all his pomp and egotism, he was the backbone of the group. He had stood up for her on many occasions, like the time in eighth grade when Angela, the class bitch, stuck gum in her hair and Caleb told her that he had never hit a girl before, but he would if she messed with Grace again. Maybe she could see some of Avery's attraction to him.

He lit a joint and passed it to Avery, who promptly took a drag before handing it to Ethan.

Ethan shook his head as he took a sip of beer. "I'm good."

"Since when?" Caleb chided. Ethan never turned down a good joint.

"Since today," Ethan shot back. "Is that okay with you?"

"No." Caleb laughed and Ethan couldn't help but chuckle.

Caleb narrowed his eyes at him. "Come on, Deadman."

Ethan glared at him. He hated when Caleb pulled that shit on him. "You're such an ass," he said, reluctantly taking the joint from Avery.

He took a hit and blew the smoke slowly in Caleb's direction, holding his stare and thinking back to the summer he and J.R. were ten and used to ride their bikes two miles from home to a field in east Timber Falls.

The field had been abandoned, though there was talk that new housing construction was to begin there. Both the Youngs and the Hudsons had banned the boys from going there. They spoke of druggies and bad kids who hung out in the fields, and wanted their prized children to be as far away from it as possible. But the boys also heard other talk of a hole in the field like a giant dirt skate ramp where kids would gather with their bikes to see who could ride it.

J.R. and Ethan would huddle with the other kids and chant on the boys, usually four or five years their senior, who would straddle their bikes at the edge of the hole and ride down the steep slope as fast as they could and up the other side. It was too deep to pedal out of. If you didn't get enough speed to ride it in one stride, then you would slide down to the bottom of the pit. And that pit they named Deadman. Deadman's Pit.

Neither J.R. nor Ethan were ever brave enough to ride their bikes, knowing if they got stuck at the bottom it was nearly impossible to get out on your own, and the ridicule you received at school was not worth the embarrassment.

Until one night.

It was after dinner, and the boys were due to be home when the sun set, but when they rode out to Deadman's Pit, they found themselves alone for the first time. At first, their instinct was to ride home, until J.R. got a wild idea to try it.

"No one is here to see if we fail," he'd said, looking over the edge, contemplating how far down it really was.

"No way," Ethan said, shaking his head. "What if we get stuck and can't get out?"

"Don't be a wuss," J.R. chided. "Kids get out all the time. I'd help you."

Ethan's eyes widened. "Hell no. You go first."

"Don't you want to prove to yourself that you can do it?" J.R. continued. "Then we can come back and show those older kids. Think about what they would say."

Ethan swayed back and forth on his bike. It was hard to reason with J.R. when he got an idea in his head, especially when he was right.

J.R. looked back over the edge, considering his plan. He really did want to do it, even if his palms were starting to sweat on his handlebars. If he could just convince Ethan to do it first.

"Let's flip a coin," J.R. decided, taking a quarter out of his pocket. "Call it," he said as he flung it in the air.

Ethan closed his eyes. "Heads." He held his breath, and when he opened his eyes, J.R. was staring at the ground with a smirk on his face.

Ethan cursed. Heads. "You swear you will do it after me?"

J.R. held out his hand. "Pinky swear."

Ethan took that promise and then backed up his bike. The knot in his belly tightened, but he pushed it aside. He wanted to prove to himself, and mostly to J.R., that he could do this.

He rocked his bike back and forth before jumping on the pedals and pumping his legs as fast as he could go. He caught J.R.'s face just as he started down the hill, and the look of awe in his best friend's eyes was worth all the terror he felt speeding down the slope. His hopes turned high as his bike began to climb the other side of the hill, and just as his front tire touched the tip of the ledge, his mouth opened in the wildest grin, knowing he had done it. But then, just as quickly as the top arrived, it faded when it became clear he did not have enough stamina to get the rest of his bike to the top. He began to slip back. His instinct was to pedal, but it was no use. He toppled off his bike and rolled down to the bottom of the pit.

He could hear the cries of J.R. through the ringing in his ears. For a moment he thought he was fine until he tried to move and his arm jolted in sharp pain. He screamed, and then to his embarrassment, the tears flowed.

"My arm!" Ethan cried. "I think I broke my arm, J.R.."

J.R. lay on his belly, leaning over the edge. "Ethan, you have to get up."

"I can't," Ethan moaned. "Help me." The pain was excruciating. At that moment, the fear of his parents finding out paled in comparison to his need for them. "You need to get my dad."

J.R. was frantic. What if they got caught out here? He would be grounded for life. No football, no video games, no arcade.

"No way!" J.R. called down. "Then he'll tell my dad."

Ethan opened his eyes and glared at his friend. "J.R.!" he yelled. "Go get my dad!"

J.R. sighed, knowing there was nothing else he could do. If he tried to get Ethan out himself, then there was a good chance they could both get stuck.

He rode home and brought back Nick Young, who got Ethan to the hospital where he had to have surgery and a cast. Both boys were grounded for a month and forbidden to ever go back. They kept that promise until Caleb showed up in seventh grade.

When Ethan and J.R. told Caleb the story, he said he had to see this place for himself. Since the housing development fell through, the hole was still there, though rarely used anymore. They took their bikes out to Deadman's Pit, and as Ethan and J.R. stood back from it, the memories of that night still lingered in their heads, Caleb jumped at the shot. He backed his bike up and set out at high speed. Ethan and J.R. called out for him to stop, but it was too late. He was over the edge and on the other side in a flash. He dropped his bike and howled at the rush of it all.

When he was back by their side, he patted Ethan hard on the back and said, "How'd you like that, Deadman?"

It was a reminder of Caleb's bravery and Ethan's cowardice. And he was never afraid to remind him of it.

Ethan took another drag of the joint and passed it back to Caleb. They shared an icy expression not seen by the others. They saw through each other in a way that was never spoken but clearly understood. Ethan had had just about enough with Caleb taking control of the reins.

CHAPTER 5

Second day gone

Nearly twelve hours after everyone cleared out of the Hudson home, they were all back, as though they never left. And the room was filling up with others. The mayor's house had become the unofficial volunteer station.

When the three boys didn't arrive for their first class Monday morning, word began to spread quickly. First, it was the whispers among the students that turned into the questions that neither Grace nor Avery could answer. Soon, the teachers were talking, which finally reached the principal. He had a call in to Mayor Hudson before the end of the first period.

To Jameson's dismay, he may have been wrong. Would his son really have had the gall to leave and not tell Anna where he was going? He thought back to only a couple days before, to the words that were shared between them, the accusations that flew with the rise of their voices. Could J.R. have let something as simple as a fight be enough of a reason to not return home?

The idea was absurd.

In his belly, he began to feel the turning as anger melted into anxiety, though he refused to show it. Anna was hardly holding herself together. What good would it do if he displayed any concern?

And then there was the chief, taking over his home and running it like a damn military outpost, separating over-eager volunteers into search groups. They had enough people to cover most of Timber Falls. Rex was looking at him now, his eyes clouded over as though he was searching for something in Jameson that he couldn't quite find yet. He probably had a hard-on from all the action in the last forty-eight hours. More police work than he had to do in all his years as chief. Jameson kept this town clean, well respected, and clear of criminal activity. Now it was his own son making waves.

Where the hell are you, J.R.?

Rex noticed the way the mayor looked back at him, and it made him fume. In his eyes, it showed his lack of confidence in his work as the chief. Maybe he was right; maybe he wasn't the best man for the job. But he was who Jameson and this town were getting, whether they wanted it or not.

Rex turned away long enough to answer a question from a volunteer, and when he looked up, Jameson was in front of him. It caught him off guard.

"Mayor." His head jerked back to look up at him. "How are you holding up?"

Jameson reached behind him, and it was then that Rex realized he was blocking the coffee station. He took two steps to the side and wondered if the mayor had even heard him speak. Jameson poured a cup of hot coffee, keeping it black, and took a sip before answering.

"My home is overtaken by the public, Chief. How do you think I'm holding up?"

Rex took notice that the mayor didn't mention anything about his son being gone, only the inconvenience of his home being disrupted. He looked over at Anna, who was nestled on the couch with her daughter Emma on one side and her youngest son, Drew, on the other. Drew was only eleven, the baby of the family, and a miniature version of J.R. and Jameson. Anna held tight to him. Rex thought she looked as though she hadn't slept in two days, and maybe she hadn't. Her face was red and blotchy from crying, her hair tangled in a clip on her head. He tried for a moment to think about what she must be feeling, but then he pushed that thought away.

He cleared his throat. "We have our first crew going out now, searching parking lots, abandoned warehouses, and the woods."

Jameson, being several inches taller than Rex, looked down at him, his lips tight when he asked, "And just what is it that you think they will find, Chief? Are you telling me they're looking for my son's body?"

"I'm hoping we find any sign of them."

The mayor shook his head. "No, what you need is people out on the road, looking for his car."

"We have that, too," Rex said patiently. "I've spoken with the sheriff and he has officers looking for his plate numbers."

"What a fucking debacle," the mayor said under his breath. And then the anger was back and he was damn certain that his son was going to walk in any minute, and he had to keep himself in check so as not to take him by the throat.

"Well, until we have a car, we see no reason to be alarmed," the chief said to calm the mayor down. He could see the flare of his nostrils and the pink of his cheeks. He felt a hand on his arm and turned to see Anna.

"I'm sorry to interrupt, Chief." But she wasn't looking at him. Her eyes, bloodshot and puffy, were tilted to her husband. "James, I think we should send the kids to my mom's." When he huffed, she continued. "The school called asking if they would be out for more than today, and I think it's important to not confuse them with this kind of chaos."

Rex found this time to excuse himself only to quickly regret it. He met the gaze of Kate Weston as she walked through the door. He took a long drink of his black coffee, hoping the potency covered up the smell of the whiskey he had poured in it. She kept her eyes locked on him, holding him in place as she headed right for him.

No one acknowledged Kate as she walked through the room. Almost mistaken as another volunteer and not a mother of one of the missing boys. Not only was Kate one of the only single mothers in Timber Falls; she was also one of the few mothers in town who worked. As a nurse at the hospital, she often worked the night shift, which left Caleb unattended most of the time. It wasn't ideal, but she wasn't left with many options. It also kept her isolated from the other women, a pariah of sorts, and friendless. She was never invited to social events or PTA meetings, even though her son was best friends with J.R. and Ethan. She never let it show that it bothered her, but deep down it gutted her.

"Oh, Rex," she whispered when she approached. Her voice sounded pitiful and his first reaction was to pull her to him, but he took another drink instead. Her light brown hair was pulled haphazardly into a low ponytail, strands of soft curls falling around her face. Her brown eyes looked hollow with grey shadows under her lashes. He couldn't help but think she was still beautiful.

"Tell me there is some news. Anything. I'm going crazy all alone in that house with worry." She was shaking. He noticed her long nails bloodied at the cuticle.

He looked away, swallowing the pit in his stomach. "I'm sorry, Kate. When I have any news, I will report it immediately."

She looked up at him as though he had slapped her. "What's going on, Rex?" She eyed him closely. "Have you been drinking?"

"Of course not," he shot back in a whispered tone. "Kate, you can't talk to me like that, not here."

"My son is missing! And you're speaking to me like I'm some..." Her voice trembled. She shook her head. "I'm not the mayor. Drop the formality, Rex, and tell me what the hell is going on. Where are all of these people going?"

He sighed. He didn't have time for this, for him and Kate. He needed to keep his head on straight, on the task ahead of him. "We have search volunteers heading out towards—"

"Excuse me, Chief," a soft voice interrupted him. Grace and Avery stood behind him, stacks of papers in their hands. "Here are the missing persons posters you wanted."

"Thank you, girls," he said, taking them from her. Avery rushed to Kate and wrapped her arms around her, instantly dissolving into sobs. Kate held her tight and whispered in her ear.

"Grace, I was hoping I could talk to you privately for a moment," Rex said.

"Sure," she said, though her wide eyes said otherwise. He sensed her discomfort, and it intrigued him. He turned and walked toward a quiet corner, Grace following his trail. When they were near the window and out of earshot, he turned to face her. She was looking away from him, back at the crowd. He studied her a moment, wondering what secrets she held. If anyone knew what was going on with J.R., it would be her.

"I know you and J.R. have been together a long time. You just may know him better than anyone."

"Possibly," she said with a shrug, finally meeting his gaze.

He thought that was a strange response, so he pressed on. "What can you tell me about J.R. before he went missing Saturday night? Do you have any insight as to why he would leave?"

"Well, I didn't see him on Saturday." She nibbled on her bottom pink lip. "I hadn't talked to him since Friday, and he didn't say anything about leaving."

"Would you call that unusual, you two not speaking?" he probed. He wanted to get inside her head. Spill the thoughts out. Was she hiding something from him? "Do you normally spend the weekends together?"

She didn't tell the chief that the last time she'd seen J.R., they'd gotten into a horrible fight, worst they'd ever been in. She'd thought for sure he would have called her on Saturday asking for her forgiveness. And when he hadn't, she'd told Avery it was over between them. She knew she was just being dramatic and didn't mean it. She never did when she said that.

She nodded. "I guess so."

He sensed her hesitation, but now was no time to tread lightly. Her eyes darted to the side, looking for Avery. She did not want to be here, answering questions that would potentially humiliate her.

"And Avery and Caleb and even Ethan? Aren't you usually all together?"

"Yes." She thought about it a moment and then said, "Usually. But not always. Sometimes I hang out with just Avery when the boys do something that we don't want to do."

"Like what?" he asked, taking a sip from his mug. He forced himself to act casual, to make her feel comfortable enough to share what he needed to know. "What are some things the boys do that you don't want to do?"

She opened her mouth to speak but then quickly shut it. She didn't know what she should tell a cop or not. Sure, he'd grown up in this town and knew what the teens did, but it wasn't the same as saying it out loud to the chief.

He leveled his eyes to meet hers. He could see the fear steaming off of her. "You won't get in trouble, Grace. It may help."

She sighed. "Well, sometimes they would go racing." She bit down on her lip to stop talking.

"Where did they go racing?" he asked as though he didn't know.

"Mostly down the old Oak Hill highway. It's pretty dead there late at night." She thought about the time when she sat shotgun in J.R.'s car with Ethan in the back. Avery with Caleb in his Jeep.

They started down the pitch black road, J.R. in the lead. They were picking up speed on the narrow highway, J.R.'s BMW bouncing with every pothole. The lights behind them went dark as Caleb slid his Jeep up beside J.R. driving on the wrong side of the road. At first, J.R. laughed, rolling down his window to call Caleb a jackass. But when it was clear that Caleb wasn't playing, J.R.'s expression darkened and his eyes narrowed to the road, his foot pressing down on the pedal.

"What the hell are you doing?" Grace said to him, grasping the door handle for support as the car bounced.

"Racing him." He was a foot ahead, but Caleb jumped down on the gas and sprung forward. J.R. swore under his breath.

"Don't let him beat you!" Ethan called out from the back seat.

"Ethan!" Grace cried. "No, J.R., slow down. One pothole and you guys could crash into each other."

"I know what I'm doing, Grace," J.R. hissed as he took the lead once more. Caleb screamed out from the thrill of it, but when Grace met Avery's eyes in the other car, she knew she was just as scared.

"Stop right now!" Grace yelled. But he ignored her. And that's when she saw the headlights coming toward them.

She spun in her seat to face J.R. "This is crazy. Please, J.R." She was begging now. His face was blank with concentration. She knew J.R. saw the car, and that what they were doing was insane and could potentially kill them all. But to pull back now would let Caleb win. And then he would never hear the end of what a wuss he was. J.R. kept his eyes on the road, but Caleb stayed next to him. Grace froze as the glare of the headlights kept coming at them, flashing at Caleb to get out of their lane. She dared one look at Caleb to see him laughing, and it was then that they all realized at once that he would risk killing himself and Avery rather than surrender.

J.R. slammed on his brakes, and Caleb took that moment to slide in front of him just as the car passed them by. She could see the sweat coming off of J.R. and that the race meant something different to him than it did to Caleb.

Still, she told him he better not ever do that again with her in the car. And that he was an asshole.

Grace decided to keep that story to herself.

"Did they do that often?" the chief asked.

She shrugged. The truth was she didn't know. She didn't want to know. She always feared the worst when the boys were off on their own. She had heard the stories from the past of the boys throwing eggs at oncoming traffic, as they hid in bushes. And even worse, when they ran out of eggs, how Caleb turned to rocks. J.R. said Caleb threw a rock so hard he cracked a windshield and then bolted, laughing the whole way home. Grace never understood why J.R. fell for Caleb's foolish pranks. She'd often dreaded the day when the call would come that J.R. was in the hospital or worse due to some stupid stunt they had pulled. But she never suspected they would go missing.

"Okay." Rex sighed. "Let me get personal for a moment if that's okay, Grace."

She nodded her head slowly.

"Would you say that you and J.R. were happy together?"

Grace thought about their fight, how bad things had gotten between them. She was afraid to answer that question honestly because the truth was she didn't know. So instead she simply said, "I love J.R., I always have."

He studied her a moment, waiting to see if she would share any more details. When it was clear she was done talking, he said, "Thank you, Grace. And you'll keep me informed if you hear anything at all?"

She nodded as she wiped her tears on her sweater sleeve.

"Chief," she said as he started to walk away. "Your daughter, Lila?"

He stopped in his tracks at the mention of her name. "Yes? You know Lila?"

"Well, no, not really. She's a sophomore," she answered as though knowing an underclassman was against the rules. "But, she's been around a bit, at parties and stuff. You know what I mean? I saw her hanging out with Ethan some. I was just wondering if you've talked to her?"

His back stiffened. "She's been at home sick," he answered. But then he pressed on. "You saw her with Ethan Young?"

"A little. It's not like they're dating or anything," she clarified.

His face went red. "No, they certainly are not."

"I didn't mean..." She could see the anger rolling off of him and wondered what she'd said to upset him. "I'm just saying she may know something."

He pressed his lips together to keep his cool. He didn't need her or anyone gossiping about his daughter. "Thank you, Grace. I'll look into that."

She nodded and walked to Avery, leaning in to whisper something in her ear. He lifted his almost empty coffee mug to his lips and downed every last drop. He'd need more whiskey if he was going to get through this day unscathed.

CHAPTER 6
Seven weeks earlier

I t was Lila's first high school party, or at least the first one that included upperclassman. She had been invited by Olivia, who had been invited by a junior she had a history class with. She was giddy with excitement, swallowing the nerves she felt and the fear of her dad finding out. She and Olivia had told their parents they were staying at Hannah's house, and Hannah, who was the first of them to get her driver's license, told her parents they were going to the movies and arcade. The only thing that could mess up this night was if her dad was on duty and the party got busted. But she had a feeling he wasn't. She knew his secret, though he would never admit it. She'd heard him on the phone and at times had accidentally picked up the line when it was in use. She'd heard the woman's voice on the other end. She didn't know who it was that he spoke to, but she knew he was with her. It was obvious the nights he would drop her off at Olivia's, only to pick her up the next morning in the same clothes he had been wearing the day before. She never questioned him. It both grossed her out and pleased her to know that he had someone. Maybe then he would stay occupied and out of her business.

He'd never brought a woman home for her to meet. She didn't know what it was like to see another woman's clothing in his closet, or smell a sweet fragrance she didn't recognize. Never saw an extra toothbrush or hair tie. It had always just been the two of them.

She had photographs of her mother. As she got older, she began to see her resemblance in her reflection. She had her mother's long, fine golden hair and moss green eyes. But her own brow furrowed a bit too hard like her father's did. And her lips were not as full as her mother's had been, but instead more of a thin straight line like her dad's.

She used to stare at her mother's photograph often as a child, speak to her and pretend she was talking back with her in conversation. Her dad had caught her on occasion but pretended not to notice, and they both preferred it that way. Now that she was a teen, she spoke less to her photo, but in a way, she craved her mother even more than when she was a child. Going through puberty with only her father was at times mortifying, probably for both of them.

And she was scared. She was slowly moving into adulthood and she had so many questions that she knew she could never ask him. She watched as her body changed, as feelings came to her in waves of such intensity that she didn't know whether to laugh hysterically or scream in a fit of tears.

It wasn't that she and her dad weren't close. They were just tight in a different way than she imagined she and her mom would have been. Her dad took her camping and taught her the constellations in the sky, how to build a fire without a match and how to listen for the fish when they cast their reel. He taught her how to change a flat tire and how to throw a good punch if she should ever need to.

But he didn't teach her about her ever-changing body, the way to talk to a boy, or, how not to die when giving birth to a child, like her mother did.

Music blasted from the house as they entered. They pushed through the crowd feeling more like outsiders among their classmates who seemed lifetimes older than them. Someone offered Lila a beer and she took it, though she had never tasted one before. The girls giggled as they cheersed to one another and took a sip. Lila did her best to hide her disgust.

"You get used to it." She heard a voice and turned to see Ethan Young standing behind her.

Her face burned. "Oh, yeah, I know," she said, trying to cover her embarrassment. "This isn't my first time."

He gave her a crooked smile, pushing his worn-in Falcons baseball hat down over his forehead. His blue eyes glistened in amusement. "Sure, if you say so."

She stood there knowing this was a defining moment for her. Here, standing beside her was *the* Ethan Young. The most gorgeous boy in school, at least in her eyes. And he was talking to *her*, though she was almost positive he didn't know her name. She could show him her vulnerability, prove that she was a young amateur who didn't belong. But one thing growing up with the Chief of Police had taught her was never to show your weakness.

"Lila," Olivia warned, resting a hand on her arm. But Lila ignored her.

She shot back the can, taking the beer down in only three gulps. When she came up for air, she could see the surprise in Ethan Young's eyes. It was worth the queasy sickness in her belly.

"Damn." His grin widened. "Impressive." It looked as though he was going to say something else, but before he could get out the words, J.R. Hudson was slamming into his side.

"There you are!" He never looked at Lila, but Grace Morgan, who was beside J.R., did. She gave Lila a look between confusion and disgust like she didn't understand why Ethan was standing next to her.

"Come on," Olivia said as she took Lila's hand and pulled her away. Lila let her friend drag her to the bathroom before she puked in front of the most popular boys in school.

"Jesus, J.R.," Ethan quipped. "You almost spilled my beer."

"Where's Caleb?" J.R. asked. He was uncharacteristically giddy. "I have some exciting news."

"I haven't seen him since we got here."

"There's Avery," Grace said, pointing in the direction of the kitchen.

"Come on." J.R. grabbed Ethan by the shoulder.

When they found Caleb and Avery, J.R. led them outside into the tepid September night, away from the prying eyes and ears.

"Okay, J.R., spill. What's the big secret?" Caleb draped an arm around Avery's shoulders, drinking his beer with his free hand.

"It won't be a secret for long, but I want you guys to be the first to know," J.R. said with a gleam in his smile. "My dad spoke with the Huskies head coach tonight."

Caleb's eyes grew wide in excitement as Ethan swallowed hard, afraid of where this conversation was going.

"He saw the tape my dad sent him of our first game against the Panthers and he's coming here to watch us play!"

"You're shitting me!" Caleb howled, pushing J.R. in the shoulder, practically toppling over Avery who was squealing with Grace.

"Swear!" J.R. stumbled back from the force of Caleb's hand. He laughed at his friend's excitement. "He'll be here in November when we play Westview."

"Westview?" Caleb roared. "We kill Westview every year!"

"Exactly." J.R. smiled smugly.

"You guys are in," Grace said, hugging J.R..

"You know what this means, don't you?" J.R. continued. "Full rides, you guys." He lifted a brow at Caleb. "Once he sees you killing it on the field, he will be begging for you." He grabbed Ethan by the neck and pulled him in. "We are getting the hell out of here."

Ethan did his best to smile. "That's awesome."

"Awesome?" J.R. questioned. "Dude, this is what we have wanted our whole lives! The three of us at UDub together." He tightened his hold on Grace. "With our girls cheering us on."

Caleb lifted his beer in the air. "To getting out of this small-ass town!"

"Imagine it," J.R. said breathlessly. "The three of us owning the Huskies field like we do the Falcons. We'll be unstoppable. Man, Caleb, you could go all the way. Straight to the NFL."

Caleb beamed with pride; it was his dream to play ball for life. First for the Huskies, then on to the Seahawks. It was an unspoken understanding that that life would never be for J.R. After the Huskies, his football career would end as he entered public service like his father, with the plan of becoming Mayor of Timber Falls.

But Ethan was the one with the unclear future. And no one knew that more than him. It was his destined path to follow in his friends' footsteps to play football in college, and up until this summer, he had seen no reason to question that life. It was Brianna who disputed it for him.

They were perched on top of a rock on Oracle Point, named for its deceptive sharp drop-offs. It was a favorite spot for Ethan and the boys, where they would come to cliff jump off shorter ledges into deep parts of the lake, but on this day he and Brianna lay out on a flat ridge that overlooked the falls. She didn't know him as a football god, as all the other girls saw him at Timber Falls High School. It was one of the things that drew him to her. He could just be himself. But just being himself had its consequences. It gave him the freedom to think on his own rather than being told what to think by J.R. and Caleb.

They had the rock to themselves, as they often did. Ethan had found this secret spot earlier in the summer and was reluctant to share its existence with anyone other than Brianna. She lay on her bare back, her bikini top undone, looking up at him as he spoke of his hesitation over his future.

"Have you thought about going somewhere else for school? Somewhere different than your friends?"

No, *he thought.* He never had. Not consciously, anyway.

"No one is holding a gun to your head, Ethan." She shrugged. "You can make your own future."

His own future. What would that look like? Did he dare tell his friends that he didn't want to play ball anymore? That he craved the day that high school was over and he could be defined as anything other than as a football player. Or, did he dare say, he could he hardly wait for the day when he wasn't known for being J.R.'s best friend.

But that was when the fear set in. Who was he if he wasn't defined by Caleb, J.R., and football?

Ethan looked at his friends now, their enthusiasm seeping from their skin. How could he possibly burst their bubble and tell them he wasn't sure it was what he wanted anymore?

"Awesome news, J.R." He smiled, hugging his friend back. "I can't wait."

He tuned out the rest of the conversation, sipping on his beer, wanting to be anywhere but there at that moment. He looked back through the window to see Lila giggling with her friends. He envied her carelessness and her free spirit. When she caught him staring, he didn't look away. Maybe it was time for him to start thinking for himself.

CHAPTER 7
Third day gone

"What do you mean, missing?" Lila asked. She was under the covers trying to talk as quietly into her phone as she could. It was well past the time her father allowed her to make phone calls. But when Olivia said they needed to have an emergency meeting tonight, she couldn't ignore the urgency in her voice. Lila called her after she knew her dad had gone to bed, and they dialed in Hannah on party line.

"Missing. Like gone. Poof," Hannah said, her voice a sharp whisper.

"You should have seen it at school today, Lila," Olivia said. "It was crazy. Everyone was running around trying to figure out what was going on. Even the teachers."

"I guess everyone was at the Hudson house," Hannah added. "They even had volunteers going out to search."

"Search? Where?" Lila asked. "They think something happened to them?" She felt a knot pulling tight in her belly. She pulled the covers tighter to calm her chills.

"Maybe," Olivia said. "But they can't find J.R.'s car."

"Do you think they just left?" Lila asked, trying not to sound hopeful. A world where J.R. Hudson, Caleb Weston, and Ethan Young had disappeared sounded like a good one to her.

"I don't know," Olivia answered quietly. "Do you think they would?"

"No way," Hannah said. "Why would they?"

"You saw how they were at Friday's game," Olivia answered. "Lila, it was horrible. It's all anyone could talk about at the party Saturday night. Which I still can't believe you missed."

"Lila, you have to come back," Hannah pleaded. "Or at least talk to us. You can't still be sick."

"Please, Lila," Olivia joined in. "We've been so worried. What is going on with you?"

Lila pushed the tear away that was falling down her cheek. She didn't want her friends to hear her cry. "I'm tired," she answered simply. "I have to go."

"Lila, don't—" Lila hung up the phone before Olivia could finish the sentence. She rolled on her side and pulled her knees to her belly and silently wept as she tried to push images out of her mind that haunted her day and night. What would Hannah and Olivia think of her if they knew the truth? Would they be able to look at her the same way? She was afraid of the answer.

But she also knew she couldn't hide out forever. Her lies would come back and turn on her if she kept them up. She had to find a way to be strong through her weakest moment.

She had to make a decision. And when the sun rose through her window, so did she. She got showered and dressed and was sitting at the breakfast nook when her dad came walking in wearing his uniform.

He was startled to see her sitting there, so normal as though the last week had never happened. He looked at the clock to see if he had possibly mistaken the time.

"Hey, Dad," she said, turning her spoon around in her strawberry yogurt, not really taking any bites.

"Hey, kiddo." He turned on the coffee pot, trying his damnedest not to make a big deal about her sitting there.

"I..." she started and then stopped. He filtered his coffee grounds and poured in the hot water. He refused to look at her in case she saw through him. "I thought I would try going to school today."

He swallowed hard. "You feeling up for that?"

"I don't know," she answered honestly. "I think so."

He nodded, keeping his back to her. When had he gotten so afraid to look her in the eye? "I suppose you've heard about everything going on?"

"Hannah and Olivia called me."

He took a sip of his steaming hot coffee while he looked out the window. An acreage of field lay in front of him, before disappearing into the blackness of the thick forest. This land had been in the Tourney family for many generations. It's where he had grown up, in this house, looking out at those woods. He had always assumed it was where he would die as his parents did, and where Lila would raise her family. But some days he just didn't know anymore.

"What do you think happened?" she asked.

His knees buckled from the fear in her voice. He straightened his back and turned toward her. "I think we're dealing with a runaway case. Sounds like these boys had some things going on they didn't want anyone to know about. I'm sure they'll turn up soon, and when they do they'll have a lot of people to answer to."

She pushed her half-eaten bowl of yogurt away and rested her elbows on the table, cradling her head in her hands. "You think they're in trouble?"

She looked so much like her mother had at her age. She sat with one knee bent underneath her as the other leg dangled over the top. He used to tease Maura when she sat like that, not understanding how it was comfortable.

"If I had to guess, I would say they are, but only they know for sure. Hopefully, they come back soon and we all have some answers."

"Hopefully," she repeated.

They sat in their silence for a moment, neither sure of what to say to the other. He finished his coffee and rinsed his cup in the sink before turning back to her. She hadn't moved.

"Do you need a ride to school?"

"Uh, no," she answered, shaken from her thoughts. "Hannah's picking me up."

"Okay." He cleared his throat. "That's good." He grabbed his jacket off the chair beside her. "I'll be at the school this morning. There'll be an assembly after the first period about all of this."

"Oh." She sat up straighter in her chair. "Okay."

"Okay," he repeated. He started to walk out of the room but stopped at the table and instinctively reached out to her and touched her head. She flinched but then closed her eyes and smiled softly.

She was pressed between Olivia and Hannah on the wooden bleachers. How many times this morning had she questioned if she had made the right decision? Her teachers welcomed her back, but she could also see the way they looked at her, how they saw the difference in her complexion. Hannah gasped lightly when she saw the way Lila's cheekbones protruded from her face, commenting that it must have been a brutal sickness for her to lose that much weight.

She wore a bulky sweatshirt to hide the fact that her jeans slipped off her hips. She didn't want any attention on her body. She only wanted to disappear into the crowd. And right now, sitting between her friends at the assembly, that was exactly what she intended to do.

There was a buzz in the air, a hum of voices though nothing that could be made out. Students were on the edges of their seats, waiting. Nothing like this had ever happened in Timber Falls.

Principal Harris was in center court, mic in hand. Gone was his light banter and easy smile. He looked stricken, tired like the rest of the staff and teachers beside him. He said something to Coach Mitchell that was inaudible to the rest of the crowd. The coach nodded, and the principal turned back to his awaiting audience.

"Thank you, Timber Falls students, for your patience. You can see that the staff here, myself included, have been pretty shaken up by the recent events. There is a lot of gossip going around. And we want to clear up fact from fiction for you." He paused as if to catch a tremble in his voice. "I'm going to pass the mic to Chief of Police, Rex Tourney, who is head of this investigation."

Lila watched her father take over the mic. She shrunk down in her seat in hopes that he wouldn't see her.

He thanked the principal before clearing his throat to speak to the crowd.

"As Principal Harris mentioned, and as most of you know, I'm Chief Tourney. I will be working with the staff today, opening our offices for anyone who would like to come forward with information regarding the disappearance of Caleb Weston, Ethan Young, and J.R. Hudson." His eyes searched the melancholy crowd until he saw his daughter sunken down. He quickly looked away.

"On Saturday, shortly before nine in the evening, J.R. left his home and went to Ethan's house. From there it was understood that they were picking up Caleb, but as far as we can tell from what information has been offered to us, that's the last anyone has seen or heard from them.

"This is where we need your help.

"You can come to Principal Harris's office or leave an anonymous tip for me at the station. We welcome all information that could lead us to them."

He left those last words hanging in the air. Silence filled the gym as students looked to each other, wondering who knew something that they didn't.

A junior sitting in front of Lila—she couldn't remember her name—, leaned into the friend beside her and sobbed. As Lila looked around the bleachers, she saw the same scene playing over and over. Students weeping in despair and fear. Could the leaders of their school really just up and leave? Or was it worse? And could what had happened to these strong boys also happen to the rest of them?

Lila's palms began to sweat. Her fingers trembled and she couldn't breathe. Suddenly, she felt claustrophobic in the sea of students and needed to get out.

"Lila?" Hannah asked, noticing her friend's distress. "Are you okay?"

She grasped at her chest, unable to respond. This was a bad idea. Just then, Principal Harris dismissed them back to class. Lila jumped up from her seat and pushed her way down the bleacher steps, knocking students over as she went. She needed to get out of the gym. She needed fresh air. She needed to be anywhere but there.

CHAPTER 8

Six weeks earlier

The air was crisp as fall settled into Timber Falls. They huddled together under the stadium lights, the boys on the field, the town in the stands. No one missed a Falcons football game. The score was pitiful, with the Falcons in the lead, and yet the crowd still went wild for every tackle and every touchdown.

The Youngs and the Hudsons sat together in their usual spot at the top of the stands on the fifty-yard line. Jameson and Nick stood as pillars on the outside to their wives who often spent most of the game chatting with their heads together. Similar to their own children, the four of them had been friends since grade school. Flashback twenty-five years and it would be Nick and Jameson on the field with Nora and Anna cheering them on like Grace and Avery did. They had talked about this day when it would be their kids running the school and living out their legacy.

Only it should have been Nick and Anna, not Jameson and Anna. But only Nick and Anna knew that.

Jameson had had his eye on Anna and staked his claim on her before he'd bothered to ask her. Had he asked her, then she would have said she liked another boy, who happened to be his best friend. And that friend liked her too, though he could never say so out loud. Nick and Anna would meet behind the gym, beginning of freshman year of high school, stealing kisses when they should have been in class. But when it came time for Homecoming, Nick hadn't had the courage to ask her, knowing that Jameson wanted her. So he'd asked Nora instead, and the rest was history. But sometimes, every once in awhile, Nick would look to Anna and catch her staring at him, and he wondered then if she felt it, too.

The halftime whistle blew and the teams dispersed under the stadium. Kids moved down the stairs or sat on the bleachers, resting their legs. Nick eyed the concession stand and asked if anyone wanted anything. Both Jameson and Nora shook their heads, but Anna stood, saying she wanted a hot cocoa.

"I can bring it back for you," Nick offered.

"No, I'll join you." She grabbed her purse and stood. "I want to speak to Patty King about the Holiday Bazaar fundraiser we're running together."

She followed him down one step at a time, by-passing rowdy teenagers. Near the end of the bleachers sat a group of girls unaware that a boy was creeping up behind them with a cup of ice water. Anna knew it was coming before she could speak. The girls screamed and jumped out of the way just as spraying cool water came crashing down on them. It splashed and would have hit Anna if Nick hadn't wrapped his arms around her and pulled her away.

It all happened so fast Anna was left dizzy, her heart racing. She could feel the heat of Nick's body against hers and she couldn't deny how good it was to feel it again. Her eyes darted between his, filled with concern, to the top of the bleachers where Nora and Jameson sat unaware of the scene transpiring below them.

"You okay?" Nick asked, his breath on her cheek. She nodded, knowing she should pull away before others noticed, but not really wanting to.

"Oh, sorry!" The boy's voice broke through her thoughts. "Dude, is your wife okay?"

Nick lifted his head and Anna waited for him to correct the boy. "Watch what you're doing." Nick snapped at him. He let go of Anna but let his hand slide behind her back to lead her forward. The boy gave her an embarrassed smile. She nodded at him and walked on.

"Little shit," Nick said under his breath when they were down the bleachers. She stifled a laugh.

"I remember you boys pulling the same kind of stunts."

Nick feigned surprise. "I would never pour ice down someone's back when it's already cold outside."

Anna smiled at a couple walking toward them. Parents of one of the boys on the team. She said hello as they passed then turned back to Nick.

"Hmm, what about that time you threw Will Akins in the pool?"

He thought about it for a moment before recollection hit him. "That was different."

"It was the middle of December."

"Was it?" He raised his brows. When she looked at him, she could still see the boy in him. He resembled Ethan in so many ways, from their soft golden hair and deep-set eyes with a ring of honey in the middle. But what Nick had that Ethan had yet to conquer was humble confidence in himself that didn't reek of boastfulness like Jameson did. Nick was successful, running the town timber plant. He didn't have a white collar job like Jameson, and though he was worth more than the Hudsons, he never talked about it. Anna knew that it drove Jameson crazy with envy that his friend was financially more secure than him, even though he had the more prestigious title. But all Anna saw was the way in which he lived his life more simply. He and Nora didn't live in a grand mayor's mansion as she and Jameson did. Nick never needed that kind of life.

"He was a jerk," Nick responded with a crooked smile. "He was asking for it."

She loved the easy banter she could have with Nick, especially on the rare times they were alone. She used to be like this with Jameson. When had that changed? Was it the stress and burden of city council?

Was it before that? When they had J.R.? Somewhere, the pleasure of their relationship had turned to mere convenience that then got swallowed into detachment. When had they last had a meaningful conversation?

Was it the same for Nick and Nora? She had never told her friend about her displeasure with Jameson, mainly because admitting it to her would mean having to say it out loud. Nothing could have been done about it anyway. But what she feared even more than the truth of her own marriage was the happiness of Nick and Nora's.

Their lives were intertwined. The Hudsons and the Youngs melded together as one extended family. Even Nora and Anna had planned their first pregnancies together. They'd known they were either making lifelong best friends, or potential spouses.

And it had been perfect, at least for the first twelve years. Ethan and J.R. had played right into their roles. J.R., much like Jameson, was the leader of the pack. Even from a young age, he was charismatic and charming. People couldn't say no to him, even teachers. He'd convinced his Kindergarten class to donate all of their unwanted books to the literacy charity Anna was running. By first grade, he'd had the whole school involved, running a booth at recess outside the classroom. That year, the charity saw more donations than in the previous three years combined. He was a natural politician. And a positive influence on Ethan, who didn't have the natural, sociable ease that J.R. did. By second grade, the two of them were heading up fundraisers for the school, and even sitting in on PTA meetings.

And then Caleb happened.

Anna should have seen the warning signs. It had started with a lack of interest in school programs, an area that had previously been a passion of J.R.'s, and more of a focus on football. Anna could understand that. But then his demeanor had changed. His tone was sharper, his words more cutting at her. Was this a sign of adolescence or of a bad influence? She'd tried to talk to him about spending less time with Caleb, whom she didn't trust, only to have J.R. lash out at her instead. Jameson saw Caleb as a good ballplayer and someone who could teach J.R. to toughen up a bit. But that was what Anna saw to be the problem. Caleb was a little too tough.

She kept a steady eye on the boy, whose mother left him alone too often and whose father was never around. He was allowed to play those violent video games that Anna condemned, and a few times she had to tell the boys to turn off that explicit music about "killing bitches". J.R. seemed enthralled with Caleb, like Caleb was a cool older brother. And he was older, by a year, because he'd failed kindergarten.

And then things had taken a turn for the worse. It was the summer before their freshman year. J.R., Caleb, and Ethan were inseparable those three months. Anna was home more with the younger children, which meant the boys spent most of their days outside.

She had just finished putting Drew down for a nap when there was a knock on the door. She opened it, surprised to see Chief Tourney standing there, but even more shocked to see J.R. next to him. Her son was trembling, his eyes red from crying, snot running down his face. Her first instinct was to cradle him. She reached out and pulled him toward her. He was taller than she was by almost a foot, but when she held him he became her small child again.

"J.R., are you hurt?"

He shook his head as he wept in her arms. She was glad Jameson wasn't here to see this. He always thought J.R. cried too much.

"Mrs. Hudson," the chief started. "I found J.R. up on the hill above Beacon road."

"What were you doing all way down there?" Anna interrupted the chief. "And where are Ethan and Caleb?"

J.R. mumbled something into her shoulder she couldn't understand.

"J.R. was alone when I found him," Rex continued. "Anna, it appears he found some old truck tires on the hill and decided to roll them down to the road."

Her head jerked up. "Excuse me?"

Rex shoved his hands in his pockets. "I was driving and that's when I caught sight of something on the hill a good fifty yards in front of me. J.R.'s head was above a bush and I could see the tire in his hands. Want to tell her the rest, J.R.?"

Anna pulled back to look her blubbering son in the eye. "Is this true, J.R.?"

"It was all Caleb's idea!" he cried. He ran his tan arm over his nose, snot dripping from his skin. "He dared me to do it, told me I was a coward if I didn't."

Anna's face went hot. Of course, Caleb would be involved. J.R. would never think to do something like this alone. Anna closed her eyes. "Did the tire hit anything?"

"No, fortunately not," the chief answered. "When I saw it come down the hill picking up speed I blared my horn, stopping all traffic just as it went sailing by and into the ditch on the opposite side of the road."

"Oh, thank god." Anna breathed. She didn't want to think about what could have happened had that tire slammed into a passing vehicle.

"J.R., head up to your room."

She watched her son stagger up the stairs and waited until she heard the slam of his door before turning back to the chief.

"Thank you, Rex, for bringing him home safely. I'll see to it that he is accountable for what he did." She leaned forward. "But let's be clear. This is not J.R.'s doing. It's that boy Caleb Weston who needs a good scaring. I say you go over there right now and talk to him."

"Mrs. Hudson," the Chief said carefully. "That may be true. But it was J.R.'s hand on the tire. Not Caleb's."

Anna stiffened. He was wrong. J.R.'s hand may have been on the tire, but Anna knew it was Caleb who was egging him on, forcing him to do something he never wanted to do.

"Chief!" Nick called out, catching Anna off guard, bringing her out of her head and back to the football stadium.

The chief, dressed in regular jeans and a pullover Falcons sweatshirt, turned around at the sound of Nick's voice. He was standing close to Kate, Caleb's mom. After all these years, Anna had never gone out of her way to get to know Kate. It was more than just Anna's distaste for Kate's son. Anna's social circle tended to surround her with women who were just as invested in the wellbeing of their town as she was. That didn't fit for a single woman who worked odd hours as a nurse.

"Hey, Nick, Anna." He extended his hand to them. Kate nodded a hello to Anna's pressed smile.

"Rex, I was hoping to run into you," Nick said. He watched the way the chief's brows rose in surprise. Yes, they have known each other a lifetime, but he could count on one hand how many personal conversations they'd had.

Anna placed her hand on Nick's arm. "I'll catch up with you, I'm going to speak with Patty a moment. Hot cocoa?"

Nick nodded at her with a smile and a "Thank you" before turning back to Rex. "I wanted to ask you about your property."

"My property?" Rex raised a brow. "What about it?"

"The acreage behind your house. Do you realize you are sitting on a timber gold mine there?"

Rex scratched his head, wondering where this was going. "Well, sure. Back in the day, my grandfather logged off a near quarter of it I believe. But it's never been an area that interested me."

"No, I can't imagine it would," Nick said with a chuckle. "Running the safety of our town the way you do and raising a girl on your own."

"So how can I help you, Nick?"

"I want to buy it from you."

"Excuse me?"

"All of it," Nick continued. "The timber and the land around it."

"Nick, with all respect," Rex said stiffly. "My house is not for sale, nor the property it's on. It's been in my family's possession since the beginning of Timber Falls."

Nick placed a hand on Rex's shoulder. "Now I'm not saying this is an easy decision, Chief. But I'm asking you to think about it. That timber is just sitting there. Think of the way it could benefit the community. I'm willing to offer you a substantial amount." He patted his shoulder. "Think about it, will you?"

Rex knew his answer, but he nodded anyway. Nick gave him a squeeze on the shoulder and a smile before walking off.

"The nerve," Kate said when they were alone again. "He thinks he can just buy the whole town."

Rex let out a deep breath. "Well, he'll be sorely disappointed that he can't buy me."

The crowd in the stadium behind them began to scream. Kate turned to see the players enter the field for the second half of the game. "I need to get back to my seat. Will I see you tonight? Caleb's staying at J.R.'s."

Rex looked to the stands to see his daughter engrossed in conversation with her friends. She probably hadn't even noticed he was there.

"Yes, Lila's staying at Hannah's."

She smiled at him, and he wished right then that the game was over and they were alone in between her sheets. This thing between them, whatever it was, was new enough that neither of them was ready to share it with anyone. Especially their own kids. He wasn't sure when he would be ready. He hadn't dated much after Maura died. He never had the will or the time. But now that Lila was older and more independent, he decided it might be time to make his desires known.

He watched as the Falcons won the game in a clean sweep. The crowd went crazy, rushing the field. It was hard to see Lila in the stands, but when he did, she caught his eye and they smiled. He waited until she left with Hannah, and then he jumped in his car and raced to Kate's house.

CHAPTER 9

Third night gone

She had been down this road maybe two or three times already. At this point, Kate was driving in circles as she followed main roads and went down unknown streets. She had this town memorized by now. But she couldn't stop. She followed the old highway to neighboring towns, familiarizing herself with their dark corners and secret pathways. It caught her breath every time she drove by a sign in the window or a poster stapled to a tree of her son's face on it with the word "Missing." She was living on caffeine and 7-Eleven burritos. She only went home to change her clothes and check her machine, which she also often did from payphones.

She was grateful for the volunteers on foot or driving around in the pouring rain. The downpour made it difficult to trek the woods and surrounding mountain trails, which seemed almost pointless when what they were looking for was not a body but a car. If they could just find J.R.'s damn BMW then they would have some answers. Kate said his license plate number over and over to herself like a mantra, willing it to come to light.

What could possibly convince them to leave town without word to anyone? It made zero sense to Kate. Caleb was all she had—he knew that! He may have been smug and at times aloof, but he wasn't merciless, not with Kate, not ever.

She had never been jealous of Anna and Nora. Not for their tight friendship or seemingly perfect lives with their perfect husbands. But for once, she envied them now. They had each other through this. And Kate had no one.

It had just been the two of them for the last seven years, since the day she left her ass of a husband and got the hell out of Sacramento as fast as she could. Dave hardly tried to stop her, and never put up a fight for Caleb, which was a relief but also made her hurt for her son, knowing his father didn't even care if he left. Caleb acted like it didn't bother him, but she saw the way he lit up on the few occasions his father would call, usually with unfulfilled promises of visits or money for a train ride back to California.

After these calls Caleb would become distant; he knew it hurt her when his father called. And then when he would realize his father was full of shit, he would become angry and lash out at the only safety net he had, his mother.

His violence became prevalent after these calls. He never meant to lay a hand on her, she knew that. She never showed him her tears, or just how badly it killed her to watch him go through this. She would call Dave when Caleb wasn't home and scream her grievances at him, but it never helped. He would only do it again, and again.

Just as he had last week.

It had been over a year since Caleb had spoken to his father, and two years before that since he had seen him last. But when J.R.'s dad announced that the Huskies coach would be in town to watch them play, Caleb's first call after telling Kate was to his dad. Kate held back her tongue and secretly prayed that Dave would pull through with his promise to make it to that game.

It wasn't until the day of the game that she received the call that he couldn't get off work. She knew it was bullshit and told him so.

"You are nothing but a coward," she spat to him over the line.

"Now wait just a minute, Kathryn." He was the only person who called her by her full name. "What do you expect me to do? Maybe if you hadn't taken our son two states away, it wouldn't be so damn hard for me to come up and see him!"

"You have never put in the effort with that boy." She was pacing the kitchen with her cordless phone. Her blood was boiling. Of course, he couldn't bother to tell Caleb himself, which left her to break her son's heart again.

She hated Dave for many reasons. The numerous affairs, or slaps across her face that she lied about for Caleb's sake, but she downright despised him for the games he played with her son.

He was a cruel man. He had charmed her when she was young and naive and didn't know any better. She'd wanted to believe he had goodness in him, but it wasn't long before she understood his heart was as black as his hair. Only then she was six months pregnant with Caleb and had nowhere to go. Once Caleb was born, she was afraid to ever leave him home alone with Dave, frightened she would return to him either not being fed or changed properly all day, or worse. During their fights, he would threaten to take Caleb away from her, that they would go somewhere she would never be able to find them. When Caleb started school, she began taking classes and got her nursing degree. It took longer than it did for most, but the moment she had that degree in her hand, she bolted.

And now she would have to call him and tell them she had lost their son.

She pulled her car over at a gas station, lifted the hood of her coat over her head and ran through the rain to a pay phone. It rang six times before the answering machine picked up. She slammed the phone down and turned back to her car before changing her mind. She inserted her long distance phone card and dialed again. This time, he answered.

"Yeah."

"Dave," she said breathlessly. The windows of the booth were fogging up from the storm outside. She wiped away the steam with her forearm and watched as cars passed the street in front of her. She didn't want to miss anything.

"Kate?" He sounded groggy and annoyed. "What the hell. It's one in the morning."

"Has he called you?" For the first time in her life, she wished her son had reached out to his father. At least then she would know he was safe.

"Who? Caleb?"

She closed her eyes. "Of course, Caleb, Dave."

"Jesus, Kate, you woke me up. What'd you expect?"

She expected a whole hell of a lot more than he had ever been able to give.

"No." He sighed. "I mean, not for a couple of weeks anyway. How did the game go on Friday?"

A black car slowed as it came toward the gas station. She lifted on her tiptoes, trying to read the license plate through the weary glass. She opened the booth door and peered out. It wasn't J.R.'s BMW. She sighed in frustration. "So he hasn't tried to call you?"

"I already said no. What's going on, Kate?"

"He's gone," she said with a shake of her head. The tears pooled in her eyes again.

"Gone?" He sounded alert now. "What, did you two get in some kind of fight or something?"

"No!" she shouted. "No. Nothing like that. He went out with his friends Saturday night and never came home."

"He's been missing since Saturday?" he bellowed. Kate held the phone from her ear. "It's Tuesday night, or...or Wednesday morning and you're just now telling me?"

"Oh, what would you have done had I told you right away?" she snapped back. "Caught the first flight up here? Right."

He didn't answer the question. He sucked in a deep breath and murmured something she couldn't understand. She didn't know if it was toward her or whoever was in his bed beside him. "Well, what's the plan?"

"We've got volunteers searching. The chief of police and the sheriff have cops out looking for J.R.'s car. That was what they were all in when they went out Saturday night. But they still think it's a runaway case."

"Christ, Kate. What'd you think was going to happen? You've never kept a tight leash on that boy. He's always been allowed to do whatever he wants when it pleases him. And now he's just up and left."

"Screw you," she spat. She hated that she had to do this, communicate with a narcissist who didn't give a rat's ass that his son could be in danger.

"Call me when he shows up. I'll come on up there and show him who's boss. He'll think twice before running off like that again."

She slammed the phone down, feeling the pit in the middle of her stomach turning rock hard. She ran back to her car and started the engine, but the tears betrayed her and she couldn't stop the sobs. She wished she could drive to Rex's house, but she knew Lila would be home in bed, and Rex had kept his distance from her since the investigation started. She knew it was what he had to do. He couldn't treat her special when there were two other boys missing as well. And she knew this case was eating him alive; she could see it in in the daze of his eyes and the droop in his shoulders. She could smell the alcohol on his breath, and he had never been a big drinker. She appreciated his dedication to finding her son, which was why she didn't blame him for drinking.

She turned her car around and headed home. A drink was exactly what she needed right then as well. She kept the fridge stocked with beer for Caleb and the boys, and never touched it herself. But she snuck a secret stash of bourbon in her dresser drawer for an emergency. When she got home to her dark and empty house, she pulled it out and poured herself a glass. There seemed to be less in the bottle than the last time she had checked, but at this point, she could just have been seeing things. She was exhausted to the point of delirium, but she couldn't sleep. Her mind wouldn't let her rest. She took her glass and walked down the hall and stood outside of Caleb's room. Out of respect, she never opened this door. There were things in there that the mother of a teenage boy didn't need to see. But now, she felt it was necessary to see if he had left behind any clues.

She opened the door and was instantly hit by the smell of sweat-soaked football gear that had yet to make it to the laundry room. She cracked open the window, regardless of the rain, and let the fresh air cleanse the room. She looked around at the mess of clothes, books, and papers, wondering where in the world to start. She eyed his messy bed, homework laid out on top of the sheets. Was that a sign of someone running away? Gone mid-sentence of a history paper? She set it down and rummaged through the top of the dresser, taking out a photo of Avery in her cheer outfit intermixed with his socks and another of the two of them taken at last year's homecoming dance. His deodorant, cologne, and aftershave all sat there atop the dresser, undisturbed and forgotten about as if he planned to leave it all behind and never come back. She stifled a sob as she looked at her grown son's belongings and remembered the joy she had felt in designing his nursery. Winnie the Pooh theme. Dave had thought it was childish and girly, but he relented. Caleb had slept with his Winnie the Pooh blanket until he was five, when Dave threw it away, saying he was too old for it.

She saw no sign of him running away. Every bit of his room welcomed his return. She just couldn't believe he would leave it all behind. Leave her without a word.

She pushed aside the paperwork, mostly old homework assignments he had gotten less-than-stellar grades on, on top of his desk, looking for anything that could tell her where he was. A piece of paper folded origami-style caught her attention. She opened it and instantly recognized the soft, feminine penmanship to be Avery's. She was not one to snoop, and under any other circumstance should not have read it. But her eyes continued to scan the print until the tone of it changed and caught her attention.

I made an appointment at the clinic. I just wanted you to know I decided to go through with it. I don't want you to come with me. Don't worry, I haven't told anyone I'm pregnant.

Avery

Kate dropped the letter on the dresser as she clasped her hand over her mouth. Avery was pregnant. Did that explain Caleb's odd behavior the last week? She thought it had to do with Dave, but this... this was much bigger than his father not coming to his football game. Or maybe it was a combination of all of it.

What was she supposed to do with this information? Would she expose Avery's secret by showing it to Rex? Or would she pretend she never saw it? Could she possibly pretend not to know?

She quickly wrapped the note back in the shape she found it and tucked it back under the other papers. Tomorrow, Caleb would show up and she wouldn't have to make this decision. He would tell her when he was ready.

She closed the bedroom window and made sure everything looked the way it had when she'd entered, and then she quickly left his room, shutting the door behind her.

CHAPTER 10

Five weeks earlier

J.R. made his wish and blew out the eighteen candles on his birthday cake. He was the last of the boys to become an adult and he was glad to finally retire the minor title. Caleb was already nineteen, and Ethan had celebrated his eighteenth birthday in August. They often teased him, calling him the baby among them, though Grace and Avery were still seventeen.

Everyone clapped and cheered as he beamed, looking at the Hudson dining room and those who filled it. His mother cut the cake as Nora, who had always been like an aunt to him, passed out the china plates and silverware. His brother and sister fought over the largest piece as Avery and Grace both kindly declined the lavish chocolate drip cake.

"I'll take Avery's slice," Caleb offered with a wide grin as he held out his free hand. "We don't need it going to waste."

"That's awfully kind of you, Caleb," Anna smirked as she gave the slice to Ethan's dad.

Caleb shrugged. "Just always thinking of others."

Avery rolled her eyes in disgust, making it obvious they were once again off.

"What did you wish for?" Emma asked J.R. as he took a mouthful.

"Play for the Huskies," he answered between bites.

"You're not supposed to share what you wish for!" Grace exclaimed. "Now it won't happen."

"Oh, it's happening," Jameson said smugly with an elbow jab to Nick. "Don't you worry about that."

J.R. wrapped his arm around Grace's shoulder. "See, baby, our future is already set."

"All your hard work will pay off," Nick added. "Once the coach sees you all, there will be no question where you will be next year."

Ethan kept his mouth full of cake, not wanting to respond. He was grateful when Caleb checked the clock and said it was time for them to head out.

"We have a surprise night planned for our baby boy," Caleb jabbed.

J.R. shook his head. "Jesus, can't we be done with that now?"

Caleb wrapped his arm around J.R.'s neck. "Never! Now get in the car and don't ask questions."

"Ethan, will you be home tonight?" Nora asked as she stacked the empty chocolate dishes.

"No, I think we're coming back here," he answered, giving his mom a kiss on the cheek.

"Okay. Well, be safe, kids," she said, looking at each one of them.

"Give them a break, Nora." Jameson laughed. "It's Timber Falls, there's no trouble to get into." He placed a hand on her shoulder. "Let's go have a drink in the parlor."

The boys piled into Ethan's red Honda Civic with J.R. sitting shotgun while Grace drove steadily behind them with Avery in her midnight blue Acura.

They drove through town, up Oak Hill and down around the outskirts that parallel the neighboring city.

"Where the hell are you guys taking me?" J.R. asked.

"Don't worry about that and just enjoy yourself." Ethan smiled. "Caleb?"

"On it." He twisted off the top to a flask and handed it to J.R. "My gift to you, my friend."

J.R. took a sniff; this wasn't the beer they usually drank. "Thanks, man." He grinned. "Or should I thank your mom?"

"She won't even know it's missing," Caleb admitted. "I don't know why she buys it when she doesn't drink it."

J.R. took a swig, feeling the burn as the liquid slid down his throat. "Dude, that is disgusting."

Caleb took the flask and shot it back. "It'll finally grow some hair on your balls."

J.R. snatched it back. "Watch it, Weston, or I'll start that rumor up again about you only having one testicle."

Ethan laughed loudly, accepting the drink when J.R. offered. "God, that was the best prank. Everyone believed us."

"You know that only worked when no one had seen my balls before, right? I have too many witnesses now." He winked, taking his turn with the flask. "More than you can say, right, J.R.?"

J.R. scowled. It wasn't a secret among them that he was still a virgin. Grace had promised him that senior year she would finally be ready. He just hoped she didn't mean the end of senior year. He didn't know how much longer he could wait.

"What about you, Ethan?" Caleb asked, sitting forward so his head was between the two front seats. "You get some action this summer with that Brittany girl that you didn't tell us about?"

"Brianna," Ethan clarified again. "And I plead the fifth." He took another shot from the flask and passed it back to J.R..

"Puss." Caleb scowled. "Turn up here on the right."

"Where the hell are we?" J.R. asked. "Are we still in Timber Falls?"

Ethan flicked on his blinker, indicating to the girls behind him that they were turning. "Nope." He drove a half mile down the unknown road before turning into a gravel parking lot, sadly pretty spacious for a Saturday night. But that's why they were there, wasn't it?

"Mickey's Tavern?" J.R. read the crooked neon sign. "How the hell are we going to get in there?"

"You know I wouldn't let you down on your birthday," Caleb said smugly. He jumped out of the car, already feeling a slight buzz from the booze they'd drunk on the drive over. J.R. sat back in the seat, incredulous. He was used to following Caleb's wild ideas without question, but sneaking into a bar led his mind to getting caught by someone who recognized him and his father finding out and newspaper headlines, and then to the loss of his potential football career. What the hell was Caleb thinking?

Avery and Grace parked beside them, their faces showing hesitation and slight distaste for the dive bar. Slowly, they stepped out onto the rocky ground, their shoes sliding into muddy puddles from the earlier rain. Avery cursed as she felt the cold dampness seep into her socks. J.R. stepped out of the car, the last to make an entrance, the most resistant to the night's plan.

"Are you sure about this, Caleb?" Grace asked as she went to stand by J.R..

"This looks shady," Avery said, folding her arms over her chest. She settled up close to Grace. It wasn't too late for the two of them to bail. She wasn't even sure if she wanted to be around Caleb. And it wasn't just that he'd pushed her aside; that wasn't new, and wouldn't last. Caleb was used to getting his way. Those on the outside would say that J.R. called the shots. He was the quarterback, he was the mayor's kid, he was the best looking, with the best shot of future success. But what those of them knew on the inside, J.R. included, was that it was always Caleb. He was the ringleader, J.R.'s puppeteer. And Avery was secretly thrilled at that, knowing she had that edge over Grace. She was the one who was with the real king. But lately, Caleb's tactics and persuasions were quick to end in anger if he didn't get his way. It was a side they were not used to. It made them walk on eggshells around him, more fearful to question his motives.

Caleb glared at her before answering Grace. "Yes, I'm sure." His voice was tight, annoyed. "I did work for Mickey over the summer, mostly roofing and some things he needed help with on the business at his house. He tried to pay me, but I told him no, that when the time came I'd be calling in a favor." He smiled with pride and patted J.R. on the shoulder. "Happy birthday, buddy!"

"Caleb, I'm the mayor's son."

"He's not the mayor here," Caleb shot back. He scratched at his head, his annoyance turning into agitation. Why didn't they trust him? It was killing his buzz. "Look, Mickey said his patrons are easygoing and keep to themselves." He omitted the part where he was warned not to draw any attention to themselves. "No one here knows who you, or any of us, are."

J.R. started to grin the more Caleb spoke. Ethan, who was leaning over the top of the car, slapped the hood and said, "Alright, let's do this."

"That's the spirit we need." Caleb's grin was back, putting the rest of them at ease. He led them to the entrance of the old brick building with a lopsided, but newly remodeled, roof. The smoke escaped into the night air as they opened the door. Through the fog, they could see a wooden curved bar in front of them with torn black leather stools. Two men who sat on the far end looked up when the door opened, only to draw their attention back to their drink as soon as it closed. Several patrons sat scattered throughout the rectangular room, men and women smoking cigarettes and sipping on bottom shelf liquor, minding their own business. Caleb could see why Mickey had said they would go unnoticed here. This was not the typical crowd that followed small-town politics or high school football.

Mickey, a burly man whose exposed arms were covered in colorful tattoos, raised his hand to wave them over. His wiry beard was thick and charcoal colored, like it'd been drawn in. His eyes were small and narrowed, giving them a distasteful slant, but his smile was unnaturally warm. He shook hands with Caleb while eyeing his friends up and down. They clearly didn't belong there.

"Just this once, understood?" Mickey said sternly, speaking just loud enough over the jukebox for them to hear. "Crystal, keep their drinks full. Tab's on me." He retreated to a room in the back, shutting the door behind him.

Crystal, a blonde with bleached yellow hair that matched her crooked teeth, stepped forward, sizing them up. When Caleb smiled at her, her mouth twisted into a sultry grin and Avery thought she was going to throw up.

"What can I get you?" she said with a lick of her lips.

If life had been better to her, she may have been pretty, Grace thought. Though she would never say that out loud in front of Avery, who was clearly seething by the way Caleb was looking at the bartender.

"Let's just get a drink," Grace told Avery, ordering the two of them a screwdriver. The boys were already throwing back their first order of shots, and Grace knew if she could just get some liquor in her friend, they could have a really good night.

Caleb, a few shots in, sauntered over to the jukebox, flipping through the tunes until he found just the right one. When the song came over the speakers, Grace grabbed Avery's hand, her inhibition loosening after a couple of drinks. "Let's dance!"

They pushed empty tables aside and made themselves a dance floor, ignoring the annoyed glances and stares by the customers around them. They felt free and happy, unapologetic for their youth. The girls danced without care of others watching them, and soon, Caleb was beside them, followed by a usually constrained Ethan. The liquor ran through their blood and they let it take control of their limbs and their minds. J.R. sat back at the bar, watching his birthday night unfold with a grin. When Caleb moved in close behind Grace, J.R. slid off his seat and gently pushed his friend aside.

"Okay, man." J.R. laughed. "You're in my spot."

Caleb stumbled back with a chuckle. "I'll get us another drink."

Grace turned to face J.R., her eyes narrowed in on his, and he saw a look come over her that he'd never seen before. Her lips parted as she danced closer to him. He had always thought Grace was beautiful, but the way she moved with her hips aligned with his and her breasts pressed against his chest made her so damn hot. His mood quickly shifted and he felt the blood pool in his groin as he wondered if tonight could actually be the night. She grinded against him as she danced, and he couldn't help but let out a moan in her ear. He was ready to get out of there if she was. Before he could make the move, she was ripped from his arms.

"What the—" He opened his eyes to see Avery grasping on to Grace, Avery's face twisted into an ugly grimace. Was she crying? Only one person could get a reaction out of her like that. J.R. looked toward the bar to see Caleb leaning up against the cracked wooden ledge with the bartender between his legs. She was doing a terrible job of trying to push him off her as he kissed at her. She laughed and turned her head and swatted at his hand on her hip, but didn't move from his grasp. Instead, she whispered in his ear, and J.R. and anyone looking on could tell just what she was offering.

"Get me out of here, now," Avery snapped at Grace.

Grace looked up at J.R. with an apologetic frown. She knew she didn't have a choice. *That fucking Caleb*, J.R. thought. J.R. was so pissed he let Grace go without a goodbye, though she tried to kiss him.

When the door shut behind them, J.R. turned to give Caleb a piece of his mind, only to find his friend pushing the bartender up against the bar, his hand around her throat as he kissed her. J.R. noticed the way Crystal's demeanor changed once she realized something he and his friends had always known: there was no controlling Caleb. She squirmed in his hold to no avail. Caleb laughed as she struggled.

"Let me go!" she choked out, pushing her arms against him. He was double her weight and towered over her.

J.R. was on him, grabbing his arm and pulling him off her. "Come on, buddy," he coached, not showing his alarm. Caleb flipped a switch and dropped his hand, jumping onto the bar counter, beer in hand. He lifted his drink to J.R., gesturing to him in a toast. "Ladies and gentlemen!" he shouted, attracting the attention of the annoyed audience.

Crystal pushed past J.R., gripping her neck as she raced to the back room.

"I just want to say Happy Birthday to the best friend a guy could ask for. This guy, right here," Caleb said, pointing a finger at J.R., his beer splashing from the glass. "This guy right here, you don't even know. He'd do anything for you."

"Damn," Ethan whispered as he approached J.R. They looked grief-stricken at the crowd where men much older and rougher than them were quickly losing their patience with Caleb's antics.

J.R. stepped forward, his buzz gone. "Thanks, buddy," he said calmly. "Come on down now."

Caleb shook his head. "You've always been there for me, man. Even when we were kids. My dad... and you had your dad." He was spinning, not making sense. He took a drink of beer and then remembered what he was standing up there for. "Let's all sing happy birthday to J.R.! Happy birthday..." he started to sing alone in an uneven tone.

A burly man standing behind J.R. stood up, taking the cigarette out of his mouth. "You kids have had enough, it's time for you to go home."

Caleb stumbled back. "Who the hell are you? I'll go when I'm ready to go."

Before J.R. and Ethan could speak up, the man took a step toward Caleb. Though he was not as statuesque as Caleb, he probably had him in weight. "The fuck you say?"

He was joined by his friend, though it was clear to Ethan and J.R. that the rest of the bar patrons had his back. They were in deep water and clearly out of their element. Caleb jumped down from the counter, creating a large thud that shook the glasses on top of the bar. A look of content crossed his face. Ethan realized to his dismay that Caleb was actually enjoying this.

"I said, I'll go when I'm ready to go, old man."

The second man to stand took a long drag of his cigarette. His battered jean jacket was rolled up to his elbows, exposing scars, deep and rugged. He pulled his other hand out of his pocket and rested it on the table. It was when he lifted his palm Ethan caught a glance of the shiny blade beneath it. "You better walk out now, son, before you get yourself into something your daddy can't get you out of."

The gleam in Caleb's eye swiftly turned to fury at the mention of his father. Ethan and J.R. caught him by the arm just as he lunged forward at the man. The back door swung open, exposing a frightened Crystal, trailing behind an enraged Mickey. He took one look at the chaos of his bar before his eyes fell on Caleb. He was foaming from the mouth that he had let this piece of trash minor come on in and risk his business and reputation.

As he rounded the corner, his hand came up and as Caleb turned to look at him, he realized he was staring down the barrel of a gun. He burst into a round of hysterical laughter. J.R. and Ethan went white, frozen in fear from what their friend had gotten them into.

"Get the fuck out of my bar," Mickey said, with eerie calm. "And don't ever think about stepping foot in here again."

J.R. and Ethan each gripped an arm on Caleb's side and all but pulled him to the front door. His laughter crippling his steps all the way to the car. They threw his ass in the back seat, both worked up in a sweat that was more from fear than the weight of their friend.

"What the hell's the matter with you?" Ethan screamed at him from the driver seat. His hands were shaking as he started the car.

Caleb was doubled over in the back seat, trying to calm his giggles. J.R. rolled down the window as Ethan screeched out of the gravel parking lot; he needed fresh air to cease the bile rising in his throat.

"Oh, lighten up, Deadman," Caleb chuckled. "Nothing but a little excitement."

"You crossed the line," J.R. said, trying to remain calm. His fingers were still trembling and he was embarrassed to show his cowardice to his fearless friend.

"Relax, quarterback. No one got hurt." Caleb's laughter turned bitter when he realized he was alone in the fun. "I promised you a good time and I delivered." He leaned forward and shook J.R. by the shoulders. "Can't say you won't forget this night, right?"

Neither Ethan nor J.R. could answer.

Ethan hit the pedal. He just wanted to get home. Fuck staying at J.R.'s tonight, he wanted away from Caleb.

"Someone's in a hurry," Caleb commented, the chuckle back in his voice as he flung against the side of the car with the sharp turn on the dark corner. They were heading back to Timber Falls, back to their own territory, and Ethan couldn't get there fast enough.

It was after one in the morning and the roads were desolate. As they reached their town, Ethan stepped on the gas, running red lights and flying through stop signs. J.R. kept his mouth shut while Caleb's hysterical laughter was back in full throttle. Ethan thought if he didn't get Caleb out of his car soon, Ethan would jump out and hit him. He was so distracted by this thinking that he missed the headlight glare pulling out of the vacant grocery lot until the red and blue lights started swirling and screaming at him.

"Shit," J.R. cursed. "Shit, shit, shit."

Ethan automatically slammed on his brakes. He knew he was screwed. He pulled into the next lot and parked, the chief's car right behind him.

"It's Tourney," Caleb said in a disgusted tone. "He's a puss, we'll be fine."

"Do us all a favor, Weston, and shut the fuck up," Ethan snapped. He watched from his rearview mirror as the chief stepped out of his car and walked his way. The chief knew who'd he pulled over; That's the thing about a small town—the chief knew everyone's cars.

Ethan rolled down the window as the chief leaned down, looking worn and tired like he'd just been awakened. What the boys didn't know was that that wasn't far from the truth. Rex wasn't usually out prowling the streets at this hour, but he'd been called in by an officer who suspected some unusual activity behind the grocery outlet. Turned out to be a false alarm.

"Ethan Young," he greeted curtly. He could smell the booze reeking off of them. He looked to J.R. Hudson whose head was down, eyes glued on his lap, and to Caleb Weston, who sat back with a superior grin and his arms crossed over his chest. "I need you out of the car."

Ethan's eyes shot up to him. "What? What for?"

"I think you know exactly what for, all of you. Now."

J.R. was cursing under his breath again while Caleb muttered something about this being bullshit and an inconvenience. But still, they stumbled out, shutting the doors behind them and lining up in a row, leaning against the car.

"How much have you all had to drink tonight?" the chief asked, studying each of them and knowing the clear answer was a hell of a lot more than they could handle.

"Who says we've been drinking?" Caleb scoffed.

Rex took two steps toward the towering football player. "I'd be happy to give you a breathalyzer test. However, I will warn you that if that number comes back at what I think it could be, things could get a lot harder for you."

Rex turned back to Ethan. He could see the way the boy trembled, and it pleased him. He needed a good scare, they all did. "What the hell were you thinking getting behind the wheel tonight?" he scolded. "Do you know the ramifications of your actions could be death, jail time, and loss of a football career?"

Ethan closed his eyes as J.R. dropped to his knees. It took the chief by surprise. "Please, please don't write us up. If I get anything on my record it's over. Everything I've ever worked for is gone." He was blubbering now, the night taking over his emotions. "I swear it, we will never do it again," he continued. His knees dug into the pavement, but his body was numb. He clasped his hands in prayer as he begged to the chief. "We will stay out of trouble, I swear."

The chief looked down at the sobbing quarterback. He knew he had more than just a few rebel teens on his hands. He had the whole town's reputation. If he followed protocol, he would be shunned and shamed as the man who had taken away the promising career of the mayor's son.

Maybe just a good scare was all they needed.

"Get in my car," he commanded, walking away from them. "I'll drive you home."

Ethan lent J.R. a hand as he quickly got up, wiping the snot from his nose. Caleb turned his back and walked to the chief's car without a word. They slid into the back seat as J.R. directed the chief to take them back to his place. Ethan would be stuck with them for the rest of the night.

"I'll have a word with the Mayor first," the chief said through the silence of the dark car as he drove. "Then I'll speak with the Youngs and Ms. Weston tomorrow."

Ethan moaned. He had hoped to get off the hook completely.

"That should be pretty easy." Caleb met the chief's eye in the rearview mirror. "A little foreplay talk with my mom?" Rex's eyes narrowed. "Oh, did you not know I knew you came to my house when I'm not there? I didn't know you two wanted it to be a secret."

"What are you talking about, Caleb?" Ethan asked, squeezed between the two football players.

Caleb kept his eyes on the chief, who had turned his attention back to the road. He wasn't going to let Caleb Weston, a nineteen-year-old kid, intimidate him.

"Nothing." Caleb smiled.

Fortunately for all, it was a short drive to the Mayor's house. Rex wordlessly stepped from his car and took the long stairway up to the grand entrance of where J.R. called home. The boys watched from the back seat as he rang the doorbell and then waited as lights eventually turned on from inside. It was Jameson, dressed in navy pajama pants and a white tee shirt, who first saw the chief. Once he spotted his son in the back of the police car, he ushered Anna back to bed.

"Chief?" He was alert through his drowsiness. Relief swept through him knowing the chief wasn't there to report his son injured or worse, but still baffled as to why his son was in the back of his car.

"Mayor," Rex started. "I'm sorry to wake you at this hour." He motioned to the boys. "I pulled over Ethan Young for driving fifty miles over the speed limit, while also running multiple red lights."

The mayor, not amused, crossed his arms over his chest. "And what does this have to do with me? And J.R.?"

"They are all drunk."

The mayor huffed. He looked past the chief to see his son sitting shamefully, afraid to meet his father's eye.

"Thank you, Chief, for bringing this to my attention, *discreetly.*" He patted him on the shoulder as if to dismiss him and stepped back into his foyer. "Boys were out celebrating tonight. Send them in and I'll take care of it from here."

"With all respect, sir," the chief continued, baffled by the mayor's response. "This is very serious. I should arrest Ethan Young, and have J.R. and Caleb written up for drinking as minors. The significance of what could have happened if I hadn't stopped them. What if someone else was on the road? I hope you take this into consideration when you apply reprimands and punish—"

The mayor spun on his heels. "I said thank you, Chief. Now, if you would please leave it to me on how to handle my son. You did your job, and I will do mine."

Rex watched as Jameson stomped his way back up the stairs to his bedroom before opening the back passenger door to let the three boys out. Maybe it was guilt from not doing his job correctly, or the way the mayor had belittled him, or maybe it was the smirk on Caleb Weston's face as he drove away that made him regret not throwing their asses in a jail cell. But who was he kidding? If anything happened to those boys, the town would only point one finger, and it would be at him.

CHAPTER 11
Fourth day gone

The halls buzzed with a low hum of speculation and gossip at Timber Falls High. Heads together, whispers in ears, tears on shoulders. It was a new air among them. Who were they without their leaders?

Rex pressed between them, walking the hall after a visit with the coach and principal. They didn't stop their chatter in his presence. Instead, they pretended that he didn't exist. He heard murmurs of runaways, Mexico and Canada, and what about Friday night's football game? They would be back for that, wouldn't they? Practice resumed last night, but with the last game of the season set for Friday night, the idea of going on without their star players seemed unfathomable. There was anger in the halls, as some accused them of running away, all for losing a game. Weakness, cowardice, they said, even selfishness.

Rex let all of these comments roll off of him. They did him no good. He spotted Grace and Avery leaning against the lockers, looking glum and uncharacteristically dull. He caught Grace's eyes, red-rimmed and glossy. He had planned to keep walking, but she waved him over.

"Chief," Grace cried out. She looked hopeful as he approached. "Is there anything new?"

"Sorry, Grace, I wish I could tell you there was."

Avery looked up then, and he was not surprised to see her eyes glazed over in tears, but her skin was ashen and pale. She looked ill, and by the way she gripped at her stomach, he thought he was pretty spot on. She shook her head and pushed past him, leaving him and Grace watching her rush to the bathroom.

"She okay?" he asked.

Grace shrugged her shoulders. "I don't know."

He eyed J.R.'s long-time girlfriend, wondering what must be going on in her head at a time like this. "How are you holding up, Grace?"

She turned her gaze to him. "It doesn't feel right being at school. Like, I hate not being out there looking for them too, but my dad said I couldn't skip anymore."

She ran a hand through her long dark curls, sweeping them over one shoulder. "My mind is going crazy thinking about where J.R. could be. Do you know that this is the longest we've ever gone without speaking, like ever?" Her lip quivered, but she took in a shaky breath to keep from crying. "I keep thinking back to the last time I talked to him, and if I said something that would make him, you know... Like if this was his way of leaving me."

Rex rested a hand on his shoulder. He felt sorry for her, he really did. She lived blindly in her own world. "No, Grace. I don't think this was J.R. breaking up with you."

"You don't know." She used the sleeve of her sweater to wipe at the tears that slipped down her cheek.

He couldn't contest that. He looked up from her to see his daughter slip between the crowd of students. Her head was down, staring at the ground. Hannah and Olivia were by her side, speaking urgently to each other. He wished he could walk over and give her a hug, but he wouldn't dare.

"Did you talk to Lila?" Grace's voice broke through his thoughts. She must have seen him watching her.

The question surprised him, and then he remembered their conversations at the Hudson house.

"You know, about her and Ethan. Does she know anything?" She sounded so hopeful. "You know, maybe he told her where they were going or something."

"She hadn't spoken to him in a while."

"Oh, okay." She sounded defeated. The buzz of the class bell rang through the hall and students picked up their speed as not to be late for class. "Well, I guess I have to go," she said. "Thanks, Chief."

For what, he wasn't sure. But he gave her a gentle smile and nod. She met up with Avery, who exited the bathroom, and the two of them disappeared among the crowd. He followed behind several feet, walked past the classrooms, and left through the back door.

"Hey, Chief!"

He turned to see two boys—juniors, he recalled—on the wrestling team, hurrying toward him.

"Chase, Jason," he greeted. Chase Everett was a stocky, tough kid and captain of the wrestling team. Up until last year, the wrestling team had been more or less a joke at Timber Falls, but Chase brought honor and prestige back to the sport and made a pretty decent name for himself. Rumor had it that big league colleges had their eye on him. Jason Sanborn was a product of family heritage in this town, like Rex himself. Rex had known Jason's parents back when they were all kids together.

"What can I do for you boys?"

They gave each other a hesitant glance before Chase said, "We have some info we thought you'd like."

Rex raised a brow. "Is that so?" He could feel their resistance and feared he would lose them if he didn't act fast. "Why don't we head to the office, or would you prefer to come down to the station with me?"

Jason shook his head wildly. "No, we don't want anyone to know we're talking. If it got back to them..."

The repercussions of being a narc. Rex had seen that enough times to know.

"Can we just talk here, like behind the building or something?" Chase said.

"Of course." Rex led them down an alley between class buildings. The day was cool but clear. They had a break from the rain, but not the crisp wind. Rex was bundled in a jacket while the boys, typical teens, wore athletic shorts and a sweatshirt. Maybe it was all the raging hormones Rex didn't miss.

When they were in the clear, Rex turned to them and said, "I want you to know that if you prefer I can keep this anonymous. No need to worry about anything getting out. And I appreciate you boys coming forward with any tip you have."

"I don't know if it's really like a tip," Chase said. "Just something weird, I guess."

"They were just acting really strange," Jason added. His eyes darted past Rex as voices echoed down the alleyway. They waited a moment for whoever was there to pass before Rex continued.

"Strange how?" The chief pulled out his pad of paper to take notes.

"Like fighting," Jason said. "We were in the locker room after practice, and I guess they just finished with practice, too."

"When was this?" Rex asked as his pen worked the page.

"Last week, maybe like Tuesday?" Jason said.

"Mmhmm." Rex thought back to just over a week ago, how that now seemed like a lifetime ago. "What were they fighting about?"

"It was hard to tell but, I heard Ethan the most. He was yelling, even though Caleb was telling him to keep it down."

"J.R. said they needed to get out of there," Chase added. "I thought they meant the gym, but then Caleb said, 'What about the Huskies?' And Ethan was all, 'Screw the Huskies.' And Caleb was telling them they were all over-reacting and to calm down. That's when Ethan yelled that he didn't want anything to do with Caleb anymore and that if J.R. can't see that then he didn't want anything to do with him either."

Rex wrote as fast as he could, catching the boys word for word. "Then what happened?"

"Then that was it." Chase shrugged. "Caleb stormed out, slamming the door behind him."

"Was anyone else in the locker room?" Rex asked.

Jason shook his head. "No, I think they thought they were alone. They didn't hear us come in."

Rex finished up his notes. "Thank you, boys, for coming forward. Is there anything else you can think of?"

"Well." Jason started, looking at Chase before answering. "It's just a rumor I think, but someone said they saw Ethan fighting with his dad on the field a couple weeks ago. I don't know if that helps or even matters but again, just strange. Like why fight at practice? Why not at home or something?"

Rex nodded as he wrote, *Nick, Ethan, fight after practice.* He would have to ask Nick about this.

"It's just so weird, you know," Chase said. "They're such cool guys, but they've been, like, kinda jumpy and almost paranoid when you see them in the halls. And then you have that shit show on Friday night... Sorry, Chief," Chase said, catching himself swearing. Rex shook his head. "You know, you were there for that game."

Rex nodded.

"You guys did the right thing coming to me with any information that could lead to finding the boys, or possibly a reason for why they left. Thank you."

They nodded, seeming relieved to have that off their chests.

"Don't you boys have a class to get to?"

"Free period." Jason smiled.

"Okay." He placed a hand on each of their shoulders. "Good job, guys. Call me down at the station if anything new comes up."

He walked out of the alley first as not to be seen with them. He tossed his pad and pen on the seat of his cruiser and turned on the engine. He was glad the students had come to him anonymously. He didn't need vicious rumors being spread about what the boys could have been fighting about. And they were right—what had Nick been doing accosting Ethan at the football field? What couldn't wait until they got home? Or, was it something that couldn't be said at home? What did Nick Young know that he wasn't sharing?

He pulled into the station, surprised to see the small blue Toyota sedan he knew so well parked near the entrance. He greeted the dispatcher at the front desk, who motioned to him there was someone waiting in his office. He nodded a thank-you and opened the door to his box of an office. The blinds were drawn, making the room darker than usual. She sat there, her back turned away from him until he closed the door behind him. That's when she stood.

"Kate," he murmured. He hadn't realized just how much he missed her until she was standing so vulnerable beside him. He pulled her to him and let her release her tears on his shoulder. He wanted to go back to before when it was just the two of them and there was hope for a future. But that was all behind them. He would hold her now, kiss the side of her cheek where the tears fell, but that was all that he could give. She felt his resistance and pulled away.

"I'm sorry." She sighed. "I didn't mean to dump that on you."

"Kate." He took her hand. "Please, don't apologize."

She released his hand and slumped back in the chair. She looked like hell, and not in a way that wasn't appealing, but in a way that made him wonder if she was even sleeping. He poured her a cup of coffee—one cream, two sugars, the way she liked it—and she took it appreciatively.

"You know, I used to love the nights when Caleb would stay at J.R.'s and I would come home from work and the house was actually quiet. The nights you weren't there, I mean," she corrects herself. "I would read or watch a movie without having to fight for the TV, and I used to tell myself to get used to this because soon he would be out of the house and at college and it would just be me, alone, most nights. It didn't seem so bad..." A sob caught in her throat. She looked up to him. "I can't go home at night, not anymore. The silence is killing me, Rex."

He leaned his legs against the desk in front of her and ran a hand through his hair as he thought of all of the things he wanted to say to her but couldn't. He couldn't bring her home with him and he couldn't stay with her. And he knew that wasn't what she was asking of him. She just wanted her son back.

He set his coffee down on the desk and knelt before her, his hands landing on her knees. "You can't give up hope, Kate. We will find him."

She stared at him a moment before nodding. "I know." She paused, looking down at her coffee before meeting his eyes again. "I think I know why he left."

Rex raised a brow. "You do?"

"I found a note in his room." She took a deep breath. "Rex, Avery's pregnant."

He wobbled on his feet before standing back up. He thought back to Avery clutching her stomach and looking sick at school early that day.

"Are you sure?"

"Pretty sure." She nodded. "I found a note she wrote him about it, sounds like they must have gotten in a fight about it."

"And you think that would make him take off?" He thought back to the stories Kate had shared about Caleb's deadbeat dad and could see why Kate would rush to think her son would respond accordingly. It's what he knew to do. Dads bail. "But what about J.R. and Ethan?"

She shrugged as though this thought had just occurred to her. She felt guilty admitting that she was so focused on her own son that sometimes she forgot about the other boys. These same boys who had saved her son. She knew Caleb was different from them. That before he met them he had been going down a road of destruction. She'd never told Rex about the time he was suspended from school in the sixth grade for bullying, or when she had caught him dissecting a dead cat in their backyard when he was ten. She was terrified of him, of what he was capable of. She knew it was his father's influence. She feared he'd inherited Dave's psychopathic genes. But she kept it to herself. She'd moved to Timber Falls to give him a fresh start, and it was through the help of J.R. and Ethan that, for the most part, Caleb stayed on a straight path.

"Maybe they were helping him sort it out or talk him through it." She wasn't sure, and neither was he. "Rex, you know they were inseparable. What one does they all do."

What one does they all do.

That struck a chord with him. It circled in his head like a chorus, around and around until it made him dizzy.

He straightened up and rounded the desk until he found his chair and sat down across from her. Avery, pregnant. It wasn't a surprise, really. But what was shocking was the timing of her pregnancy. He felt the bile turn in his stomach, aching to climb up his throat. He pushed it back down, taking a swig of his coffee that now tasted bitter in his mouth. He will have to have a discussion with Avery, and now thinking of it, he wondered if Grace knew or if this secret was strictly between Avery and Caleb.

"Chief!"

Rex jumped in his seat as the door to his office swung open with such force he felt the wind on his face. Kate, just as shocked as Rex, swore as she spilled coffee on her jeans.

Officer Maloney hung in the door frame, his eyes wild and frenzied, his hair dripping with sweat. Rex could see it in his expression before he even uttered the words. And he wished to god Kate would disappear and wasn't sitting in his office right now. But she was, and when Maloney spoke the words, it was her cry he heard over the chaos in his head.

"We found J.R.'s car."

CHAPTER 12

Five weeks earlier

C aleb knew the rumors that were said about him. Some he had even started himself. Like when he'd first come to Timber Falls in the seventh grade and told Micah Dunn how he'd beaten up a senior in high school and ended up in Juvie for a month. It had spread like wildfire.

Everyone eyed him carefully as they passed him in the hall, wondering if it could be true. He walked with his head high, a smirk on his face and gleam in his eye. No one would mess with him, not a student, a teacher or his old man.

It was J.R. who cornered him in the locker room one day after P.E. with that little apostle, Ethan, and actually had the nerve to ask him if the rumor was true.

"Did you really do that?" J.R. was the man on campus, Caleb was quick to learn. If Caleb was here to impress anyone, it would be him. And here was J.R., looking at him as though he was a god. "Was he a big guy?"

Caleb seemed unfazed. "Biggest guy in school."

"Why?" Ethan asked. Caleb could see the skepticism written all over his face. "What'd he do?"

Caleb shrugged. "He was messing around with this younger kid at the skate park we all hung out at. I told him to knock it off or else. He didn't believe me, so I had to show him."

What he didn't say was that he was the one kicking around a young kid, and it was the older guy who pulled him off and gave him a black eye. Told him not to show his face around there anymore.

J.R.'s eyes widened. He had never met anyone like Caleb. Caleb was the kind of guy you wanted on your side, not against it. "Have you thought about playing football?"

No one questioned his motives after that, and when new rumors were spread about him, he never bothered to correct them whether they were true or not.

But standing in the hall that Monday after J.R.'s eighteenth birthday, he knew he had to do damage control. For the first time, he saw doubt in J.R., like he didn't know who Caleb was. And J.R. was the closest to knowing who he really was. He'd seen the times Caleb would slip and show his weaknesses, like when his dad bailed on him, or how the nights he would be left alone with only his deranged mind while his mom worked all hours of the night affected him. He never shared that with Avery or Ethan, but J.R. had a way of bringing out his truth. He loved and hated his friend for that. He always knew he'd never fully won Ethan over, but he was too shackled to J.R.'s ass to question Caleb's motives.

And then there was Avery, who wouldn't even look at him as she passed him in the hall. Disgust clear on her face as she tossed her head away from him. They both knew he always fucked around, that she wasn't the only one, but this was the first time he had blatantly shoved it in her face. The bartender wasn't even hot! What had he been thinking?

He reached out for her as she slid by him, wrapping his large arm around her tiny shoulder and pulling her to him. She tried to resist, but her defiance to him was always weak. They both knew that.

"Let me go, Caleb." She pushed her hands against him. But one thing they both knew was Caleb never took no for an answer.

He turned her so her back was against the wall, pinning her with the strength of his body. "Come on, baby. You know I was just messing around. Nothing happened between me and the girl."

She glared up at him. "Because you got kicked out of the bar!"

He rolled his eyes. "They were a bunch of losers." He laid a soft hand on her cheek. "I would have never gone home with her, swear. I just got wasted and lost a little control, that's all. And when I went looking for you, you'd left. You know I went looking for you, right?"

She softened a little in her stance. "No."

"Come on," he groaned. "You can't stay mad at me. Let me make it up to you, okay?" She cocked a brow at him and he couldn't help but smile. Her cute little angry face was just a farce and he knew it. Avery could never really stay mad at him. "Come over after practice. My mom's working tonight and we'll have the house to ourselves." He could tell she wasn't yet sold on the idea of a hook-up night, so he added, "I'll make us dinner."

She was taken aback by that. She met his eyes now and a small smile crept over her strawberry pink lips. "You'd do that?"

"Of course." He slid his hands around her waist and pulled her to him. This time, she didn't resist. Her shirt slid up over her belly and he could feel the soft warmth of her skin on his hands. He sweetened the deal by covering her mouth with his, and slowly he felt her melt into him. She loved when he kissed her in public.

"Avery?"

The voice was sharp and loathing. They knew it was Grace before they pulled from each other's embrace to see her standing beside J.R. and Ethan, arms folded stiffly across her chest. Caleb sighed. Apparently, Grace would need some convincing as well.

"Let's get to math." Grace turned on her heels and stomped away as Avery gave Caleb an apologetic smile.

"See you tonight," he whispered in her ear. And he would. And after ordering pizza, he would show her just how much she needed him and how much he owned her.

"That didn't last long," Ethan huffed. He was still sour over Saturday night. He hadn't waited for the other boys to wake on Sunday before bailing and walking home, not answering calls for the day.

"It never does," Caleb smirked. He pushed off the wall and followed in step with his friends to history. "Dude, your dad saved our asses!" He slapped J.R. on the shoulder. "Things got a little out of control Saturday night, but I did deliver, didn't I?"

J.R. stopped in his tracks. "What the hell are you talking about? It was a disaster, and thanks to you we almost ended up in jail."

Caleb threw his head back and laughed. "Listen to you. *Almost* ended up in jail. Who else gets to have that story for their big eighteen? Huh? I told you I would give you a night to remember."

"That's fucked up, Caleb," Ethan spat at him. "You know what could have happened."

Caleb grinned at Ethan. "It was you driving the car all crazy that got Chief Puss all on our asses."

He swung his arms around each of his friends' shoulders. "Come on! Think about it. Ten years from now, are we going to be saying that's the night we regret? Or will it be the wild night we *got away* with?" He looked at J.R., who was starting to sway in Caleb's direction. "You know you had fun. At least for most of it."

J.R. looked at the ground and cracked a smile. "I guess it was pretty wild. Nothing we've done before, for sure." He didn't share that what he was most pissed about was how close he had gotten to Grace before Caleb fucked up his chance of finally getting laid that night. From the sound of disappointment in Grace's voice over the phone last night, he thought she felt the same way. When he'd asked if he could sneak over tonight, she hadn't hesitated to say yes.

Caleb squeezed his shoulder then turned to Ethan who was less amused. "Come on, Deadman. You know you were loving letting loose a little, for as much as you can let loose." He tightened his grip on Ethan's shoulder and gave it a little shake. "It's a good look on you."

"Alright, knock it off," Ethan said, shifting out of Caleb's grip. "You're right, maybe I am overreacting a little." He shrugged, tightening his Falcons baseball hat down over his forehead. "Nothing bad happened. Chief Tourney could have taken us in but instead was super cool and took us home."

J.R. gave Caleb a crooked smile. "Never thought I'd be in the back of a police car."

Caleb laughed loudly. "Stick with me and it won't be your last."

Ethan jabbed him in the ribs but laughed with him. "Man, your dad was awesome about it, J.R. My dad would never be that cool. And he swears he's not gonna tell?"

J.R. nodded. "He didn't see the point in us getting in trouble." But that was far from the truth. What Jameson didn't want was the dishonor that came with his son cavorting around town and breaking the law.

J.R. had known it the moment he woke, even with the killer hangover clouding his head. As soon as Caleb was out the door, Jameson had laid into him, yelling about what an ass J.R. had made him look like in front of the chief of police.

"How dare you humiliate me," Jameson raged. "You are my son. What you do reflects on me. Do you have no care for how you're perceived in this town? You have a reputation to uphold! You are the example. This was all Caleb's idea, wasn't it? I don't know why you ever befriended him in the first place. He's not your stray cat, J.R. He is not your golden ticket. You have always been his."

"That's not fair," J.R. shot back. Sure, he was pissed at Caleb right now, but he also knew that Caleb would never intentionally sabotage him.

"What if it hadn't been Tourney who found you? What if it was some other hard-nosed cop who didn't give a shit about your football career? What if word got back to the Huskies Coach? What then? You think anyone would want you? No one wants a fuck-up, J.R."

"I am not a fuck-up," J.R. spat. He had never spoken back to his father this way before. Maybe it was the booze still in his system, or maybe he was just done staying silent. "I am sick and tired of living under your shadow, and I can't wait to get out of this town so I don't have to be reminded whose son I am every damn day."

Jameson raised his hand to strike his son, only to be stopped by the cries of his wife as she raced into the room.

"Enough!" she screamed, jumping between them. Though J.R. resembled his father in looks and stature, it was his mother he took after the most. Jameson hated this about his son. Both of them so meager and cowardly, allowing others to make up their minds for them rather than being true leaders like Jameson was. He should have felt pleased to see them both standing up to him, finally for once speaking their mind. But instead, he only felt revulsion.

Jameson stood there, his hand still in the air. J.R.'s eyes widened in fear as he realized how close his father came to hitting him.

"Get out of my sight," Jameson seethed, dropping his hand to his thigh. J.R. spun on his heels and bolted up the stairs to his room. He wanted as far away from his father as he could get. And if he just kept his head down and do what needed to be done on the field, then that time would soon come.

"What?" Jameson sneered at his wife's anguished face. "You going to go coddle him now? He's not a kid anymore, Anna. Stop babying him."

She was at a loss for words over her husband's animosity. For the first time, she felt she was being asked to choose between him and J.R. If she left now to check on her son, she would lose any respect her husband had left for her. But what kind of mother lets her husband get away with almost striking her child? What would have happened if she hadn't been there?

"Are you crying?" he exclaimed. "Jesus, Anna." He pushed past her, leaving her alone in the room as he slammed the door to his office.

It was past eleven on Monday night when J.R. rolled his car to a stop, headlights off, just down the street from Grace's house. He was able to leave home unnoticed as his father still wasn't speaking to him. His mom had been out of the house most of the evening only to return at ten to kiss him goodnight. He had heard his parents fighting earlier and could see on his mother's face that it was left unresolved. He felt a calm camaraderie with her, knowing she was on his side, not his father's.

He had always lived in the shadow of Jameson's expectations. And usually he delivered. When he was younger he thrived on his father's attention, reveled in the fact that he was his father's golden boy. But somewhere over the years, he learned for himself that it wasn't love and pride that drove his dad's adoration of him, but envy instead. Jameson wanted to relive his past through his son. His youth, his football career, even his girl.

Grace was expecting him and had left the back door open. If there was a piece of paper between the wood and latch, then it was safe to come in. When he cracked the door open, there was the paper, falling to the floor. He crept up the stairs he knew so well that he had no problem finding his way in the dark and slid her door open quietly, shutting it behind him.

He could see the outline of her body in between the sheets, and it instantly made him hard. God, he needed this. He needed a release after all the bullshit the last couple of days. And just like Grace to read his mind, she pulled back the covers, inviting him in.

As his eyes adjusted to the darkness, he could see the shape of her face, the way her hair fell over her bare shoulder as she lifted up on her elbow and the whites of her eyes when she looked at him as a smile crept over her beautiful mouth. She moved to make room for him and he slipped into her sheets, covering his body and then his mouth with hers.

His lips had only touched hers in three years. There had been many temptations, but he prided himself on never acting on one. They had this year together, this last final year before things changed. And though they never talked about separating, he knew it was inevitable. He was driven on his path to UDub, preferably without her.

"Slow down, J.R.," she whispered between his fervent kisses. But he couldn't. He'd wanted this so bad and for so long he pushed on, pressing his hardness against her thigh. She moaned as he slid his tongue against her neck, his hands pawing at her breasts that hid beneath her tank top. She was willing, he could feel it in the way she opened her legs to him and let him fall between them.

"J.R.," she moaned. And if she wasn't careful, he would come before he even entered her. "Please, slow down."

He tugged at her shirt, pulling it over her head and exposing her taut breasts to him. He took one in his mouth and felt her jolt with excitement.

"J.R.," she hissed. Her hands found his shoulder and she pressed against him, almost like she wanted him off.

"It's okay, Grace," he breathed, his fingers gliding down her belly to the edge of her pajama bottoms. "Relax."

"J.R." She pushed against him more firmly. "Stop."

He lifted his head, searching her eyes to see the fury in them. "What?"

"Do you think I wanted you over here for sex?"

What was she talking about? Why else did she think he was there? For late-night conversation? Cuddles? He loved her, it wasn't like he was using her. It was time... He had put in his time. "Well, yeah."

She grunted as she pushed him all the way off her and pulled her shirt back on. "I can't believe you."

He sat back, dumbfounded. "What? What'd I do?"

Her shoulders shook while she cried. He was afraid to touch her, still not sure of what had gone wrong. He stared down at her purple floral comforter, the one she'd gotten for Christmas last year. It had these itchy white flowers that drove him crazy; he didn't know how she slept with it. His fingers twirled the fabric, tugging on the flower patch.

"Do you want me to go?"

"No!" she whispered harshly, burying her head in her pillow. He wished he could reach for her and comfort her, but his frustration held him back. It was so typically Grace to turn from him and shut him down just when he thought they were getting somewhere.

"Then what, Grace? Are you not ready? 'Cause you sure as hell were acting like you were on Saturday night."

She turned her head and glared at him. "That's not fair." She looked embarrassed as she added, "I just thought our first time would be more special, you know?"

"No, I don't."

She sighed, brushing the tears away with the palm of her hand. "I always pictured it would be somewhere special, not like in a car or just in my bed all sneaky like this." She shrugged. "It feels unmemorable this way."

He was moving from confusion to irritation at an alarming speed. "Where the hell do you think we could go, Grace? I don't have money for like a hotel or something."

Her eyes widened as she shook her head. "Oh, no, not a hotel. I'm not some hooker, J.R."

He ran his hand down his face, his hard-on long gone as he realized she was once again turning him down. "Grace, we can't keep doing this. You promised me senior year."

She crossed her arms over her chest. Though he could still see the hardness of her nipples through her shirt, he was no longer turned on. "Or what, J.R.? You'll find someone else who will give it up to you?" She tossed her head away from him. "Whatever, I'm sure the list is long."

She was right, of course. He knew that. There was not a shortage of girls at Timber Falls who would jump at a chance to go to bed with him. And maybe if he'd realized it before, he wouldn't have waited so long on Grace. But he had. Because for all the times she teased him with her body or the sensualness in her words she was, and had always been his Grace. The one person who continued to be his rock and greatest champion. He could always count on her to lift him up or have his back when it seemed like everyone else around him needed him to be more.

He reached for her hands. "That's not what I'm saying."

She pulled her hands back. "Just go." She lay back on the bed and turned away from him. He watched her for a moment, wondering what he could say that would get her to change her mind. When it was clear he was on the losing end, he sighed and left her crying into her pillow.

CHAPTER 13

Fourth day gone

Rex did his best to keep Kate from coming with him, but a tormented mother could never be stopped. They hopped into his patrol vehicle the moment Officer Maloney said they'd found J.R.'s car, and raced toward the scene.

It was a hiker who had called in the car when he recognized the make and model atop the scenic Oracle Point. Oracle Point sat nestled deep in the dense woods about fifteen miles south of town. Though, because of its popularity in the summertime, Timber Falls claimed it as their own. The falls itself were pressed back from the main road, making the gravel drive steep, and during the late fall and winter, a risky one. The moment summer arrived, the kids piled into cars and made their way up to the top of the falls to sightsee, hike, and even climb down to the lower cliffs to jump into the pristine lake below. The top of Oracle Point stood at five hundred and seventy feet, making it a beautiful place to look at the valley around them. No one dared to jump from the top of the falls—not even the most rebellious of kids could defy death in that way. Once you hiked down a few hundred feet, there were cliffs meant for jumping into the lake below, the most popular being a fifteen-foot drop, and then the more dangerous twenty-five-foot jump that the boys could be seen at all summer long.

The drive was silent between them as Kate nervously gnawed at her cuticles, looking out the window in hopes she would magically see her son walking out from the trees. Rex spoke to other officers through the radio, driving at a speed he rarely hit in his small town.

Outside became darker the deeper into the woods they drove. Trees hovered around them, welcoming them into their secrets as they crept up the gravel drive. Kate could feel her heart pounding in her ears, and Rex had the urge to reach over and touch her knee to calm her, but resisted. He was shaking just as much. Could they have really found them?

The landing to Oracle Point was eerily still. Officers moved in and out of the trees in slow motion rather than with the haste that Kate wanted or expected. Rex pulled his car to a stop beside the sheriff who was walking toward him now. Among the shallow landing there sat two other patrol cars, but to Kate's dismay, no black BMW.

They sat in a clearing above the cliff, though you could see the edge of it straight ahead. When Rex was a kid, there was nothing but grass and edgy rock that separated the gravel parking area to the lake below. It was three years after he graduated high school when a freshman, a brother of a friend of his, fell over the unprotected brink and was killed. After that, the town partitioned a stone half-wall boundary. Since then, Oracle Point had remained mostly safe besides some minor mishaps here and there.

"Where's the car?" Kate asked as soon as they parked, as though she expected him to know.

He cut the engine. "I'm not sure, Kate." He turned toward her. He could see the franticness in her eyes, and once again he cursed himself for allowing her to get in the car. "I think it's a good idea that you stay here until I get some things sorted out."

But she wasn't listening to him. She was out the door before he had a chance to open his. He sighed and reckoned he didn't blame her. If it had been Lila out there...

"Chief," Sheriff Harvey Gibson said as he approached his car, eyeing Kate as she walked by him.

"Caleb Weston's mother," Rex said to him. "She was at my office when the news came in."

"So much for discretion for the families," he answered, shaking his hand.

"No discretion in Timber Falls." Rex watched as an officer exited his car with a German Shepherd K9 on a leash. He wished he'd had the drive alone to sneak a drink or two in.

The sheriff gave a slight nod. "No, I suppose not. Come," he said, leading Rex toward the wooded entrance. "We got the call about an hour ago from a man named Jared Lepinksi. He's right over here."

Rex shook Jared's hand, sizing him up. He was a young man, maybe in his early twenties if Rex had to guess. He was nervous but cooperative, although quick to remind them he needed to leave soon for his busboy job.

"I'm sure your boss will understand, Jared," the sheriff said in a way that implied he would be there for as long as they needed. "For the record, if we could have you explain to Chief Tourney the events, that would be helpful."

Jared scratched at his head, more of a nervous habit, Rex guessed, than a necessity. "Sure. I, uh, I came up here for a hike. I like it this time of year 'cause no one's around." He nodded toward the woods. Rex's eyes followed his, and he caught sight of the shape of black paint. "I saw a car in there, which I thought was really weird. I didn't know if someone was in it, so I ignored it at first and walked down the south path. But when I came back up it was still there, so I went to go check it out. And that's when I noticed it was the missing car. I've seen the posters around but hadn't paid too much attention, except I knew it was a black BMW."

"Good memory," Rex encouraged. He kept one eye on Jared and one on the unfolding scene before him. The K9 entered the woods just as Kate was walking out, escorted by an officer. Her face contorted in distress when she saw the dog. The officer stopped and spoke to her, blocking her from the entrance to where the car was. She should have stayed in the damn patrol car like Rex told had her to do.

"So then I got in my car and drove down to the payphone at the gas station about a mile back and then waited back up here until the sheriff arrived. I never saw the guys, though. Three of them, right?"

Rex nodded. "Did you see signs of them along the trail? Maybe footprints or food or trash, something that indicated they've been around?"

Jared thought about it a moment before shaking his head. "No, it's just me, didn't look like anyone else has been here." His eyes widened. "Do you think they could have been attacked by like a bear or something? I thought I heard a growl in the woods but never saw anything. Maybe I need to get a gun."

"We are certainly looking at all angles, but before you jump ahead of yourself, I think if it was animal attack you would have seen evidence of such."

Jared shivered at the idea.

"Do you come out here often?" the sheriff asked. "When was the last time you hiked this trail?"

"I try to come out once a week, but it'd been a couple weeks since I'd been able to, you know with work and stuff."

"Great, thanks, Jared." Rex shook his hand. "You did the right thing."

The sheriff reached out his hand and Jared shook it awkwardly. "Thank you, Jared." The young man was excused as the sheriff pulled Rex towards the entrance of the woods.

"Rex, if I could be blunt here," he said, stone-faced. "What we are looking for here are not three boys camping out in the woods but the remains of their bodies."

Rex fell back a step. "What leads you to believe that? Isn't it possible they're somewhere along the trails Jared didn't explore?" He knew it wasn't true as he spoke it. Camping at Oracle Point was just as odd as leaving an abandoned car there.

The sheriff stopped walking and pulled a piece of folded paper from his pocket, handing it to Rex. "We found this on the dashboard of J.R.'s car."

Rex scrunched his face in confusion as he slowly opened the torn paper. The words were simple, the meaning not to be left misunderstood.

I'm so sorry. Please forgive me.

Ethan

Rex drew in a deep breath. "A suicide note?" He turned the paper over in his hands, looking for more.

"That's what we're looking at here, Chief. Three boys who for whatever reason drove up to Oracle Point to end their lives."

Rex felt a chill down his spine. "But why only one note?" he asked. "Why didn't J.R. or Caleb leave one as well?"

The sheriff shrugged. "Maybe they never planned on leaving a note and Ethan left it without their knowledge. Maybe that's why it's so short. Teenage boys do unexplainable things, Chief."

Rex nodded, folding the paper back into its original form and slipping it into his back pocket. He took in a shaky breath, running a hand through his hair. "I need to see the car. Have they found anything else in it?"

"We've got the dogs sniffing it out. No drugs, just booze." The sheriff led them toward J.R.'s BMW. It sat straddled between two trees awkwardly as though they had sped through the woods and landed in an odd angle. "The evidence of the alcohol and by the angle of the car, it suggests they were driving under the influence."

Rex stepped up to the car, taking a moment to collect himself before looking in. As the sheriff said, beer cans scattered the floor of the car like an afterthought, left out in the open. A Falcons sweatshirt, football shoulder pads, and an empty bag of fast food littered the back seat, leaving only a small clearing for one boy to sit. Rex lifted a Huskies sweatshirt from the passenger seat, recognizing it as one he had seen on Caleb a week before they went missing. Kate had surprised him with it when she'd found out the coach was coming to watch them play.

He heard her cry out to him from the entrance to the woods. He lifted his head to the sound of her to see she was being held back by an officer but putting up a good fight. She wiggled out of his arms and ran to Rex. Ripping the sweatshirt from his hands, she fell to her knees and buried her face in the smell of her son, muffling her sobs.

"She needs to get out of here," the sheriff muttered, in no mood for distractions.

Rex took her by the arm and gently lifted her to her feet. "Can she?" Rex asked the sheriff, referring to the sweatshirt. The sheriff nodded. Neither of them wanted to be the one to take it from her. Besides, the unspoken truth was that they weren't looking at a criminal investigation.

He led her out of the woods to the clearing where he instructed one of his deputies to take her home. "I promise when I know something more I will call you."

She nodded as she clung to her son's clothes. She didn't want to leave, but she didn't know how to be there, either. Would she be emotionally prepared if they were to find something more than a car? The idea made her woozy and she needed to sit. The deputy helped her into the car and Rex shut the door behind her. He smiled gently, but inside he was more than a little relieved to watch her go. That feeling didn't last long—the moment she was out of sight, the squeal of tires raced to the landing and out stepped the mayor from his gold Mercedes.

"Where is my son?" he cried out in a demand to anyone who could hear him.

How the hell word had spread to him so fast, Rex didn't know. He sighed in frustration as he walked toward the father of a missing boy, who looked as though he would tackle anyone who got in his way.

"Mayor." Rex approached him cautiously. "I'm going to ask you to leave. We are working—"

"Let me remind you, Rex, just who you work for," the mayor snapped, pushing past him. "Where's the car?"

Rex felt the rage of humiliation as though the mayor had just slapped him. He stepped back and lifted his hand to show Jameson the direction of the BMW. He watched him stomp off, deciding to hang back rather than follow the storm.

His feet sunk down into the mud that hung there after the rains. It made him feel like he was sinking in quicksand, unable to move. His eyesight blurred as he watched officers lean over the concrete barrier and peer down the cliff. Would they find them there?

"Chief." Officer Maloney caught him off guard. "You alright?"

He cleared his throat, embarrassed he'd been caught staring off. "Of course. What'd you get?"

Maloney was a good man, the best right hand Rex could ask for. He was always on the right side of the law, something Rex himself envied. He didn't let the mayor push him around, or make his decisions for him as Rex had on multiple occasions. It's also why Rex knew deep down, the mayor had chosen him as the Chief of Police over Maloney. Sometimes, he wondered if Maloney knew it, too.

"Cleared the area up here. We caught scent of the boys near the edge of the cliff, so we have a crew heading down to search." He looked out toward the stone wall that made a barrier from the edge to the lake below. He shook his head, and Rex could see his affliction. It was an emotion his officer rarely showed.

"What is it?" Rex asked him.

"It just don't seem right, Chief," he said with a shake of his head. "Why would they do such a thing?" He almost sounded choked up when he added, "They had their whole lives to live. And their parents..." His voice dropped off and Rex knew he was thinking about his small children at home, as Rex often thought about Lila.

"I know." Rex patted him on the shoulder. They may have been officers, but living where they did, they did not have the thick skin as big city cops must. Crime, disappearances, and death were not something they were used to.

"But best not to let our emotions get to us, Maloney. We can't let that affect the job we have to do."

Maloney nodded, shaking out of his stupor. "Right, well, I'll get to it, then."

But Maloney didn't move. He swore under his breath as he looked straight ahead, causing Rex to turn and see what had him all distressed. It was an officer walking toward them, a leash for his K9 in one hand and in the other a worn-in Falcons baseball cap.

Ethan Young's hat.

CHAPTER 14

Four weeks earlier

I t was the gold Mercedes Nick recognized first, a gift from Anna to Jameson on his fortieth birthday. Nick had gone with Anna to the dealership and had helped her pull off the surprise of a lifetime for her husband. Jameson had been beyond thrilled. He prided himself on having all things bold and shiny and expensive. A gold Mercedes screamed all of those things. As Nick pulled up beside it in his old Toyota truck, he was not oblivious to the fact that their cars spoke volumes about who they were. Nick hated to wonder if they had met later in life, and not as kids, would they have chosen each other as friends?

As he pulled in to park, he was surprised to see Jameson's car outside of town, and that it wasn't Jameson sitting in the driver seat but Anna instead.

She didn't see his truck appear beside her, or when he got out of the car and stood at the passenger window. Her head was down, and it was when she lifted a delicate hand to her cheek Nick realized she was crying.

He gently tapped on the window, and her head sprung up in surprise and then in shame. She never wanted anyone to see her cry, especially Nick Young.

She unlocked the doors, and Nick slid into the seat beside her. She kept her head turned from him, hurriedly swiping at her damp cheeks.

"Do you often sit in strange parking lots and cry? Or did I just catch you on the right day?"

She swatted at him, a laugh escaping her lips. He smiled at the sound of it. She knew if it had been Jameson who had caught her indulging in her tears, he would have scolded her weakness. What a refreshing change to have someone try to make her laugh instead.

"What are you doing here?" Nick asked, referring to them sitting in a parking lot two towns over from home. "I thought the Hudsons didn't leave Timber Falls."

She broke out into a wide grin. When she looked at him, he could see the shimmer of residual tears in her eyes. It made the blue of her irises sparkle. "Confession," she said sheepishly. "I prefer The Grind Coffee House's London Fog tea above any in Timber Falls." That and she wanted to feel she could be herself in peace if only for just a moment instead of being watched by the whole town.

Nick's mouth dropped in feigned dismay. It only made her laugh harder. "Stop," she teased.

"So, you're telling me that you drive thirty minutes for a cup of tea?"

"*The* cup of tea," she smarted back. She met his eye and held his stare. Was she flirting with him? She wasn't sure she remembered how.

"Well," he sat back, dumbfounded. "I think I am going to have to try this London drink."

"A London Fog, and it won't taste as good now that I've hyped it up." She didn't mean to sniffle when she spoke, but a sob caught in her throat and escaped her. She pressed her lips together in a tight line.

Nick was looking at her; she could feel it even though her head was turned away from him.

"Come have a cup with me, please," he asked softly. "I don't have to be back at the office for a while and would love the company."

She knew in her heart he was saying it for her benefit over his, but she couldn't say no. She simply nodded and got out of the car. As they walked toward the coffee shop, she realized she didn't know why he was out of town either.

He opened the cafe door for her as he answered, "I had to meet with the head of operations down at G.E. Mills. Finished up quicker than I expected. I was heading back when I saw Jameson's car."

"Oh, right," she said foolishly. Of course he had pulled over looking for his best friend. Would Nick call Jameson later that evening to tell him he saw his wife crying on his steering wheel? "Jameson took my SUV this morning, saying something about needing the cargo space."

They ordered their drinks along with a pumpkin scone he bought them to share, and nestled into a quiet corner in the back. It was nice to be somewhere people didn't know her name. Or interrupt her private conversation to talk town politics.

She tried to remember the last time she had been alone with Nick. Beyond football games, chance encounters on the streets, or when, for only a moment, Nora and Jameson were in the other room, she couldn't recall a time it had been just them. Maybe since high school. The way he compressed his face in concentration made her wonder if he was thinking the same thing.

He took a sip off his scalding tea latte. "Man, you weren't kidding. This is good." He tore off a piece of the scone and popped it in his mouth. His eyes rolled back as he moaned. "Okay," he said through bites. "Now I'm sold. You better have some before I eat it all."

She normally wouldn't dare eat a pastry—she usually just liked to eye them from behind the glass wall—but today she didn't feel like saying no to Nick Young. She took a bite and agreed, it was the best pumpkin scone she'd ever had.

For a moment, sitting here with Nick, a smile now pressed on her lips, she almost forgot what had made her cry earlier. Until Nick asked her.

"I don't mean to pry," he said when the scone was gone between them and their drinks had cooled. "But I do pride myself on being a good listener."

There had been many times, when they were younger, that Nick would find her crying in the hall or behind the bleachers after a fight she'd had with Jameson. It was frivolous really, kid stuff like him not paying enough attention to her or her accusing him of flirting with one of the other cheerleaders. Jameson had always had a way of turning it back on her, excluding himself of any blame. She was needy, she was jealous, and it was not his problem. Then Nick would swoop in and let her cry on his shoulder, until the day that Nora had caught notice, and then it abruptly stopped. She wasn't sure if it was she who had quit leaning on Nick or Nick who had stopped trying to save Anna. But that was back when they were kids. Dealing with adolescent issues.

Nick did something then that surprised them both. He reached across the table and rested his protective hand over her slender fingers. "Talk to me, Anna."

She stared down at his hand on hers but didn't move. She tried to remember the last time Jameson had touched her like this. It was so simple and yet electrified her down to her bones. Did he touch Nora this way often? She had always kept her jealousy at bay when it came to her best friend, never letting on just how much she envied the life she lived. She always felt torn between feeling happiness at her friend's seemingly perfect life and complete and utter malice toward it. It shamed her to think such thoughts, and she often prayed that Nora was blissfully ignorant.

Here, her best friend's husband sat across from her, his hand tenderly on hers, his eyes pleading with her to bare her soul, and she felt nothing but comfort and contentment.

She was a horrible friend. She didn't even want to think what kind of wife it made her.

She took in a deep breath. "Sometimes, I suppose, I find that I am trying so hard to be everything to everyone that I end up being nothing at all."

He cocked a brow. He could feel her pain seeping out of her, yet he couldn't relate to what she was saying. To him, Anna had always been the rock and the glue of them all.

She brushed crumbs off the lap of her shift dress. "I think I got so wrapped up in trying to be the person everyone needed me to be that I lost who I really am. And now, it feels like it may be too late."

"Why would you think that?"

"The way that Jameson looks at me." Her voice dropped off.

He knew exactly the way Jameson looked at her, and it made him sick to his core. Absentmindedly, he rubbed his thumb over the back of her hand. He didn't realize he was doing it until he caught her staring down at the movement. He should have stopped, but he didn't.

"I never wanted to be a politician's wife," she said for the first time out loud. "I don't mind the service to the community, I actually enjoy it. But what I didn't realize at eighteen was that to be with Jameson meant giving up any of my own dreams. At the time, I thought motherhood would fulfill that."

Nick thought back to all those private conversations under the bleachers. "You used to talk about being a lawyer."

She smiled sadly. "I would have been a good lawyer, back when I had a voice." She looked up to him now. "When did I get so weak?"

His heart plummeted. "You are one of the strongest women I know, Anna."

She shook her head. "No, Nick. You just see what's on the outside. What I show to the world. You aren't there when Jameson chastises me and I don't speak up. Or when he yells at J.R. for not being good enough and I don't speak up." She gave a shaky sigh. "When did I lose my voice? When did I become so afraid? Jameson can be cold and standoffish, and just when I think I've had enough, he flips on me and is warm and engaging. It makes me feel like I can't trust him, or even worse, my own mind."

"Whiplash."

She could feel the tears welling up in her eyes again. "Imagine what it does to the kids, Nick. I see it in J.R. the way that he will do absolutely anything for his father's approval, but he is stronger than I am. He is learning to have a voice, but it only makes Jameson angrier. I'm afraid for him, and I'm afraid I can't protect him." Her eyes widened as though she had said too much.

"Protect him from what?" Nick asked, not hiding his alarm.

She shook her head. What was she thinking spilling her fears to her husband's best friend? Was she so foolish to think he wouldn't tell him?

"Nothing, Nick." She pulled her hand away from his grip and pressed her fingertips to the corners of her eyes. "I'm so sorry to do this to you. It's not fair. Jameson is your friend, your best friend. And I never want to put you in an awkward position to make you feel as though you have to keep secrets from him."

If only Anna knew the number of secrets he kept from Jameson.

"I have never had an alliance with Jameson over you, Anna," he said calmly. Yes, there were things he knew about Jameson that he had never told Anna, but that was to keep from hurting her rather than to protect Jameson.

She nodded, gratefully. They sat staring at each other a moment longer than either realized they should.

"I should go," she finally said, breaking their silence.

He stood to walk her out. He didn't want to leave. He wanted to stay in this bubble of just the two of them a little longer. The thought should make him feel guilty but it didn't. He'd admitted to himself long ago that choosing Nora was choosing second best.

He tried to fight that feeling for many years. He would push any thoughts of Anna out of his mind and put so much focus on Nora, willing himself to love her as much as she loved him. To the outside world, they seemed like the perfect pair. And Nora was perfect. She was beautiful, kind, humble, and a good partner to him. He wished desperately that that was enough. When he let Jameson win Anna, he knew he was walking away from the one person he loved above all else.

It had never been Anna who was the weak one. It had always been him.

He could have prevented her unhappiness. Hell, if he had known how miserable she was with Jameson, he would have whisked her away long ago.

Their cars sat as silent as the air between them in the vacant lot. She turned to him when she got to the door and thanked him for the tea.

"I hope that wasn't too much," she said apologetically. "I admit I'm a little embarrassed about what I said back there."

The way he stared down at her made her throat dry up and fingers tingle. He was so close to her that if she breathed in heavily, her breasts would brush against his chest. She yearned for the way that would feel.

"Anna, you never have to feel self-conscious when you talk to me."

Her eyes dropped from his. She felt too much when she looked at him.

He gently placed her chin in his hand and forced her eyes on him. "I see you, Anna. You may feel weak when you don't speak up, but you are a fighter trying to survive the best way you know how. Your strength is your willingness to not give up. You see what others need, and you set aside your own needs to give everything you have to them. That is not weakness, Anna. And your children? They see that. That voice J.R. is exhibiting is not a reflection of Jameson's anger but the essence of your strength pouring out of him."

He had more he wanted to say. The words he had always wanted to share with her poured from him so easily now with no restrictions or inhibitions. But before he could speak again, he felt her body lean into him as she reached up on her tiptoes and pressed her desperate lips against his.

CHAPTER 15

Fourth day gone

Nora hadn't left the house since Monday morning. She feared being away from her phone in case Ethan was to call. She refused to let her mind think of the other reasons why the phone would ring.

She barely slept at night, tossing and turning and eventually getting out of bed rather than allowing images to seep into her mind that she silenced during the day. She could feel Nick's restlessness as well and wished desperately for him to reach for her and pull her close to him, but he didn't. She relied too heavily on Connor for her need for affection, and at age nine he was still willing to give it. She could see how terrified he was that his older brother was gone, to the point that every night when she got out of bed, she found him lying on the floor with a blanket and pillow just to be close to her. She needed him near, just as much as he needed to be. She couldn't bear the idea of losing two children.

Anna and Jameson had sent their youngest kids to stay with her parents. She understood the logic behind it, keeping them protected from all the craziness, especially when the Hudson home was also used as the volunteer search station. But Nora couldn't part with Connor, even if it meant he heard things he shouldn't. She clung to him every moment she could.

So when Connor asked to go back to school that morning, Nora was torn between allowing her youngest some normalcy and not wanting him to be more than an arm's distance away from her. It was Nick who encouraged her to let go of the reins a little.

"It will be good for him, Nora," Nick said as he slid a pair of jeans on. She was still in her robe, the one she'd been wearing since Sunday. She sat on the edge of the bed, watching her husband dress.

"I'll take him in," Nick continued as he slipped an old Falcons tee shirt over his head. "You do your best to get some rest."

"Will you be back?" She tried not to show the alarm in her voice, but the idea of being alone right now when she was so vulnerable terrified her.

"After I drop Connor off I'm heading to the Hudson house. I want to jump in on the search team, see which areas haven't been covered." He ran his hand through his hair, ruffling the strands that had fallen out of place when he slept. Nick had always been a night showerer. Something Nora didn't understand. She needed the water to wake her up, he needed it to unwind after a long day. The one good thing was there was no fighting over space in their master bathroom.

She pulled her robe closed like it was her security blanket. She should have been out there too, like the other parents. But the idea of being away from the phone made her numb with anxiety.

"Also, I need to head to the office for a bit this afternoon," he added as he slipped on his sneakers.

Her eyes widened. "You're working?"

"No," he answered as he tied the string to his shoes. "But I have a few things that need tending to. I left things with the guys a mess, and I need to get a few things organized for them in case I'm out for a while."

Nora caught her breath. The only reason Nick would be out of work longer would be because their son was still missing, or dead.

Nick hung his head, realizing the words that had just escaped his mouth. It took everything in him to stay with the task at hand and not let the emotion of what he was feeling take control. He swore under his breath before looking up to his wife who was curled into a ball. He could hear her weeping, though she hid her face from him. He got up from the bed and placed a hand on the back of her shoulder.

"I'm sorry, Nora. That wasn't what I meant."

She didn't move or react to his touch. Eventually, he stepped away, and hours later, when the phone did ring, she was still curled up in her robe where Nick had left her.

In the silence of the house, the sound of the phone made her jump. She looked around her bed, frantically searching for the cordless phone she had left near her. On the third ring, she answered, willing her son's voice to be on the other line.

"Hello, hello?" she answered eagerly. She had always told the boys that if they got into some kind of trouble and had no money for a payphone to just call collect. She would never be upset with them for reaching out to her if they needed, even if it meant adding money to their phone bill. She waited to hear the operator's voice.

"Nora?"

But it wasn't the operator asking her to accept a collect call. And it wasn't the voice of her son, either. To her relief, it also wasn't that of Chief Tourney. She sighed and responded to the mayor.

"Yes, Jameson. It's me."

"Nora, they found the car."

Her ears began to ring. She couldn't hear what he was saying. He was speaking so fast her brain couldn't keep up. *They found the car.* J.R.'s car. Did that mean they had found the boys with the car?

"Are they okay?" Her voice came out in a gasping sound as she choked back a sob.

"No, Nora, you don't understand." He sighed impatiently. And then all too soon she did understand. They found the car but not the boys.

"Where?" She cried out, the tears escaping her eyes. How could there be a car and no sign of the boys? Had there been an accident and they had left to go find help and gotten lost?

"Oracle Point," he answered. "I'm heading there now. Tell Nick to meet me up there."

Oracle Point. What...? Why would they be there?

"Nora, do you hear me?" he asked. "I have to go now. Tell Nick to find me up there."

Nick. "But he was at your house. Or was." She realized she had no idea what time it was.

"He left here a long time ago, Nora," he said, his patience dwindling. "I have to go. Oh, and if you hear from Anna, please tell her to call my car phone."

She was nodding even though she knew he couldn't see her. "Okay, alright, I will."

She hung up the phone and immediately dialed Nick's office. Several rings later, she hung up and tried again. When she didn't get an answer, she threw the phone down and jumped out of bed. Her fingers were shaking as she tossed off her robe and grabbed the first pair of jeans she could find off the floor.

She was in her car and backing out of the driveway not two minutes after her conversation ended with Jameson. She had to find Nick. She needed to get to J.R.'s car, but couldn't do that without the help of Nick.

What could have possibly led the boys to Oracle Point this time of year? They never talked about hanging out there, except in the summertime of course. It wasn't as though Ethan or any of the boys were avid hikers. This had to be a Caleb idea. She never trusted that boy. There was just something wrong about him. She could see it in his cold, blank eyes.

When Caleb had first arrived in Timber Falls, Nora had felt sorry for him. What mother wouldn't? That didn't mean she wanted her child to befriend him. He had this air about him that made him even a little scary. She had caught him on more than one occasion watching her in a way that gave her chills. And then there were the times when he was younger that she had walked into her room only to see him sifting through her panty drawer. She scolded him of course, but to her surprise, it was she who was embarrassed, not him. He stood back with that smug grin, shrugged his shoulders like he didn't even care that he had just been caught red-handed. She told herself the next time it happened, she would call his mother. When she told Anna the story, Anna said she too had had odd experiences with Caleb, like the time she finished her shower and entered her room to see her door slightly cracked.

"I saw his little black eyes looking in at me," Anna had said. "Scared me to death. I just stood there a minute in shock before slamming the door in his face and telling him to beat it. Thank god I had my towel on."

As the years went on, Nora never got more comfortable with Caleb, but she adjusted to the fact that he wasn't going anywhere. Whenever she would say something to Ethan, he would just roll his eyes and tell her he wasn't that bad.

Maybe he wasn't. But then, maybe he was, and both J.R. and Ethan were blinded to it.

She pulled into Timber Falls Timber Company driving faster than the suggested ten miles per hour. She screeched into a parking space just outside the west building's entrance. Her husband's office was the corner window, three stories up from where she parked. She couldn't wait for the elevator. The adrenaline pumped through her veins in such velocity that she ran the stairs two at a time. She caught her breath just as she zipped past his secretary and threw his door open.

Her mouth was open, his name escaping her lips before she had a chance to take in the scene before her. Her husband was there, as he'd said he would be. But he wasn't alone. He sat with his back to her, still dressed in the same clothes she'd seen him leave in. But on his shoulder was fine blonde hair spilling down his back, as his arm draped around the back of her chair, holding her close to him.

They both startled at the sound of her entrance. There were tears in her friend's eyes. She could see her obvious sadness, but there was something else she hadn't seen before. Guilt.

"Anna?" Nora could feel the heat rising in her cheeks. She hadn't caught her husband cheating. He wasn't kissing her best friend behind closed doors. No, he was just comforting a mother who was missing a child.

But then, why didn't Nick comfort Nora in the same way? Why didn't he hold her when she cried for *their* missing son? The answer was so clear, it had always been there. Nick had never loved Nora the way he had always loved Anna.

Anna stood quickly, though Nick stayed planted in his seat. He watched the way his wife's eyes jumped back and forth between them and the conclusions she was coming to.

"What are you doing here, Anna?" Nora asked calmly, though she felt anything but.

Anna was shaking her head. Her words stumbled as she searched for the right words to say. "We were just talking, Nora. I was upset... And Jameson wasn't... and I just thought I could talk to Nick."

Nora eyed her oldest friend. "You mean you were looking for comfort from my husband, rather than coming to me?"

Anna bit her lip as tears started to form in her eyes. Nick stood then and walked to his wife. He needed to do damage control. Now was not the time to tell Nora what he and Anna had been doing. That he felt comfort in her best friend and leaned on her in a way he couldn't with his wife. That he longed to hold Anna while they suffered rather than hold his wife. He could see in Nora's eyes that she had already discovered all of this for herself in the mere seconds that she was here. Which led him to the gut-wrenching question of what had gotten his wife out of bed.

"What do you know, Nora?" Nick asked as he moved toward her.

Her eyes flickered between his and Anna's before landing on him, bringing her back to why she was there in the first place. "They found J.R.'s car."

Anna's hand flew to her mouth as she gasped. Nick swore as he fought the urge to reach for Anna. Instead, he took his wife's hand. It felt limp and lifeless in his as she didn't respond to his feigned affection. "Nora, oh, my god. Are the boys okay?" he asked, repeating the same line she had given Jameson.

She shook her head. "It's just the car, Nick. Jameson called me at home. He was looking for you two…" Her voice trailed off, and instantly Nick was hit with remorse that his sweet and innocent wife had been left to answer that call alone.

"Oh, Nora," he sighed as she slipped her fingers from his grasp. "Where is the car?"

"Oracle Point."

"What?" Anna cried. "Why?"

Nora couldn't look at her best friend when she answered. "I don't know. But your *husband* is there now, and I'm going, too."

Both Nick and Anna felt the intended infliction Nora had thrown at her. But now was not the time for explanations or excuses. Anna grabbed her coat. "I'm coming with you."

Nick led the girls out of his office and into Nora's sedan, where she instinctively took the passenger seat and Anna slid in behind Nick, who was driving.

"Someone should call Kate," Anna said as she buckled up.

Nora felt guilty that she had only thought of herself and of Nick when she had gotten the news. Of course she should have reached out to Kate. Just another way that Anna was a better person than she was.

"Let's just get up there and see what's going on," Nick said as he pulled out of the parking lot. "I can always find a payphone and call her."

"Jameson has the car phone," Nora added, looking out the window. "Which he had asked me to tell you to call him on, Anna, if I was to find you."

"Thank you," Anna said softly. Her heart hurt for more reasons than she could explain. But right now, the only thing that mattered to her was finding her son. If his car was at Oracle Point, it only meant he wasn't far from there. She knew in her gut that J.R. hadn't left. That maybe Jameson was right all along and that the boys only needed to blow off some steam. Had her son been camping in the woods all this time she had feared he was gone, or worse, dead? Slowly, her fears began to turn to anger, which then turned back to fear. If she was furious that her son was out meandering in the woods without letting her know, she could only imagine what Jameson was feeling. She needed to get to her son before her husband did something he would regret.

They sat the rest of the trip in silence. Nick didn't dare look back at Anna or extend his hand to his wife. He was lost in his own mind of what-ifs. When he traveled up the steep gravel road and onto the landing of Oracle Point, he was more than a little surprised to see the flurry of activity in front of him. Multiple police cars, K9 dogs, Chief Tourney, as well as the county sheriff.

Anna's reasoning that they had been camping in the woods began to disappear as she looked around at the activity before her. There was her husband standing next to the chief. His back was turned to her, but she could see the way his shoulders slumped.

Nora shut the door behind her, not waiting for her friend or her husband as she broke out in a run to get to the chief and any news that her son had been found and they were bringing him to her soon. But her steps faltered almost as though her legs were made of stone and could no longer move. She fell to her knees, her jeans soaking through the mud. It was the chief who saw her first, turning toward her, and in his hands was her son's favorite hat.

CHAPTER 16

Three weeks earlier

I t was Chinese night, and Ethan's turn to pick up for the family. He placed his order at the counter, their usual to go. Mr. Chung smiled at him and wished his family well as he congratulated him on last Friday's win. He reached into the jar of fortune cookies by the register and handed one to Ethan.

"I think this one is just for you."

Ethan took it with a smile and thanked the old man before turning to take a seat while he waited for his food to cook. And that's when he saw her. Sitting in the waiting area, one leg tucked under the other as she twirled a loose string from the bottom of her flannel shirt. He smiled to himself as he took up the empty seat beside her. She was just a sophomore, but there was something about Lila Tourney that intrigued him. Maybe it was the way her nose scrunched up in frustration as she pulled on the yarn, not caring what others would think of the face she was making. Or maybe it was the way she walked in the halls at school. She had this briskness about her that made her look a little tough, like she wasn't there to put up with anyone's shit. He thought it was kind of hot. And maybe, to be honest, it was because she wasn't a cheerleader.

"Hey, Shotgun," he quipped when he sat down beside her.

She startled a little at the sound of his voice and then at the nearness of his body to hers. She looked up to see the teasing in his eyes and then felt sorely disappointed—he must have thought she was someone else. "Sorry," she said with a shake of her head. "That's not me."

When he shifted in his seat to rest his elbows on his knees, she could smell the scent of Ivory soap on his skin and see the dampness of his hair under his Falcons hat. He must have just showered after practice.

He laughed. "No, I mean you. I don't often see a girl shoot back a full beer in a few gulps."

Her face blushed at the mention of the party she had seen him at a couple of weeks ago. She could still taste the bitterness of the beer in her belly; it brought a weird sensation up her throat. She groaned. "Don't remind me." But she was thrilled that he remembered.

"Picking up dinner?" he asked. He liked the way she turned her body toward him. She sure didn't look that much younger than him.

She tucked a strand of fallen hair behind her ear. "Yeah, my dad has odd hours some days and isn't the best cook." Though he had tried many, many times, something she was proud of him for. But he often ended up burning, undercooking, or somehow ruining the meal. Their top drawer in the kitchen overflowed with take-out menus.

Ethan cocked his head toward her. "I forgot about that. It's just you and your dad, isn't it? I see the chief around but never really think about—you know, his wife. Sorry, is it hard to talk about?"

She shook her head. "No, it's okay. I never knew my mom, so it's not like I'm sad."

"You can still miss her, even if you never met her. I couldn't imagine not having one of my parents around. I don't think I could handle it being just me and my dad or—oh, god, me and my mom. She'd probably never let me leave the house." He scrunched up his face, and it made her laugh.

"A little overprotective, huh?" she said. "Imagine living with the chief of police."

His shoulders shook when he laughed. "You got me there."

She smiled. "He's not so bad, actually. He's pretty cool considering. What are you doing?" she asked as she watched him rip into the clear wrapper. "Don't you know the fortune cookie etiquette?"

He cocked a brow at her as he snapped the cookie in half. "Fortune cookie etiquette?"

"Yes," she exclaimed. "You can't eat the cookie until after you finish your dinner. And you can't read the fortune...oh, now you've ruined it." She laughed as he pulled the piece of paper from the cookie and turned it over.

"Be patient," he read. "Good things are coming in your future."

"That's a good one," she said and then shrugged one shoulder. "Too bad it won't come true now. You just tested fate."

He jabbed her in the side with his elbow. He was starting to like this girl. "You don't think good things are coming in my future?"

"I'm sorry, Ethan," she said solemnly, trying not to smile. "Your future is now doomed."

He stared at her trying to make sense of what he was feeling. Her cheeks turned pink and felt hot under his gaze. She didn't know why he was looking at her that way.

"Lila!" Her name was called out from the counter.

"That's my dinner," she said as she stood. He didn't want her to go, but didn't know if it was wise to keep talking to her this way.

She grabbed the plastic bag and swung it onto her wrist. "Stay away from danger, Ethan," she teased as she pushed through the door.

He was still thinking about her on the drive home. He couldn't help but smile as he thought about the easy banter between them. But not only was she too young for him, she was also the chief of police's daughter. Rex Tourney would never allow his daughter to date an older guy. Lila was right; his future was doomed.

He pulled up to a red light, adjusting the station on the radio when something just ahead of him caught his eye. It was his dad's truck. But what was strange about that was where it was parked. Tucked near a tree where it hoped not to be seen in a motel parking lot. Ethan felt a knot in his belly as he tried to reason why his father would need to leave his car at a motel. Had it broken down and he'd had to ditch it and have his mom pick him up? Had it been stolen? Jesus, could someone have actually taken his dad's truck?

Just then, as though he was being summoned, Nick Young opened the door to room seventeen. Ethan began to sweat as his brain tried to rationalize why his father would be there. The light turned green but Ethan was frozen in place as he watched his father remove the keys from his front pant pocket, a fucking smile plastered to his face.

The car behind him honked, but Ethan couldn't move. His father jumped in his truck and started the engine, reversing away from the parking spot. And that's when Ethan saw her. Her blonde hair glowed from the exterior light fixture just above the door she was exiting. Her head was turned away from him, but he knew who it was. He didn't have to see her face to know it was Anna Hudson. His best friend's mom. Ethan gripped the steering wheel so tight his knuckles turned white. He had an urge to throw his stick into drive and run through room seventeen.

The car behind him blared his horn again, catching Ethan's attention, and the attention of his father, as he pulled his car to exit the motel parking lot. Nick's smile faded from his lips as he caught the eye of his son. But it was too late for excuses. Ethan could see clearly what was happening, and Nick knew he would have to confront him about it. But not at home. If he could just get Ethan alone, away from Nora, and explain. To his relief, Ethan never came down for dinner. He told his mom he didn't feel good and went to bed. It wasn't a lie. Ethan had never felt so sick.

Nick had no choice but to track down his son after practice the next day. The team was just finishing up their last drill as Nick sat on the bleachers. Ethan knew he was there, but refused to meet his eyes. He was still sickened by what he had seen yesterday, and if his dad was here to lie his way out of it, he didn't want to hear it. It was hard looking at J.R. all day knowing what he knew. If J.R. knew their parents were fucking around, he sure didn't show it.

It left Ethan in a sour mood. He wanted to be left alone and spent lunch in the library going over tomorrow's ethics test. But he couldn't concentrate. He ended up doodling on a scratch piece of paper until the bell for the next period rang. When Caleb came up behind him and swung an arm around his neck, he reared back on instinct and slugged him in the stomach.

"Whoa." Caleb laughed. "What's got your panties in a bunch?"

"Fuck off, Caleb," he muttered as he walked away. J.R. spun around and caught up with his best friend. He grabbed him by the arm and ducked as Ethan swung around, ready to strike again. "Whoa, whoa, buddy. It's me."

Ethan took a deep breath to calm down. It didn't work. He couldn't look at J.R. right then, not with the knowledge he had.

"What's going on, man? You're not like yourself today."

Ethan shook his head. "I'm fine," he lied. "Just stressed about tomorrow's test." He took a step back. "I'll catch up with you at practice." He knew his friends didn't deserve his wrath, but he also knew he couldn't tell them what was bothering him. He left them, the boys and Grace and Avery watching him with great disdain as he pulled away from them. When he turned around, he ran smack into Lila.

She held up a hand to his chest to steady him. Her smile was large and inviting, and it was just what he needed at that moment.

"I need to get out of here," he said breathlessly, looking only at her and not the two girls standing next to her. "Want to go for a drive?"

Her face twisted in confusion. He could see she was contemplating what he was asking her, and he wouldn't pressure her. He just couldn't be in these halls right now, and he didn't really want to be alone. He just needed to be with someone who didn't know him well enough to know when he was lying.

"Sure," she said hesitantly, looking at her friends for encouragement. They smiled eagerly at her and her voice got stronger. "Sure, yes. I'll go for a drive with you."

"Great." He took her by the hand, aware that his friends were still watching him as they walked out of the building.

He pulled the car out of the school parking lot and turned in the direction of Oak Hill highway. He didn't know what he was doing or where he was going, but he just needed to be on the open road. Lila sat silently next to him, still not sure why he had invited her to go. But he looked different today than he had last night, and not in a good way. It made her edgy and nervous. She lifted his CD case into her lap and started flipping through the pages until she found a band she liked and slid it into the player. The beat surrounded them. He turned up the volume, a small smile finally fluttering across his face.

"Good choice," he said.

She began to relax when she saw that he was, too. She rested her head against the back of the seat and looked out the window as the burnt orange and auburn leaved trees flew past them.

"Do you know how to drive?" he asked her.

She looked over at him, a little embarrassed by her answer. "I have my permit. But it's not very cool learning to drive in your dad's patrol car."

He laughed as he slowed the car to a stop. They were in the middle of the vacant road when he unbuckled his seat belt.

"What are you doing?" Her voice was filled with alarm.

"Teaching you to drive. Get out."

She shook her head. "Oh, I don't know."

"Come on, it'll be fun. You need it, and I need something to clear my head."

She looked at him and saw the desperation in his face. Whatever he was feeling was wearing on him, and she couldn't say no to him.

She was exhilarated and terrified as she did what he asked. What if she totally bombed? Would she look like an idiot, or even worse, like a kid?

"Okay," he said when she got into position. "You ever drive a stick before?"

"Uh." She looked down at the clutch by her foot. "No."

He chuckled. "Okay, this will be fun."

She glared at him but then quickly smiled in return. She couldn't wait to tell Hannah and Olivia she had spent the afternoon learning to drive in Ethan Young's Honda Civic.

"Right foot is for the gas and brake and the left foot is for the clutch. The key is to slowly slide your foot off the clutch at the exact speed you accelerate on the gas."

"Sounds easy," she said as she did what he told her. The car began to lurch forward before jerking to a stop.

"Totally easy," he teased.

She shot him a glare and tried again.

"Slowly," he encouraged. The car began to roll forward again before it slammed to a halt. She hit the steering wheel with her palm.

"I suck at this."

"Everyone does at first," he agreed. He rubbed her shoulder to calm her frustrations. It only made her more nervous. But after a few more tries, she got the car out of first gear and was cruising down Oak Hill Highway at an exhilarating speed. Ethan liked the way her face softened as she relaxed, even bouncing a little to the music as she drove. It was in that moment he forgot their age difference and let them just be.

"Do you have a date for Homecoming?"

She hit the brakes, accidentally causing them both to dive forward. He grinned at her embarrassment.

"No," she said. "Not really. I'm planning on just going with Olivia and Hannah. My dad won't really let me go with a guy until junior year. Really lame."

He shrugged. He was bummed he couldn't ask her to the dance, but also happy she wasn't going with another guy. "Do you want to *not* go with me?"

She looked over at him and chuckled. "What is *not* going with you?"

He shrugged. "You know, like unintentionally going together. You go with your friends and I'll go with mine and we can like meet up there and hang out and we'll know that we're there together but no one else will."

She thought about this a moment, trying not to let her thrill of excitement show too much on her face. "Okay, I'd like to *not* go with you to the Homecoming dance."

His smile widened. This had worked out even better than if he could officially take her. He wasn't sure of the teasing he would endure from his friends if they knew he was taking a lower classman to the dance. "Okay, great. Also, there's a party after at Bryan Lawson's house that we always go to every year. Do you think you'd be able to come?"

She felt a thrill go down her back. She reminded herself to keep her eyes on the road. "Uh, yeah. I can just tell my dad I'm staying at Hannah's that night."

"Cool."

He took back control of the car and led them back to school. He felt lighter after spending the hour with Lila. The edge was gone, like he'd smoked some good dope. But all of that was short lived when he saw his dad sitting in the stands after practice.

He grabbed the last of the balls from the field and tossed them into the netted basket. When he turned, his dad was standing all chummy with Coach Mitchell like he wasn't a total fucker. They approached him, and he knew instantly what his dad's tactic was: get him in public where he wouldn't dare make a scene.

"Take a walk with me," Nick said to his son.

The coach patted him on the shoulder. "Good work out there, Ethan. We'll see you in the locker room."

Ethan nodded in the coach's direction. Nick watched the way his son refused to meet his eyes, and it crushed him. He never wanted to hurt his son. It was just all deeper than Ethan could ever understand.

"I'm sorry for what you saw last night," Nick said when they were the only ones left on the field.

Ethan huffed, taking the helmet from his head, dropping it on the ground. "Right. You looked real sorry."

Nick deserved that, he knew it. "It's not what you think. It was a one-time thing, Ethan. I'm not leaving your mom."

"Oh, that's a relief," he said sarcastically. Did his dad really think he was that stupid? "Dad, you're fucking her best friend!"

Nick raised a finger to his son. "Watch it, Ethan. I know it's wrong. I know you don't understand it, but that doesn't give you the right to speak so crassly about it."

Ethan crossed his arms over his chest, feeling defiant over his father. "I can speak however I want about it." He glared at his dad. "I can't even look at you. You make me sick. That's J.R.'s mom. She's like family, Dad, it's gross. How could you do this?"

Nick let out a sigh. "There's many things you don't know, Ethan. Anna and I have a history together..."

The anger boiled over in Ethan. He let out a loud grunt as he swiftly kicked his helmet like a football. "So you *have* done this before."

Nick jumped back out of the way of the flying helmet. "Keep your voice down," he snapped. "No, I told you it hadn't happened before. And it won't happen again. I need you to believe that."

Ethan brushed by his dad, who grabbed him by the arm and pulled him back to him. "Please, son. If this gets out, it will ruin all of us."

Ethan gave his dad a deathly stare. Of course Ethan wouldn't tell. If he did, not only would it risk his parents' marriage, but his friendship with J.R. But he didn't want his dad to know he had that kind of power over him. "You should have thought about that."

This time, when Ethan pushed past his dad, he wouldn't be stopped. He left his dad standing on the field, drenched in his own sweat.

CHAPTER 17

Fourth day gone

Nick stood dumbfounded, staring at the hat in the chief's hands. His legs were heavy, bolted into the muddy ground as it sucked him in. Everything but the Falcons hat blurred around him. Objects moved in and out of focus, swaying like the leaves on the trees. Sounds faded in and out of comprehension. He couldn't decipher between Jameson's antagonizing shouts and his wife's piercing sobs.

His body was telling him one thing, but his brain was saying another. There was no actual sign of danger. His son's hat only meant that his son was in the vicinity. And maybe he still was.

He pinpointed his focus on Jameson, who seemed to be having the same thoughts as he was.

"I want people all over this damn forest," the mayor commanded the chief. "Get your team up here and let's scour the area. If the boys are hurt and haven't been able to get back to the car, we will need stretchers and paramedics." His demands were strong, but his voice broke enough for Anna to be alarmed. He pulled her to him, though she wasn't sure if it was to comfort her or to keep himself from shaking.

"Don't worry, sweetheart," he said. He hadn't called her that in so long, she almost didn't realize he was talking to her. "We'll find them."

Nick watched the way Jameson clung to Anna. It didn't make him jealous as much as worried. If Jameson was showing weakness, it only meant one thing: he didn't believe his own words to be true.

Nick reached for Nora's hand. She had forgotten to be worried about their marriage, to concern herself with Nick and Anna. All that mattered right then was her son. She gratefully took her husband's hand for strength and looked up at him with teary eyes.

"James is right," Nick said to her and then to Anna. "The boys are out there, and when we find them, they'll have a good explanation as to what they were doing in the woods." Nick could feel Nora take in a deep breath. "There's no reason to get worked up yet. They're smart boys, and if they got lost or hurt, they know how to survive."

Anna nodded. Nick was right. They had been on heightened emotions since realizing their sons were missing, but this was a break. They knew their sons were here. Now, the only obstacle was to get to them.

"We can split into teams. There's a path that runs down the eastside—"

The chief cleared his throat, causing Anna to stop and look his way. He didn't look well. "Chief, are you alright?"

He stared at the hat in his hand before gently handing it over to Nora. She took it graciously and cradled it to her chest, as though it was her son instead. She felt a shiver go up her spine when the chief finally met her eyes. He looked vacant.

"There's something I need to show all of you." Rex reached into his back pocket. "I didn't want to do this here. We're still in an ongoing investigation, and it would be better if the four of you would head home until we have more answers."

"An investigation," Anna murmured, feeling woozy. What was the torn paper he had folded in his hand?

"Yes," the chief responded. "We have reason to believe this wasn't an accident." He hesitated a moment before handing Nick the paper. "Nick, I need you to confirm that this is Ethan's handwriting."

Nick looked confused as Rex handed him the folded square of paper. There was something holding him back from opening the note. Something he knew would change this all if he saw what was inside. His hesitation scared Nora, who ripped the paper out of his hand. She unfolded it as fast as she could and then gasped. Her fingers trembled as she covered her mouth. A small "No," escaped her lips.

"Nora, what is it?" Anna asked, her own voice trembling.

Nora just stood there, shaking her head. Nick took the note back from her and read his son's words. He had to read it twice before he understood.

"Is that Ethan's handwriting?" Rex asked again. He knew the answer by the way that Nora wept and Nick's fingers shook.

"Nick?" Jameson stepped forward, letting go of his wife as he took the paper from his friend's hand. His eyes glazed over as he read. "A suicide note?"

Anna gasped. "No, no," she kept saying. "That can't be."

Nora let out a wail, but Nick was back in his fog, unable to move or to hear around him.

I'm so sorry. Please forgive me.

Ethan

His boy, his baby boy. Nick felt the world spin around him.

Oh, Ethan, he thought, *tell me this isn't true.* Why would he do such a thing? What could have made his son feel so desperately hopeless that he felt he needed to end his own life?

Nick dropped to his knees, the dampness of the ground soaking into his jeans. This was all his fault. He had pushed his son away. Ethan hated him, and that hatred had seeped into his gentle spirit and made him feel useless and alone. Any despair he must have been feeling, he couldn't talk to his own dad about because he despised him. All of this was because Nick was in love with a woman other than his wife.

Anna held Nora as she sobbed. She couldn't look at Nick. She knew the guilt he was feeling, because she felt it, too. He had broken down and told her earlier that day that Ethan knew about them, and of his fear that their fight had driven a wedge between them. It terrified Anna to think that Ethan may have told J.R. and that the two of them had devised a plan to leave Timber Falls as her and Nick's punishment. When she looked back on the last couple weeks and the changes in J.R.'s behavior, it now made so much sense. He had known all along about her affair. And she couldn't even protect him from it. She was too selfishly wrapped up in her own confusing emotions to think what her actions were doing to her children.

"Chief," Jameson said, carefully aware of his friend's distress. "Are there more notes?"

Anna perked up. She desperately wanted a note from her son just as badly as she didn't. If there was no note, then maybe J.R. hadn't committed suicide.

She was a horrible person to admit it, and she hated herself for thinking she wished it was only Ethan and that her son was alive in the woods, waiting to be rescued.

The chief shook his head. "No, not that we've seen. The sheriff found this on the dashboard of J.R.'s car. So far, it's the only sign that leads us to believe that the boys took their own lives. We have no reason to suspect foul play was involved. But until we recover the bodies, we won't know for sure."

Nora felt her stomach churn and was afraid she would throw up right there. *Recover the bodies.* How was this happening? None of this made any sense. Ethan would never end his life. She felt a rage building inside her that she couldn't ignore. Her son would never be a culprit in a plan like this.

Caleb.

She knew in her gut that he was behind this. He always was. When the boys were in trouble, when Ethan broke a rule or told a lie, it was all for Caleb. He was the bad seed who grew in her son. He was the one who planted the danger and the deceptiveness in her boy. She should have never let her son become friends with that evil monster.

As if Anna could read Nora's thoughts, she spoke softly. "Kate should be here. Someone needs to call her."

"She's already been here," Rex admitted. "She was at the station when I got the call and followed me up against my orders. I sent her home moments before Jameson arrived."

"Does she know about the note?" Anna asked. She watched as Nick lifted his head, running a hand down his face. She wanted to go to him, wrap her arms around him and help him up, but she couldn't. She would never be able to touch Nick the same way again.

Rex shook his head. "No."

Jameson's head was spinning. No note meant that his son could still be safe. He wasn't going to wait around for someone to tell him otherwise. He pulled off his blazer jacket and handed it to Anna. He didn't give a shit if his dress shoes were ruined by the mud; he was going deep into the woods and wasn't coming out without his son.

"James..." Anna started, but knew there was no stopping him.

"Mayor," Rex started. "I think it would be best if you stayed back..."

Jameson spun on his heels and jabbed a finger in the chief's face. "Don't you tell me what's best," he snapped. "That's my son out there, Rex. *My son.* Keep your limp dick out of this."

"James!" Anna gasped.

He turned to look at his wife. "You think this guy is going to find our boy, Anna?" He returned his glare to the chief. "If you'd been doing your job instead of sitting on your hands, you would have been up here day one! Instead, my son has been sitting in the woods probably scared shitless cause you can't get *your* shit together." He laughed wildly. "And now, you want us to leave so you can do your *job.* Tell me, Chief. How would you have handled this if it was Lila in the woods instead?"

At the mention of his daughter, Rex lost all restraint he had with the mayor. He knew Jameson's words came out of fear. He knew that since the day J.R. had gone missing, Jameson hadn't wanted to believe his son was in any danger, or had left of his own accord. He didn't want to take any blame for J.R.'s actions. Especially if it ended in suicide. Rex could handle that. But he wouldn't stand for him to speak of Lila in that way.

Rex grabbed the mayor by the collar, and with unimaginable force, shoved him to the ground. He was soaked in mud. His white shirt stained shit brown. He looked dismantled and shocked by the chief's reaction, but Rex was done playing nice guy.

"Don't you ever talk about Lila." The chief towered over Jameson. The venom in his voice was thick. "Do you understand?"

The mayor's eyes were wide with surprise and then quickly clouded in fury. Officer Maloney was at his side, helping the mayor off the ground while eyeing the chief suspiciously.

"Get your hands off me," Jameson said, shoving the officer off him. He stood up and adjusted the button-down shirt that was stuck to his skin. He ran a hand through his hair, collecting his rage as he turned to the officer who had knocked him to the ground and growled, "That just cost you your job, Tourney."

"Jameson, no!" Anna cried out. They needed the chief. Of course Jameson understood that. He was just scared, and acting on impulse.

"James," Nick started. He stood from the ground, using Nora's hand to steady himself. "Let's not make any hasty decisions right now. Everyone is emotional and..."

But Jameson wasn't hearing him. He kept his glare on Rex, who only returned the fire. "Get the fuck out of here, Tourney. I don't want you anywhere near my son."

Officer Maloney rested a hand on the chief's shoulder. He had no idea what could have caused him to shove the mayor to the ground, but also knew he didn't deserve to be fired over it. Through his hand he could feel the short, quick breaths Rex took. He had never seen his friend so worked up before, to the point of explosion. It was a side of the chief he had never expected to see. He feared Rex would attack the mayor again and decided that pulling him from the scene to calm down was probably the best choice.

"Come on, Chief," he said, making sure the mayor heard him use Rex's title. He wouldn't let Jameson fire the chief without a fight. "Let's go cool down."

Rex resisted at first. He was not going to feel threatened by the mayor. And if he ever heard him speak of his daughter again, Rex would kill him. That he was sure of.

He felt Maloney tug on his shoulder and eventually caved in and followed him. Maloney was right. Rex needed to calm down. Let the mayor go searching for his son. One thing he'd gotten right: If it were Lila, he would never stop looking until he found her.

"Come on," Maloney said. "The sheriff has things under control right now. Let's get you some water."

He needed something stronger than water. A lot stronger. There was a flask waiting for him in the glove compartment of his patrol car. If he could just get to it without Maloney, he would feel better. He pulled his arm from his friend's grip and did his best to smile.

"I'm fine, really," he said to Maloney's wary look. "I think this case is just getting to me, and I lost control for a moment."

Maloney let go of his arm. "I hear ya, Chief." He leaned in closer. "Between you and me, I haven't been sleeping much. Too much running through my head, you know?"

Rex nodded. He did.

"We gotta keep it together, though," he continued. "I tell myself all the time if I'm struggling, just imagine what these families are going through. That helps me keep my head on straight."

Rex placed a hand on his friend's arm. "You're a good man, Maloney. You'd make a good police chief."

Maloney looked taken aback. "I'm not taking your job, Chief."

Rex looked back at Nora and Anna, huddled together as they watched their husbands trek off to the woods. Maloney may not have had a choice in the matter. If the mayor were, in fact, to fire Rex from being the chief of police, Rex would lobby for Maloney to take over. If by chance the mayor changed his mind and let Rex keep his job, Rex may still have decided to walk away. He was not the man for this job.

"Go help the sheriff," Rex encouraged. "I'll go grab a coffee and calm down. Keep me informed if there is any new information."

"Of course, sir."

Rex caught Anna's apologetic eye as he walked to his car. He didn't want her pity or her apology. He nodded back at her and slid into the driver's seat, noting the time. Lila would be out of school by now, and probably at home. He had half a mind to go home and tell her what was happening, but the other side of him pulled stronger. He drove down the steep gravel drive until he met concrete. From there, he turned from town and drove along the lake that met the bottom of Oracle Point. He found a place to park, away from the road and wandering eyes. He put his car in park and lifted the flask from the glove department. He shot back a drink, his eyes never leaving the scene ahead. From where he sat, he could make out a clear view of the top of Oracle Point.

He kept his radio on, though it mostly fell silent as all of the officers in the area were on scene and in search of the boys. They would have spread out, taken various trails down to the lake below as well as searched the deep of the brush in case one of the boys had gone off trail and become lost. There was just as much possibility of finding the boys together as alone.

He drank in the silence, his nerves rattling as his mind filled with images making him sick to his stomach. Ethan, Caleb, J.R., Lila.

Lila, Lila, Lila.

It was foolish of him to have allowed the mayor to shake him as he did. But he couldn't help himself. The rage that he held deep in his belly was slowly seeping out, and he didn't know how to contain it any longer.

He drank while the evening sun began to set over the hill, and still, no word came from the mountain above. He should have gone home, but he wasn't sure if he could see straight enough to do it. His head wobbled as he struggled to keep it upright and straight. He should have been on the mountain. He shouldn't have been on the mountain. He was a fuck-up. Everyone knew that. His head slid to the side as he eyed the gun on the passenger seat. He picked it up and weighed it in his hand. Would anyone even care?

Lila, Lila, Lila.

He swore under his breath as he placed the gun back on the seat. He took another drink, emptying the flask. Crap, now what was he going to do? He closed his eyes and began to drift when the two-way radio shifted on, startling him.

"Chief. Come in, Chief, this is Officer Maloney."

His fingers wobbled with the cord, causing the CB to fall from his hands. He picked it up and cleared his throat. He tried his voice before pushing the button to return the message.

"This is Chief Tourney." How much longer would he be able to say that? He waited in silence for a reply. It seemed to take forever. He wished he had more to drink.

"Chief," Maloney's voice came back over. "We found a body."

CHAPTER 18

Three weeks earlier

Ballots for Homecoming King and Queen were passed among students. It would be no question that J.R. and Grace would hold the title, but they had to earn it rightfully through a vote. Avery and Grace had plans that upcoming weekend to travel north to Seattle to buy their dresses, a tradition of theirs since freshman year. They hadn't officially been asked to the Homecoming dance yet, but that was just a technicality. Of course Grace would go with J.R., and Avery—well, she thought Caleb better get his act together soon and ask. She'd been dropping hints whenever they were around each other, whether that was when they were making out in the back of his Jeep or when he was ignoring her and talking to the boys at the lockers. She made sure he heard her. He was doing this on purpose, she knew. It would just be like him to make her sweat it out.

She watched him now, the way he eyed that freshman ass as it waddled by. He was a disgusting pig, and she hated that she loved him. He leaned against his locker all cocky. The girls giggled when they walked by and caught him staring. She was sure they felt special. Avery knew by experience that they weren't. She rolled her eyes and then glared at the girls when they passed. Their smiles quickly vanished from their faces.

Ethan walked up between her and Caleb, and twisted the knob to enter his locker combo. She looked up at him. Why hadn't she ever gone for Ethan? He was just as hot as Caleb, maybe a little prettier and not so rough around the edges. She wondered what he would be like in bed, if he would actually care about her needs.

"Ethan," she said sweetly, leaning into him.

He didn't look at her when he answered. "Yep?"

"Go to Homecoming with me."

Grace, who'd been wrapped up in J.R., spun her head Avery's way. "What?"

But it was Caleb who caught Avery off guard. It was meant to make him jealous, and instead, he was laughing so hard he had tears in his eyes. Asshole.

"Uh," Ethan stammered as he shoved his math book to the back of his locker. "Thanks, Ave, but I'm not going with anyone this year."

Her face turned as red as her hair. "Who goes without a date to Homecoming?"

Ethan closed his locker and turned to face her, one shoulder against the cool blue metal. He shrugged. "I don't like to be tied down," he teased. "Besides, don't you already have a date?" He rolled his eyes back toward Caleb behind him.

She leaned against the locker and crossed her arms. "No."

"Come on, Caleb," J.R. said. "Don't be a jerk."

Avery was so embarrassed. She did not need a pity date. She was sure there were plenty of other guys in this school who would be happy to take her to the dance if Ethan and Caleb wouldn't. She'd been told her number was plastered on all of the boys' bathroom stalls.

Caleb was still chuckling when he came to stand in front of her. She rolled her eyes and looked away when he dropped to one knee in front of her. It caused other students to stop and watch. He took her hand.

"Avery Abigail Quinn, will you escort me to the Homecoming dance?"

"You're a prick."

He cocked a smile. "Is that a yes?"

"Fine," she retorted. But she couldn't help but smile. Everyone was watching them when he lifted her up off the ground and kissed her hard on the lips.

"You've made me the happiest man on the planet."

She swatted at him. "Put me down. You better take me to a really expensive restaurant."

"Aren't you making me dinner?"

"Yeah, Ave," Grace chimed in. "I was thinking it would be really fun to make the guys dinner this year. My mom said it was okay and they'd leave the house for us. And Ethan, you can come, too."

"Pre-party shots on me!" Caleb cried out.

Avery sighed. "Fine." She wouldn't argue about getting sloshed before the dance.

"And the after-party at Bryan's," J.R. said, smiling at Grace. What he was thinking about was the old cabin playhouse deep in the backyard of Bryan's house. Every year, Bryan auctioned the room to the highest bidder, and this year it was J.R.. A few candles and incense burning would hopefully be what Grace needed to feel special and get her in the mood.

"Bryan throws the sickest Homecoming parties," Caleb exclaimed. "Remember last year?" He winked at Avery. It was Caleb who had won the cabin last year, where he'd taken what he'd assumed was Avery's virginity.

Everyone remembered last year, Ethan thought. And everyone but Caleb had known that Avery wasn't a virgin. She'd lost it to Marcus Freshman year. How'd Caleb miss that? But no one corrected Caleb when he boasted about it, especially Avery.

Ethan lifted his head to the crowd of students rushing from one class to the next. A few guys stopped, as they always did, to high five the star athletes and comment on the previous game. Walking toward them, he recognized the golden hair nestled between two brunettes. As she stepped closer, their eyes met and he held her stare and smiled. Lila bit down on her lower lip, trying to suppress her wide grin.

The exchange didn't go unnoticed.

"The chief's daughter?" Caleb exclaimed. "Damn, Ethan, are you hitting that?"

Ethan's smiled faded as he glared at his friend. "Shut up, Caleb."

Caleb whistled. "Isn't she like fifteen? I mean *I'm* all for the young girls, you know, but didn't know you liked to babysit." He winked at his friend.

"You're disgusting," Avery snapped at him. She pushed off the locker and grabbed Grace's hand. Grace planted a kiss on J.R.'s cheek as she was yanked away and led to class.

"Don't talk about her that way," Ethan warned. "And it's not like that."

"What's it like, then?" J.R. asked. He seemed sincere, which Ethan appreciated even if he was chuckling at Caleb's jabs. "She wasn't looking at you like it's not like that."

Ethan shrugged. "We've just talked some, that's it. And I took her for a drive the other day."

Caleb smacked his friend playfully in the arm. "Damn! You're getting some from the chief's daughter. You know he hooks up with my mom?"

"I'm not *getting some* from Lila," Ethan repeated. He wouldn't deny that the thought had crossed his mind. It actually crossed his mind *a lot* late at night when he was alone in bed.

"What are you talking about, Caleb?" J.R. asked. J.R. had never seen Kate with a guy before. It was strange to think of her with anyone, especially someone well known in this town. "Is your mom dating the chief of police? I thought you hated him."

"He's a douche." He nodded. "She doesn't talk about it and I don't want to hear about it. And it's never when I'm at home. But I've seen the evidence of him being there." He smiled at Ethan. "What if it got serious and they like moved in together? Maybe Lila and I could share a room..."

Ethan's face went red. He didn't like Caleb talking about Lila like she was another one of his playthings. "Knock it off, Caleb."

"Oooh, did I hit a nerve?" Caleb laughed. "Hey, I'm just saying if you're not hitting that, then she's fair game, right? Can't blame me if we're stuck in the same house."

Ethan shoved off the locker and stormed off.

Lila watched the scene unfold from a distance. She didn't know what had happened to make Ethan go from happy and smiling to brooding and looking pissed. He turned the corner and out of her sight, headed down the English hall. She looked back to see Caleb Weston and J.R. Hudson laughing at an inside joke, and she had the sinking suspicion that maybe the joke was her.

She wanted to fall into a sinkhole.

"So, are you going to tell us what's going on with you and Ethan Young?" Hannah asked her, breaking her thoughts.

Lila looked at her best friend, the one she told everything to. "I don't know what you mean. Nothing's going on."

"Come on, Lila," Olivia pressed. "We're not stupid. And where'd you disappear with him to the other day?"

"He took me on a drive," she answered. A small smile crept up on her lips. "Actually, he let me drive his car."

"What?" Hannah exclaimed. "You drove Ethan's car? You don't even have a license."

"Duh." Lila sighed. "He knew that." She kept her answers short. There was something pressing inside her to keep her feelings for Ethan a secret. Deep down, she knew it had to do with him not returning her obsession.

"Are you ditching us for Homecoming?" Olivia asked.

"Right." Lila rolled her eyes. "Like my dad would even let me go with a date to Homecoming."

"So you do want to go with him!" Hannah declared, loud enough to get stares from passing students.

Lila looked away from her best friend. She didn't know how to lie to her and get away with it. "No."

"Liar!" Hannah cried out.

Lila brought her finger to her lips to hush her friend. But a smile broke through anyway. The truth was that she hadn't been able to stop thinking about Ethan since he'd taken her for a drive. They'd had small exchanges in the hall between classes, and even once at lunch. But as far as she knew, he'd forgotten his invitation to *not* go to homecoming together.

Lila looked her friend straight in the eyes and kept her lips from smiling. "I swear that there is nothing going on between Ethan Young and me."

Hannah eyed her, looking for any cracks. But it was Olivia who spoke. "I don't know, Lila. He was looking at you like he likes you."

Lila bit down on her lower lip. So she wasn't imagining it. "Well, it's not like my dad would ever let me go out with him."

Hannah shrugged. "So don't tell him."

Lila rolled her eyes. "You try keeping a secret from the chief of police and let me know how that works out for you."

"Tell him you're staying at my house," Hannah suggested. "He'll believe you."

Hannah's parents had always been the lenient ones. Being an only child, Hannah pretty much got whatever she wanted, whether that was no curfew, or a brand new car she wasn't even able to drive yet. Olivia and Lila soaked up Hannah's privileges, and Hannah was all too eager to share. Lila was an only child too, but lived a vastly different life.

"Actually," Lila said. "Can we stay at your house on Homecoming night? There's this party we got invited to."

"Whose party?" Hannah asked. "You don't mean Keith's, 'cause his are always super lame."

Lila shook her head. "No, Bryan Lawson."

Olivia's eyes widened. "You got invited to Bryan Lawson's *Homecoming* party?"

"We did," Lila clarified.

Hannah held up a hand. "Wait, what? How?"

Lila shrugged, trying to be nonchalant about it. "Ethan invited us."

"Girl, there are things you are not telling us," Hannah quipped.

The bell to class rang above them, but the girls didn't move. Hannah was going to dig the truth out of her best friend, even if it meant missing her math exam.

Lila sighed. "I told Ethan I was going to Homecoming with my friends. And he said that there was this after-party we should come to."

Hannah eyed her suspiciously. "That's it?"

"That's it," Lila confirmed.

Hannah looked at Olivia, dumbfounded. "Okay," she said. "I guess we're going to Bryan Lawson's party."

Lila smiled. She couldn't wait to *not* go to Homecoming with Ethan Young.

CHAPTER 19

Four days gone

The words rang in Jameson's head like a gong being hit with a mallet over and over again. It made him dizzy, unable to focus. "We found a body!"

Nick gripped Jameson's arm, though Jameson wasn't sure if it was to keep himself steady or Jameson from falling. Thank God they'd sent the women home. He wouldn't want Anna to hear this, to wonder if the body they found was their son's.

He had been kept back from the scene, a shadow in the background. He wasn't supposed to be there, but it was made clear that neither he nor Nick would be leaving the mountain without their sons. There had been a bit of a frenzy after he kicked Tourney out, but then they all got their asses in gear and sorted out that there was an important job to be done. He wanted his son found.

It had taken all of his strength to hang back, leaning against his car and watching others as they took over. He was used to being in charge, and when your child goes missing it's the responsibility of the parent to find them. He should have been the one out on those trails, searching through brush, looking for clues as to where his son might be hiding. He saw it in Nick too, the way his body leaned forward, ready to pounce. They didn't say much standing together, but they each felt what the other was feeling. And just being there, with his best friend of over thirty-five years, gave Jameson the slightest bit of comfort, knowing he wasn't alone.

When the words he dreaded to hear echoed through the trees, he thought he would run toward the sound. That his first instinct would be to see if what they had found was, in fact, J.R., but his body betrayed him. He froze, like a coward.

"Sheriff!" One of the officers called out as he made his way through the clearing. The sheriff trotted towards him "We've got a body," the officer said, out of breath. "He's about a hundred and fifty feet down from the ledge. We found him on a rocky cliff that juts out from the mountain."

"Do you know who it is?" Sheriff Gibson asked.

The officer shook his head. He looked distraught as though he had never seen anything like this. "No, he's face down, and he's hard to reach. I need the fire department to help us get him. Most likely, we need to rope down."

The sheriff wiped at his brow. "Christ. Okay, I'll get them out here." He stopped the officer from walking away by adding, "Do we need paramedics? Any chance he's still alive?"

The officer looked over at Jameson and Nick before turning back to the Sheriff. "No, sir."

An odd sound escaped Nick's throat, one that Jameson couldn't place and had never heard before. It was guttural, like a wounded animal, and it made Jameson sick to his stomach.

The sheriff hung his head, his hands shoved deep in his pockets as he took the news in. Slowly, he made his way to the car where Jameson and Nick stood frozen. Unlike the Timber Falls police department, this was not his first time dealing with death and having to speak with family members. What he wasn't used to was those family members hanging around where they didn't belong.

"Mayor." He sighed. "Mr. Young. I think it's time you consider going home to your wives. There is no good that can come from you being up here. If you prefer, I can set up a space for you at the station where we will have full access—"

"If you think I am leaving this mountain without my son," Jameson spat, coming back to life. "Then you are wasting your breath."

"I'm not trying to suggest that you—" the sheriff tried again.

"We aren't going anywhere," Nick said firmly, interrupting him.

The men stared hard at each other, individually using their force to convey their message. Ultimately, the fathers won.

"Alright." The sheriff sighed again. "Can't say I'd be doing any different in your position." He pulled out his CB radio. "I'm calling for the fire department to back us up. Let's get that boy off the ledge and find the other two." He stalked off, defeated, while making his commands into the radio.

Jameson fell back against the car, running a hand through his hair. He shivered in the cold. It didn't help that his shirt was soaked with wet mud. What he would give to have a drink. He watched as Nick paced back and forth, his arms crossed tightly over his chest. He thought back to last Saturday, the last day he'd seen his son. His body clenched as the words that were spoken between them played over in his head. He had not wanted to take responsibility for this. He had put the blame in every direction but his own. He had been afraid to admit his own fault in this, where he had failed his son.

"I told him to go to hell," Jameson admitted.

Nick stopped pacing and turned to face him. "You what?"

Jameson kicked at a pebble by his muddy dress shoes. "That was the last thing I said to J.R. before he left on Saturday."

"Jesus, James."

"We'd been fighting," he added. "It seems like that's all we'd been doing lately, and I lost my temper. I said some things that had been building inside of me, this anger I felt for his lack of integrity." He looked his friend in the eye, pleading for him to understand. "I didn't mean it. Nick, I have to make this right with him."

Nick sucked in a deep breath and came to stand next to him. "Don't do that, James. Don't put this on yourself."

"Come on, Nick," Jameson huffed. "You and I both know I'm not as good of a father as you are. You would never say something like that to Ethan, no matter how angry you were."

Nick's cheeks reddened. "I'm not the man you make me out to be, James. We all have our faults."

"I doubt your faults could compare to mine." He ran a hand on the back of his neck. "There was something off with J.R., I sensed it. But instead of talking to him man to man, I became accusatory. I pulled a lot of strings to get the Huskies coach to Timber Falls. A place like this wasn't on his radar. And then for J.R. to throw away his future like that. I should have seen that there was something else going on. But how was I to know? What did we miss, Nick?"

Nick shook his head. He thought back to his son's behavior prior to Saturday. Nick had chalked it up to his anger at his and Anna's affair. Could it have been something more? "I don't know, James." His train of thought was broken by the sound of the fire truck alarm blaring up the hill. They watched in awe as the men jumped from their truck, carrying rope and a rescue stretcher.

Minutes stretched to hours as daylight faded in to dusk. Neither man moved from their post as they waited for answers. Silence hung between them as they both wallowed in their own grief and guilt. They waited anxiously for the fireman to return to see the boy who lay on the stretcher. But it was the sheriff who appeared, worn and aged since they had seen him last. Both men knew the news would not be good. They had thought they had mentally prepared themselves for anything, as long as they had an answer. But as the sheriff opened his mouth to speak, Jameson found himself turning away, as though the words would not exist if he didn't invite them in.

"I wanted to warn you, they are bringing the body up now." He paused for a moment. "It appears to be Caleb Weston."

Nick sucked in a deep breath. "Appears? How do you not know? Every one of those officers down there knows Caleb."

The sheriff cleared his throat. "Mr. Young, with all respect, we are dealing with a body that has been in the wild for days, and though we are to assume his death is in relation to a fall off the top of the ledge, it seems as animals may have found the body before we did."

Nick swore under his breath.

Jameson collapsed in half and vomited what little he had in his stomach.

"That's not all, I'm afraid," Sheriff Gibson added. He placed a hand on Nick's shoulder, and Nick's face went white. "Mr. Young, we found Ethan's body at the base of the mountain on the water's edge. They are bringing him..."

Nick pushed off the car and was running toward the forest entry before the sheriff could finish his sentence. The sheriff raced after him like he was in a hot pursuit until he was able to catch him and tackle him to the ground. Nick screamed profanity, flailing his arms until another officer was able to help hold him down. The sheriff placed his hands behind his back to keep him steady. Nick's head hit the soft dirt as he began to sob.

The sheriff was panting and out of breath when he said, "I'm sorry, Nick. This wasn't the outcome I wanted to give you."

Jameson was there, kneeling by his side. "Come on, Nick," he said softly, reaching out a hand to pull him up. "I got you."

The sheriff stood as Jameson attempted to lift his friend off the ground. When it was useless, he plopped down beside him. He looked up at the sheriff, appearing more like a young lost child than the mayor. "Where's my boy, Sheriff?" he choked out.

The Sheriff squatted down, resting a hand on his shoulder. "We will find him."

Nick reluctantly sat up, his eyes glossy and frantic. "How do I tell Nora? James, this will kill her."

"Please go be with your families," the sheriff begged again. "They need you right now, and no good can come from you staying here."

Jameson lifted his friend to his feet and half dragged him back to the car. He would drive him home, where Anna would be sitting and waiting for news on Nora's couch with her. They would tell their wives what they had heard, they would comfort them while they cried. And

Jameson would hold on to every last bit of hope that somehow he was the lucky one. That his son made it out alive.

But when an officer came knocking on the door looking for him after four in the morning, every last ounce of hope was lost. The body of J.R. Hudson had been found.

CHAPTER 20

One week earlier

Avery had a secret.

Caleb could tell in the way that she tightened in his arms, not wanting to meet his eyes as they danced. Grace sensed it in the way she'd stayed silent all through the dinner they'd made for the boys. J.R. knew something was going on when she never took a drink of the wine that Caleb brought over for Homecoming dinner. But it was Ethan who heard her puking in the Morgans' bathroom and knew this was bigger than what any of them had dealt with before.

He was standing with his back against the wall, his hands shoved into his tan dress slacks, when she stepped out of the bathroom. She startled to see him there and took a step back. She fumbled with the spaghetti strap of her short, metallic silver dress, which normally would look amazing on her if she didn't look like death.

Ethan gave her a knowing look that stopped her in her tracks.

"What?" she asked, trying to avoid his eyes.

"Aves," Ethan said softly and low enough that he wouldn't be heard in the other room. "Are you okay?"

"I'm fine," she said, shrugging him off. "I think my stomach didn't like the clams or something." She lifted her eyes to him. The fear she was trying so hard to hide lived there.

"Avery," he continued. "I don't think it's the clams that are making you sick. Do you need to talk to someone?"

"No," she snapped. She pulled out her lip gloss from her purse and leaned into the hall mirror. Her fingers trembled when she tried to apply the stick to her lips. Meeting Ethan's eyes in the mirror, she said, "Just don't say anything to Caleb, okay?"

He held her glance. "I won't say anything to him," he answered. "But I think you should."

Her eyes began to gloss over. She couldn't look at him. Ethan, the good one. He would have never carelessly knocked her up. She knew the exact night it had happened. It was a month ago when Caleb had promised to make her dinner after practice. He'd ordered pizza and then bent her over the couch while they waited for the delivery guy to show up. It all happened so fast she hadn't realized until afterward that she'd never heard the tear of foil. When she'd asked him about it, he'd shrugged it off, saying he was out of condoms but that he'd pick some up tomorrow. He'd kissed her anger away, as he always did.

And now she was pregnant.

"I'm fine, Ethan," she repeated. "Let it go."

Grace eyed her best friend as she re-entered the room. Her eyes looked shiny like maybe she'd been crying, but she couldn't remember anything that Caleb could have said to upset Avery that night. Grace draped an arm around Avery's bare shoulders, wishing she could crawl into her friend's head. Avery gave her a small smile before pulling away.

"Who's ready for the dance?" Avery asked, forcing a smile on her shimmery lips.

"One more round of shots," Caleb announced, pouring them all a glass.

"I'll pass on this one," Ethan said, resting a hand on his belly. "I don't think my stomach liked the clams."

Avery jerked her head his direction. Was he making fun of her? But when he gazed at her, she knew that wasn't true. He was protecting her. She could cry again right here in front of everyone. She pulled it together and said, "Yeah, me too."

"What's wrong with the clams?" Grace burst out.

"Nothing, they were delicious," Ethan corrected. "I'm just a little sensitive to seafood."

"You're a little sensitive to more than just food." Caleb laughed, but then said nothing else as he skipped over Avery and Ethan and poured himself, Grace, and J.R. a shot.

Avery looked over at Ethan, and when she caught his eye, she gave him an appreciative grin.

They piled into three different cars. J.R. drove Grace in his black BMW, Ethan followed behind in his Civic, while Caleb drove Avery's Acura that she was adamant they bring over his dirty Jeep. Caleb jammed to the music the whole time, completely unaware of Avery's silence. J.R. had one thing on his mind and that was to get through the dance and to the after-party.

He took Grace's hand and led her to the dance floor. Her flimsy silk baby blue dress felt more like something she would wear to bed, and it only made him more excited. He wrapped his arms around her and pulled her to him so she could feel just how ready he was. Tonight would be the night. He'd done everything he could to make this special for her.

Ethan looked across the gym. He bypassed all of the eager eyes from the girls who'd known he'd come stag until his sight landed on the one thing he wanted.

She was standing in the middle of the room, her long blonde hair falling in soft ringlets. Her tight black dress hugged her hips as she swayed to the music. She was squeezed between the two friends he always saw her with, smiling and laughing, but her eyes were searching. He stood back and watched her, the constant conflict that resided in him when it came to her.

She was too young.

She was the chief's daughter.

He would be gone soon and shouldn't start anything with a girl he had no future with.

But...

She got him, in a way that not many people did.

She made him feel nervous when he was used to being confident and in control.

And she was hella hot.

He decided right then that he would let the night take over. If she wanted him the same way, then they could see where this would lead, even if it was only temporary. He knew the likelihood of him being able to date her was slim, but for tonight they could pretend. He would let down his guard and not let the voices of Caleb or J.R. into his head.

He walked toward her, a lion on the prowl for its prey. He was so hungry for her he wanted to devour her. She looked up as she saw him approach, and her body stopped moving. She held his stare as he came upon her, her friends speechless as he reached for her hand and pulled her to him.

"Hi," he said in her ear as he wrapped his arms around her. He could feel her tension begin to ease as they stepped into the rhythm of the music.

"Hi," she whispered back, her arms reaching back behind his head.

He breathed her in. She smelled delicious, like raspberries and cream. "You look beautiful," he told her as he fingered the curls that trailed down her back.

He felt her smile against his shoulder. "Thank you. So do you...I mean..." She caught her last word with a chuckle.

She was nervous and it made him laugh. "You think I'm beautiful?"

"That's not what I meant." She laughed with him.

She felt good in his arms. He looked over her head to see her entourage looking back at them as they whispered between themselves. "Are your friends going to be jealous if I don't give you back tonight?"

She stiffened in his arms, and he couldn't tell if it was from fear or excitement. But then he felt that smile again.

"They won't mind," she answered. "I did tell them about the party, though. I hope that's okay."

"Sure," he said. He knew she was a package deal. "As long as you're there, I don't care." He was getting more brazen in the way he spoke to her. He knew they probably only had this night, and he wanted to make it count.

She relaxed in his arms, resting her head on his shoulder, holding him closer to her. They danced without parting as one song bled into another. When a fast song came on, he asked if she wanted to get something to drink. She followed him to what she thought would be the punch bowl, only to be led behind the bleachers. She was surprised to see Caleb, J.R., Grace, and Avery huddled together. She instantly felt nervous, but then Ethan took her hand as if to tell her she belonged with him.

"Ethan, there you are," Caleb called out. "We thought we lost you to the underclassman section."

Ethan brushed him off and took the flask from his hand. He took a shot of whatever crap was in the bottle and then handed it to Lila. "You don't have to if you don't want to. It tastes like shit but gets the job done."

She shrugged and took the flask from him. She wasn't sure what was in there, but just like when she'd shotgunned the beer, she did it because she had something to prove. She wasn't going to look like a child in front of the most popular kids in school.

She took a sip, trying not to smell the foulness that crept out of the bottle. The liquid burned in her mouth, and it showed on her face when she swallowed.

Caleb roared with laughter. J.R. jabbed him in the side. "Shut up or you'll get us caught back here." He reached for the flask from Lila.

"I love this song." Avery moaned. "Come on, let's go dance. I don't want to spend all night behind the bleachers. It's gross back here."

"One more," Caleb said as he took the flask from J.R. when Grace passed on a drink. She knew she'd be called on stage for Homecoming Queen soon, and the last thing she needed was to make a fool of herself up there. She just wished J.R. would do the same.

Caleb shot back the drink. When his head came forward, his eyes were on Lila. Everyone but she missed the way he licked his lips at her, and gave her a salacious grin. It made her uncomfortable, the way he belittled her. He only saw her as a little girl. He would never look at Avery or Grace that way.

She straightened her back and reached a hand out, asking for the flask. He lifted a brow at her and placed it in her palm. This caught Ethan's attention. He watched as she swigged back a drink, and when he thought she was done, she shot back one more.

"Okay, okay, Shotgun," he said, taking it out of her hand. "Take it easy."

Caleb's eyes were wild with enthusiasm. Not often did someone provoke him, and that's exactly what the chief's daughter was doing. Little did she know, he was up for the challenge.

CHAPTER 21

Five days gone

K ate was inconsolable.

It had been nearly twelve hours since Officer Maloney showed up at her door saying they had found Caleb's body. Twelve hours since her whole world had been destroyed and any hope she'd had left of finding her son was gone.

She'd fallen to her knees right there in the doorway. Officer Maloney had leaned down and helped her up, cradling her in her arms while she cried. She'd demanded to see to see him, but Maloney calmly explained to her it was still an ongoing investigation and they needed all family away from the scene. At that point, only Caleb's body had been found and the department was still searching for the other missing boys.

She hadn't known about the suicide note that Ethan had left, or why it had been Maloney at her door instead of Rex. She hadn't known how her son had ended up mangled halfway down a rocky cliff or what he'd been doing up on the ledge in the first place. She had so many questions and no one to answer them. Which was how she ended up at the bottom of Oracle Point before the sun rose. She pulled her car to the steep drive only to have her lights shine on the yellow tape, blocking her from entering. On the side of the road stood two officers, one of which approached her car.

"Ma'am, this road is off limits," he said as he leaned in through her window.

"My son is up there," she said frantically. She realized this officer wasn't from Timber Falls and had no idea who she was. She searched for his nametag. "Officer Fisher, please, I need to see him."

"Your son?" he asked in confusion.

"Caleb Weston," she answered. "They found my son, and I need to be up there."

Recognition of Caleb's name made the officer nod and sigh. "Ma'am, I'm sorry. We are not allowing anyone, family or otherwise, on Oracle Point. I can have Officer Maloney come speak to you."

She was shaking her head wildly. "No. Get the chief. Tell him I'm here and I need to see Caleb."

The officer dropped his head and looked back at the other cop blocking the entrance. He took in a deep breath and said, "That's not possible, Ma'am. The chief isn't here." He could see she was barely holding it together. "Look, let me escort you home. I can—"

"No!" she yelled. "I'm not going anywhere until I see my son!"

"That's not possible," he repeated patiently, but it was useless. She shoved him aside as she opened the door to her car and stepped out.

"You don't have the right to stop me!" she screamed at him. "That's my son up there!" She pushed past him. If he wouldn't let her drive up, then she would damn well walk up the half mile it took to get to the landing.

He swung around and grabbed her by the arm, pulling her back.

"Get off of me!" she screamed, thrashing around to loosen his grip. The other officer was now at his side helping him aid in calming Kate down.

"Ma'am! I need you to stop." He grunted as she jerked around. One of her arms flew loose, nailing her fist to his mouth by accident.

He could have had her arrested; that would have given her time to chill out. He gripped her by the shoulder, forcing her arms to go limp. "Stop," he commanded. "I know you're scared. I know you want to see your son. He's not here."

"What?" Her lips slackened as she came to a stop.

The officer licked the blood on his lower lip that was swelling as they stood there. She had a good right hook. "He's not here. The coroner took him. They need to do an autopsy on the boys to rule out foul play."

Kate stumbled back. His words made her dizzy. It was then that she also realized that the other boys, her son's best friends, were dead as well. Her hands flew to her eyes as the tears burst out of them. She just wanted to see her son, to hold him one more time. The officer bent down to her and held her shoulders to him. "I'm so sorry, Ms. Weston," he said sincerely. "I truly am."

"He can't be dead," she sobbed. She crossed her arms over her chest, holding her heart in, afraid it would escape her.

He nodded at the other officer to head back to guard the entrance. He held tight to this stranger he felt immense pity for. He let her cry on his shoulder without speaking a word until her sobs fell to soft whimpers. When she lifted her head up, he said, "Let me drive you home, Ms. Weston. It's best to wait there and we will contact you when we have more details. Is there anyone home, a family member or friend?"

Kate felt gutted. She was utterly alone. Rex had abandoned her through this, and now the only soul she loved was dead.

She shook her head. "No." She sucked in a deep breath to keep the sobs away. "There's no one."

"I'd be happy to stay with you if you need someone to talk to."

She tried to give him a smile of gratitude, but she couldn't quite muster it. "Thank you, but no." She pushed the tears away with the palm of her hand and straightened up, embarrassed by her display. "I'll be okay."

He helped her back into her car where she thanked him again. "When you see Rex—I mean the chief—will you please have him call me?"

He nodded. "Will do, Ms. Weston."

She pulled out of the drive as the sun came up over the trees. She didn't want to go home, but she had nowhere else to go. She pictured her son blue and cold in a body bag tossed to the side like trash. It made her sick to her stomach and she had to pull over on the side of the road to vomit, though there was nothing in her belly. She had barely eaten in days.

She saw the Acura as soon as she turned down her familiar street. She wondered how long Avery had been parked there waiting for her. When Kate pulled into the driveway, she saw the trembling girl sitting on her front porch, her body wrapped up in one of Caleb's football sweatshirts. The sight of it caught Kate's breath. She parked and slowly exited the vehicle, her body suddenly exhausted and worn. Avery stood, the tears rolling down her face when she saw Kate.

"Is it true?" Avery hiccuped a sob. "Did they find his body?"

Kate walked up to the girl and swallowed her up in her arms. It felt so good to hold someone who loved her boy like she did. Avery fell in her arms and began to sob. Kate breathed in the scent of her son on the sweatshirt, and it was enough to make her feel faint. She pulled Avery down to sit on the porch step. She needed this, to feel strong for someone else while her world fell apart.

"I'm so sorry, love," Kate said into her hair as she wept with her.

"No, no, no," Avery cried. She lifted her head to look at Kate. "How? What were they doing up there?"

"I don't know." Kate shook her head as she brushed a damp strand of hair away from Avery's cheek. "I hope we are able to get some answers soon."

Avery used the sleeve of Caleb's sweatshirt to dry her tears. Kate felt a wave of unflattering anger come over her, feeling ownership to all things belonging to her son. As much as she adored Avery, she wanted to rip the article of clothing from her body so that it only ever smelled like Caleb. It was irrational, and Kate knew it. But it didn't change how she felt. She wanted every last thing that belonged to her son in her possession. And it was then, as the girl beside her trembled in grief, that she realized Avery was carrying the greatest gift of all, a piece of her son.

"Avery," Kate said as she lifted a hand to brush away the fallen tears on the girl's face. "Honey, is it true that you're pregnant?"

Avery's eyes bulged.

"It's okay," Kate said with a smile. She was terrified to feel hopeful, but the look on Avery's face confirmed what she was thinking.

Avery slowly nodded. She hadn't confessed her pregnancy to anyone but Caleb, and she knew where that had gotten them. Had he told his mom? Would he have after the way he'd reacted to her telling him?

"Oh, honey," Kate cried, pulling the girl in close. "This is the best news."

Avery stilled in Kate's arms.

"What?" Kate asked, pulling back. She saw the fear in her eyes and her own fear multiplied. "Honey, you are planning on keeping the baby now, aren't you?"

Avery couldn't look at her. She dropped her gaze to her hands. She thought back to Caleb's rage when she told him. She'd said that she wanted to keep the baby and he straight up told her he wanted nothing to do with it. So she changed her mind, realizing the best option would be to get rid of the fetus, and wrote Caleb a note saying she would take care of it. She was alone, and scared and questioned if it was the right choice. She had never been more confused in her life. She never made it to the clinic. "I don't know. I thought I was going to, but then Caleb..." She shook her head. "I don't know how I can do it."

The idea of having a piece of her son so close to her and then possibly being destroyed sickened her. "No, love, you can't think like that. This is a part of Caleb, too. You can save him by having his child. Don't you see that?"

"But my parents will kill me!" she cried. "And how am I supposed to do this on my own without him?"

"You have me, Avery." Kate was adamant about it now. "Please, don't make any drastic decisions yet. If you're not sure you can keep him, then I will take him for you. I will adopt him."

Avery realized how Kate referred to the baby as him, before they even knew. She so deeply wanted a redo when it came to Caleb.

Avery, for as much as she had given herself to Caleb, knew he'd had his demons. He was more dark than light, salt than sugar. She was terrified of bringing a child with his genes into this world. Could she raise a boy to not be like his father?

She saw the desperation in Kate's eyes, the way she must have seen this as a way to get her son back. Avery didn't know yet what it would feel like to be a mother, to know the kind of love that blinds you to their faults. To make you look past their evil and see only the good. But Kate did. And if Avery wasn't strong enough to bring this child into the world, then Kate would be there to guide her, or if she should choose to, take her child and raise it as her own.

Avery nodded at her. "Okay."

She would do this, all for the love she had never wanted to feel for Caleb, for the love she was beginning to feel for their unborn child, and to ease the pain for the woman who had just lost her only child. She would have this baby.

CHAPTER 22

One week earlier

L ila couldn't stop giggling. She sat atop the counter in Bryan Lawson's kitchen guzzling from a beer bong being held up by a group of senior boys. They chanted her name as she chugged, and when she started to laugh again, a little dribble came out of the side of her mouth. Ethan reached up and wiped it away with a soft finger. She came up for air and caught his eye. His grin was wide, and she saw something else in it as well. Fascination, maybe?

She teetered on the counter as the world around her began to swarm. Ethan rested a hand on her shoulders to steady her and she nestled up against him.

"Mmm," she said. "You smell good."

"So do you."

She shook her head, lifting a heavy lid to him. He was all out of focus. She closed her eyes and then tried again, looking him in the eye. "No," she groaned. "I smell like beer. You smell yummy."

He chuckled softly, pulling her closer to him. "I think you smell yummy, too," he said in her ear. He was so perfect. He was Ethan Young, and he had his arm around her. She still couldn't believe it.

She didn't know where her friends were, and she didn't care. She was having the best night of her life and she didn't want it to end. His mouth was close to hers, and the way he was looking at her lips made her wonder if he was going to try to kiss her. She'd only been kissed by Robbie Ferguson a few times last year when she told him she'd go out with him, only to have him dump her after a month cause her dad never really let her go anywhere with him. No one wanted to date the chief's daughter. It was like she held a big neon sign over her head that said, "Don't even think about it." But Ethan didn't look at her that way. He didn't see the restrictions she came with or the invisible neon sign. He leaned into her until she could feel his breath gently caress her cheek. She closed her eyes and waited for that sweet moment when his lips would touch hers for the first time, only to have a hiccup escape her throat.

Her eyes flew open to catch him jerk back his head. She went to speak but was betrayed by another hiccup. That's when Ethan started to chuckle again. She was horrified but not enough to keep the giggles at bay. She covered her mouth with her hand as hiccups and laughter escaped.

"Ethan!"

Lila and Ethan turned to see Grace pushing through the crowded kitchen toward them. She gave Lila a once-over before turning her attention to Ethan. "Have you seen J.R.?"

Ethan shook his head and went to speak before his eye caught the figure coming through the back door. "Over there."

Grace whipped her head around to see her boyfriend walking toward her. "Where have you been?" she accosted him.

He came up behind her and wrapped his arms around her waist. "It's a surprise."

"A surprise?" she asked warily.

He leaned into her ear to whisper about his plans for them in the playhouse when a loud boom came crashing in, startling all of them.

Caleb swung through the kitchen door with such force it broke off one of the hinges. The look on his face was pure rage as he pushed his way past partygoers, spilling their drinks against their sequin dresses and silk ties. "Get the fuck out of my way," he sneered at a group of boys, and they spread out like a swarm of bees jumping to get out of his way.

J.R. caught Ethan's eye, and both of them had the same reaction. They were used to seeing Caleb in a frenzy, while on the field or even on the occasions when his dad bailed on him. They'd watched him punch through walls, break windows with baseballs, and even smash trophies into T.V.s, but there was something on his face that his friends had never seen before. J.R. lept into motion, pushing through the crowd to get to his friend. No one dared to say a word as they watched him with mouths hung open as he reached the door to the backyard and slammed it shut behind him. The silence hung thick like fog in the air until Lila broke out in a drunken giggle.

"What's his deal?" she said a little too loudly to Ethan. He hushed her, but not before Grace threw her a solid glare.

"Caleb!" Avery screamed as she flew through the broken door. Her eyes were smudged black from crying, her cheeks red and blotchy. She looked wild and scared as though she was the prey running from her hunter and not toward it. She grabbed at her fallen spaghetti strap of her dress, searching the crowd for him. When her eyes landed on a worried Grace, she raced toward her friend.

"Where did he go?" Avery asked frantically. Her eyes were everywhere but on Grace.

"Avery." Grace gripped her friend by the shoulders "What's going on? What happened?"

Avery lifted on her toes, shaking Grace from her grip. "I need to find Caleb. Where did he go?" She looked at Grace for the first time. "Did you see him?"

Lila pointed to the back door. "He went that way."

Avery looked up, just now noticing the underclassman sitting on the countertop a little too close to Ethan. What was she doing here? And why was she the one telling her where Caleb was? Avery went to speak but was caught off guard by J.R.'s return. He went to stand next to Grace, but it was Avery who reached out to him and grabbed him by the arm. "Did you see him? Do you know where he is?"

"Avery," J.R. said, taking his arm from her grip. "He's really pissed. He won't talk to me."

"I have to go," she said frantically. This time, J.R. reached out to her, holding her back. "He doesn't want to talk to you, Avery. And I wouldn't try changing his mind right now. I've never seen him like this. I don't know what you two were fighting about, but he needs some time to cool off."

Avery took one step back. One foot in flight and one in surrender. She lifted her eyes to look at Ethan, and that's when he realized what the fight was all about. Apparently, Caleb hadn't taken the news of Avery's pregnancy well. He sighed and rested a hand on her shoulder. "Let it go tonight, Aves. You can talk to him tomorrow."

She searched his eyes, finding the comfort she needed in them. She nodded slowly, and then the tears began to fall again as realization hit her. Caleb wanted nothing to do with her or the baby she was carrying. The only way to keep him would be to terminate her pregnancy. She started to sob in her hands. She felt the warmth of Grace's embrace and fell into her friend's arms.

"I have to get out of here," Avery said to her. She was so humiliated. She wanted this night over and to be as far away from Bryan Lawson's house as possible.

"Okay, Aves," Grace cooed as she patted her friend's hair. "Want me to come with you?"

J.R. flinched at the request. "Grace?" She wouldn't just leave, would she? Not when he had planned for them what he had.

Avery nodded. "I don't want to be alone."

"Okay." Grace kept hold of her friend and turned toward J.R. "I'm sorry, but Avery needs me."

J.R. stood there with his mouth hung open. "Grace," he hissed, grabbing her by the arm. "I got us the cabin. You can't leave now!"

Grace was taken aback by the force in J.R.'s tone. She looked her boyfriend up and down, disgusted by his selfishness. "I'm not going to bail on my friend who needs me just so you can get laid!"

"That's not what—"

"Grace," Avery said, cutting J.R. off. "You can stay. My car is here. I can go home."

"No," Grace said sternly at her friend before turning her glare on her boyfriend. "Why is it always about sex with you, J.R.?"

"Grace," he warned. "That's not fair, and you know it. You asked me to make it special, and I did. I spent time and a hell of a lot of money to make it special for you."

"Screw you, J.R.," she snapped. "I'm not a hooker you can buy. Come on, Avery." She grabbed her friend's hands and stormed off, leaving a livid J.R. behind.

J.R. swore loudly, startling Lila, who then started to giggle, which made him turn and glare at her. Ethan placed a hand on her knee, giving her a gentle shake of his head as though to tell her to keep her tipsy mouth shut. It made her smile, and she tightened her lips to show him she could be a good girl. She never knew alcohol could make her so loose and at ease. She would never have had the nerve to react this way if they had been at school. She wouldn't even have had the courage to talk to them, let alone laugh at them.

She liked the feel of Ethan's hand on her leg. It did something to her insides she hadn't felt before. She wished he had kissed her before she'd screwed it up, and now wondered if there would be a chance for him to try again. All too soon, his hand was gone as he leaned in to talk to J.R., one hand resting on his shoulder to calm him down. She overheard J.R. say something about finding Caleb and Ethan saying to not worry and he'd take care of it. She gripped the edge of the counter as her body swayed like it was in its own romantic slow dance. She heard her name being called and turned to see Olivia and Hannah walking toward her, the same sloppy smiles plastered on their faces. They came carrying red solo cups filled to the brim. Lila squealed at the sight of them and opened her arms to embrace them as they approached.

"Oh, my god, Lila, this is insane," Olivia started. "I just won a game of beer pong in the garage."

"By won, you mean lost." Hannah laughed, the beer in her hand sloshing around. "She drank more than the senior guys."

Olivia leaned forward to whisper in Lila's ear but spoke loudly when she said, "Andrew Brickner grabbed Hannah's ass."

"Olivia!" Hannah gasped, looking around to see if anyone was in earshot. Lila and Olivia giggled wildly knowing the crush Hannah had on Andrew. When it was clear no one else had heard, Hannah smiled. "He did."

Lila watched as J.R. said something angrily to Ethan before storming out the back door. Ethan turned back to her as she jumped down from the counter. He reached a hand out to help her as she stumbled forward.

Hannah handed Lila her cup. "Here, I need to sober up."

Lila took it and lifted it to her lips, but the smell of the sour beer made her tummy turn. She set the almost-full cup on the counter behind her.

"Are you leaving?" he asked.

She liked the look of disappointment on his face. She bit her lower lip to keep from giggling, but the smile she couldn't hide. She shook her head. "Nope."

"Good." He slipped a hand around her waist. "I told J.R. I'd shut down the cabin for him. Want to come with me?"

Lila felt a rush of adrenaline flow through her. Even as a sophomore, Lila had heard rumors of Bryan Lawson's cabin that was tucked away in the trees of his backyard. She felt a nudge on her arm and turned to see Hannah smiling. "Of course she will."

He wasn't asking her for sex. He was simply asking her to take a walk with him to clean up for his friend who had been denied sex. And maybe, in their moment alone, away from prying eyes, he would try to kiss her again. This time, she wouldn't screw it up.

She nodded her head. The nerves that set fire to her veins kept her from speaking. He took her by the hand to steady her step, and she followed him out the back door. The cool night air caught her by surprise and she shivered. Ethan let go of her hand and wrapped his arm around her shoulder, pulling her closer to him. If he was drunk, Lila thought, he held his liquor well. She could smell the booze on his breath, but his walk was steady. He held on to her as her heels dug into the soft dirt, catching her shoe a couple of times. They walked, unnoticed by a group mingling in the hot tub. Girls swam in their bra and panties while the boys sat in their boxers, feet dangling in the water. One of the girls straddled a boy, and they didn't seem to care who watched them make out. Lila blushed at the sight of it.

"I should have grabbed my coat for you," Ethan said, cutting through her thoughts. "You're freezing."

"I'm okay." Her teeth chattered, but if she had his coat, Ethan wouldn't hold her as close.

"It's just a little farther up here," he said as they entered the dark woods. The moon was bright tonight, guiding their way down a small trail.

"You've been here before?"

He knew what she was implying, and the answer was no, he had never paid for the cabin before. But that didn't mean he hadn't made out with girls in there.

"We used to have slumber parties here in middle school." Slumber parties where the girls would sneak out from their sleepover and there would be a couple in every corner until the sun came up.

"Oh," she said, relieved, and then smiled to herself.

She wobbled and fell against him. She started laughing again as he stopped to swing her onto his back, but she couldn't hike her dress up enough to straddle him. So he picked her up and cradled her as she wrapped her arms around his neck. "You are going to break an ankle," he said with a chuckle as he continued the walk through the trees. She rested her head against his shoulder, breathing him in. They were completely alone, away from all the sounds of the party when he arrived at the cabin and gently dropped her back to her feet. There was a warm glow that flowed from the draped curtain windows, and when Ethan opened the door, the heat hit their face in a nice welcome.

Lila took one step forward, her mouth dropping at the sight of the room.

"Wow," Ethan whistled.

"Uh huh," Lila agreed as she took it in. J.R. had gone to the extreme to impress Grace, and if Lila had been her, she would have loved this room for herself. White pillar candles sat atop any surface that would hold them, mixed with lavender burning incense. The room was small. It held a sink, a futon couch with a table stand next to it, and a coffee table in front. In the corner was a T.V. with a VHS player attached to a makeshift stand of wooden crates, but what caught Lila's attention the most was the bed.

The queen-sized bed took up most of the room, becoming the focal point of the cabin. But it wasn't the fresh sheets and down comforter that caught her eye, but what lay on top. J.R. had taken the time to lay rose petals in the shape of a heart that nearly covered the top of the bed. He then had scattered the rest of the petals around the floor, one below Lila's pointed heel.

"Man," Ethan said. "I can see why J.R. was so pissed."

"Yeah," Lila murmured.

Ethan walked to the sink where a bottle of champagne sat open and inviting. He took the two cups and filled them to the top, handing one to her. "We can't let this go to waste."

She sipped at the fizzy drink, her belly feeling the odd sensation again as she smelled the liquor.

Ethan took a taste and then set his cup down. He was watching her, studying her and the way she lifted her eyelashes to him. It was her and the booze and this room that made him reach out to take her hand and pull her close to him. She went willingly, tilting her face up to him, inviting his lips to join hers. And when they did, she let out a soft moan that almost made him lose it. He gripped at her dress, pressing her body to his, and deepened the kiss, his tongue slipping in to meet hers. Her whole body trembled in excitement. He walked her back until her knees touched the edge of the bed. He lay her back, never breaking the kiss, and climbed on top of her. His hands were everywhere, in her hair, on her neck, down her leg and then up her thigh. She kissed him back with the same intensity, but when his palm clasped hold of her breast, peeling back the fabric that covered her, she froze.

"You okay?" he asked as his lips slid down to her throat.

Was she okay? They were just kissing, and now her breast was exposed and she had never been with a guy like this before. Her head spun and she couldn't think straight. If she told him she wasn't okay, would he call her a tease?

She felt the queasy sensation build in her tummy. The nerves, and the booze, took over with the fear that she wasn't ready for what he was doing to her.

"Oh, god," she groaned as she shoved off of him and ran to the sink. She made it just in time before she vomited the alcohol that was sloshing around her belly. She heard Ethan swear and jump up from the bed just as she puked again. She had enough sense of mind to be mortified by what was happening and held a hand up at him. "Don't," she said between hurls.

"Lila," he started. He wanted to help, but he didn't know how. "I should go get your friends."

She slumped down to the floor against the counter, her body breaking into a sweat. "No," she moaned. "Don't leave me." She wanted him there even though she would never be able to look him in the eye again. There went any chance of being with Ethan Young. She started to cry.

"Lila." He leaned down beside her, ignoring the stench that came from the sink. "Let me help you get into bed." He lifted her arm around his neck and picked her dead weight up. She groaned as her head fell back against him.

He laid her atop the sheets and searched for the trash can to put next to the bedside. She appeared to be asleep, so he snuck to the door and softly opened it.

"Don't go!" she cried out.

He flinched at the sound and turned around to see her trying to lift her head. "I'll be right back," he promised.

"My dad is going to kill me," she muttered as her head hit the pillow.

She closed her eyes, wanting the spinning world to fade away. She didn't bother to pull her dress down or adjust her breast that was still hanging out of the top. And when she heard voices that seemed so distant and yet so near, she had a fleeting thought that Ethan couldn't already be back with her friends that quickly, could he?

But as the door opened to the cabin and footsteps walked in, she forced a lift of her lid just enough to see it was not Ethan, or Olivia or Hannah who had found her. When the shadow appeared over her, she opened her mouth to speak before a hand clasped it shut.

CHAPTER 23
Fifth day gone

"Chief, Chief!"

Rex rolled his head to the side, moaning as a burning jab shot up the back of his neck. He reached a frozen hand to the back of his collar, rubbing the strain of tension. He shivered in the cold causing the affliction to shoot up from his neck to his head. He swore under his breath as the pain clouded over his brain like a prickly blanket.

"Chief!"

Banging on glass distorted his thoughts. He wanted to open his eyes, but the pressure on them was unbearable. He felt the queasiness in his stomach roll around in an acid bubble bath and he needed to take a piss, bad.

He groaned as the banging continued, and he heard his name again. Only he wasn't the chief anymore, was he? Not after the mayor had fired him at Oracle Point.

Oracle. Point.

The memory brought him back to life. His eyes shot open and he was surprised to see he was still in the driver seat of his patrol car. The evening sky had dimmed to a beautiful melody of orange and pink. He must have passed out for a couple of hours. He noticed a shadow out of the corner of his eye and turned to see a distressed Maloney pounding his fist on his window. Rex reached for the handle on the door and began rolling the window down. Maloney was speaking about ten volumes louder than Rex could handle before the window was even cracked.

"Hold on," he muttered.

Maloney leaned in, resting an arm on the opening and meeting him at eye level. His nose scrunched from the smell coming out of the car. Rex remembered the flask sitting in the passenger seat. He should try to cover it with something, paper or a hat, but then it was pointless; Maloney's eyes darted right to it.

"Chief, I've been looking all over for you." There was that distress in his voice again, Rex noticed. "I've been trying to reach you on the CB."

That's why he was so cold, he thought. He cleared his throat, feeling a burning sensation rip down his esophagus. "Sorry, Maloney, I turned my car off while I caught my bearings. What's going on?"

"Chief," he continued. "It's not good." Maloney looked stricken.

Rex sat up straighter in his seat. The way that his officer was looking at him right now made even his blood run cold. He was afraid to ask the next question, almost certain he knew what the answer was.

"What did you find, Maloney?" he asked.

Maloney dropped his head, pressing two fingers between the bridge of his nose. Rex wanted to tell him to get his shit together and tell him already, but he waited until Maloney lifted his gaze back to him.

"We found the bodies, sir." Maloney choked out his words. "Caleb, J.R., and Ethan are dead."

Rex's vision clouded over as he took in this information. His fingers trembled as he stretched them out over his face and slid them down to his chin.

Maloney was still talking. "Caleb was found first on a rocky ledge about one hundred and fifty feet down. Ethan's body was discovered at the water's edge, and J.R. was found early this morning floating face down in the lake about a mile south. It looks as though they may have fallen from the top of Oracle Point."

"Jesus." Rex exhaled. And then he whipped his head toward Maloney. "Did you say this morning?" That couldn't be right. He was only out a couple of hours. He turned his car on, the light of the clock on his dash illuminating it was after six. This wasn't sunset he was seeing, but sunrise.

"Chief?" Maloney jerked back as Rex threw his car into drive.

Lila.

He'd left her alone all night without word. How could he have been so foolish, so careless? He'd only meant to rest off the drink for a couple of hours.

He flipped the lights on his hood on and blared his siren, cautioning anyone on the road to get out of his way. He sped back to town, dodging lights and stop signs until he screeched to a halt in front of his dark house.

He wasn't a praying kind of man. But at the moment when he stepped out of his car, he asked God to please let his daughter be peacefully asleep in her bed. He steadied his breath as he unlocked the front door and quietly stepped in. He turned right, toward her side of the house, and stood outside her closed doorway, one hand on the knob. He closed his eyes, feeling the beats of his heart pound in his chest. Carefully and as quietly as he could, he opened her door. She would be asleep, her alarm for school not going off for another forty-five minutes. His eyes took a moment to adjust to the darkness of her room. Her dark purple curtains blocked out all of the natural light. When his eyes came into focus, he narrowed in on her small twin-framed bed, expecting to see ruffled sheets, with one leg hanging over the side as she often did when she slept. Since she'd been a child, she would start at the top of her bed, head on pillow, only for Rex to find her most mornings curled up in the middle, her pillow abandoned. What Rex found now was not his daughter in a peaceful slumber but a vacant bed, still made from the day before.

"Lila!" he screamed. Panic rose through him as he pushed off her doorway and raced back down the hall. He flipped the lights as he entered. The bathroom, his room, the living room, calling for her as he ran.

A soft whimper caught his attention, causing him to turn on his heels toward the kitchen.

"Lila, Lila, Lila," he murmured.

There she was, his fragile child, his soft and broken girl curled up under the kitchen island. She sat pressed against the wall, the cordless phone by her side. Her body was bent in half as her face lay down in her arms on top of her knees. She was shaking. Her whole body trembled.

How could he have done this to her? How could he have been so stupid? All he ever wanted was to protect her, the one person who mattered to him. The only person he loved. And he'd failed her.

He dropped to his knees and pulled her to him. She fell into his embrace, a sob escaping her lips as she threw her arms around his waist. He brushed his hand through her hair like he had when she was just a girl and she'd still allowed him to comfort her when she was hurt.

"It's okay, sweetheart," he breathed. "I'm here."

Her body shook as she cried into his chest. He held her tight, whispering over and over again. "I'm so sorry. I'm so sorry."

And he was. To her, and to everyone he had wronged. He couldn't be what the mayor needed him to be, what Kate needed him to be, and most of all what Lila needed him to be. He was weak and his weakness had driven him to crumble.

And still, he was sickened that he felt relief that they had found the boys. The search was over. He was freed from a responsibility he couldn't deliver. He was no longer needed. And there would be no more questions as to their whereabouts. Timber Falls could now be free to grieve these three boys.

As he held his daughter, he wondered how he would break the news to her. He wouldn't be able to send her to school with the gossip and rumors that would obviously follow. She needed to hear it from him, but he didn't know how to speak the words. Instead, he held her as her cries deepened, her body going into hysterics.

"Shh, Lila," he comforted. "It's okay, it's all going to be okay."

Her head jerked up, almost knocking him back. Her face was red, her eyes puffy and swollen. She must have been crying for hours. His heart hurt when he thought of his daughter sitting here alone, in the dark with her fears and her sadness.

"Stop saying that!" she cried out. He was taken aback by her anger. "It's not okay, Dad! They're dead!"

His mouth dropped. "Lila," he managed. His head spun with confusion. "How did you... Where did you hear that?"

She wiped her arm across her running nose. "Caleb's mom called, looking for you. She was hysterical saying that Caleb was dead."

"Oh, Lila." He leaned back against the island wall. "When did she call?"

"Last night. I think at like ten?" She gave him the accusatory look he deserved. "Where were you, Dad? I called the station, but they said you'd left the scene that afternoon. They couldn't find you."

He shook his head. How could he tell his daughter he was passed out drunk in his car when she needed him?

"I was out looking for them," he lied. "I never heard the radio call me in."

She was crying again. "Hannah called an hour ago and said she heard they found J.R. and Ethan's body. Is it true?"

He nodded.

She moaned. "No, no, no."

He reached for her, but this time she pushed him away. "Don't. Don't comfort me. This is all my fault."

He jerked forward, grabbing her by the shoulders. "Don't say that. This is not your fault, Lila."

She glared at him. "You don't know," she sobbed. "Oh, god." Her head fell back against the wall. "I did this, Dad. It's all my fault. I wished them dead." She covered her face with her hands. "You don't know."

Slowly, he pulled himself up and knelt in front of her. Carefully, he took each of her hands and lifted them from her face. She tried to fight him, but he wouldn't let her.

"Look at me, Lila," he said softly.

Her eyes darted away from him, but he held still, waiting. He would wait as long as he needed. He wasn't going anywhere. Finally, her gaze settled on him.

"This is not your fault."

She opened her mouth to argue, but he cut her off, this time speaking clear and strong. "This is not your fault. Do you understand me?"

She stared at him a while before slowly nodding her head. He pulled her close and she collapsed onto him, sobbing. He would hold her for as long as she needed. He would never let go if she allowed it.

CHAPTER 24

One week earlier

J.R. found Caleb sitting in the dark shadows near the side of the house. He was slumped over, nursing a beer, his eyes vacant as he stared off into space. J.R. pulled up a seat beside him, an old rickety lawn chair that hadn't been dusted off in years. His mom would probably yell at him for dirtying up his dress pants, but for the way this night was going, he no longer cared about anything.

He took a drink from his cup. "Want to tell me what happened tonight?"

"Nope," Caleb answered, staring straight ahead. He took another drink and then threw the empty bottle against a wooden post. Neither of them flinched as the glass shattered into pieces.

Caleb sat back and fumbled in the pocket of his tan slacks. "Where's Grace?"

"She left with Avery." J.R. took another drink. He didn't want to think about Grace tonight. He wanted her pushed to the farthest corner of his mind. Maybe Caleb had been right all along in that he should have never tied himself down to her. All these years, he could have been playing around like Caleb did. Using his name as a way to get laid.

"Sucks, man, sorry," Caleb said, pulling a small baggy out and placing it on his leg.

J.R. looked over, intrigued. "What is that?"

"Something to make us feel better." Caleb took out two small green tablets from the bag and handed one to J.R. "I had these for Avery and me tonight, but that shit didn't work out. Anyway, I think you could use it more." He popped the pill in his mouth and swallowed hard.

J.R. looked at the small tablet with the letter X embedded at the top. He had never taken anything stronger than weed before and had no idea Caleb had drugs like this.

Caleb caught him eyeing the pill suspiciously. "Trust me, dude, you need it."

Maybe on another occasion, he would decline, but this night, on the shittiest of nights, J.R. needed something to take the edge off. He popped the pill in his mouth and shot it back with a swig of beer.

"Come on, I don't want to sit here anymore," Caleb said, standing. They walked back inside and grabbed another beer. The music pounded from the other room as teens kept the dance party alive and thriving from Homecoming. As the drug began to dissolve into J.R.'s bloodstream, he felt himself loosening up and drawn to the music. He melted into the crowd, feeling more alive than he ever had. As he danced, he felt he was one with the music, like it was a living, breathing thing inside of him. He couldn't get enough. He didn't care that Grace had left. He loved everyone in this room more than he had ever loved her.

A brush of a leg slid up beside him, and he grabbed hold of the girl it belonged to, not caring who it was. He grinded against her, feeling the overwhelming sensation of arousal that made him want to fuck her right in the middle of the crowd. She giggled when he pressed his cock against her, and he thought it was the most beautiful sound he had ever heard. He grabbed her face and pressed his lips to hers, only to be pulled away a second later by two hands on his shoulders. He turned to see Caleb standing next to him. Had he been there the whole time?

He swung an arm around his friend. "Caleb! I love you, man. Have I ever told you that? It's true, I swear."

Caleb grinned. "Come on, let's get Ethan and get out of here."

"But I like being here," J.R. protested. He wanted to dance and kiss that girl who had just been there with him. He looked around him. *Where'd she go?*

"Where's Ethan?" Caleb asked. He seemed agitated as he scratched at the back of his shaved head.

J.R. thought a minute. "I think he went with that sophomore chick to the cabin. I told him he could have it since I obviously wasn't getting laid in it." He laughed uncontrollably at his own demise.

"Come on," Caleb commanded, leading J.R. out by the arm. When they got outside, he said, "It's too crazy in there. I...I need out of here."

"Whoa, wait up." J.R. stumbled behind him, trying to keep in pace with Caleb's frantic steps.

Caleb spun, searching around him. "Where the hell is the cabin?"

"Dude, you've *gotsta* chill," J.R. said with a sloppy grin. "Come on, it's up here." He took the lead, heading them to the dark trail. J.R. wanted to skip through the trees like he had when he was a child. He felt a rush as though someone had poured liquid joy into his bloodstream. Why wasn't Caleb buzzing like he was? They had taken the same drug. When he looked at Caleb, it was like his friend had taken a negative spiral down. He was jumpy at every sound in the trees, his eyes darted around him in an anxious flurry, and when they focused on an object, they turned hard and black. It made J.R. want to wrap his friend up in a big bear hug and squeeze the ugly out. The dim light of the cabin came into view, and Caleb picked up the steps. He called out for Ethan, but there was no response. He banged on the door once before pushing his way through. J.R. was hit with the familiar lavender scent and felt a rush of arousal come back to him. He was supposed to be here, alone with Grace. But instead of Grace on the bed, naked and waiting for him was another girl, her dress pulled up high to expose the softness of her inner thigh, her bare breast, plump and inviting, waiting to be touched. He was spinning in lust.

The sensation so strong he was afraid he'd come in his pants before he was even able to touch her.

"Close the door," Caleb demanded.

J.R. did as he was told and watched Caleb walk over to the girl, alone as though she had been waiting for him. He leaned down just as Lila opened her eyes. She looked as though she was about to speak when Caleb softly covered her mouth with his large hand. He hushed at her as she started to squirm.

"You've been playing me for a while, haven't you?" Caleb told her.

Caleb climbed onto the bed, straddling her small frame between his legs. J.R. couldn't see the fear in her or the tears that slipped from her eyes as Caleb kept one hand on her mouth and the other slipped her panties and nylons down. He could barely make out the soft whispers Caleb said to her about having wanted this since the moment he'd first seen her, and that he knew she'd been wanting it too. J.R. closed his eyes and listened to the moans that came from the bed and the way the mattress pounded against the wall. He didn't feel shame in standing there, a witness to this intimacy. He didn't feel alarmed that Ethan wasn't there and that Caleb had taken it upon himself to seduce the girl Ethan liked. He didn't feel guilty that he was imagining himself with her instead of Grace. So when he heard his name being called, he smiled as he opened his eyes and saw Caleb rolling off of her and inviting him over.

"Your turn," Caleb said with a smug grin.

J.R. felt the fire in his veins that flooded his groin and an overwhelming sense of love to his friend for sharing this gift with him.

Caleb kept his palm over her mouth as he stood at the edge of the bed. He leaned forward, meeting her eye. "You going to be a good girl if I take my hand away?"

Her whole body shook as she nodded her head at him. Slowly, he pushed away from the bed, watching her intently for any sign that she would scream. She kept her promise and tightened her trembling lips.

She was shivering, so J.R. took off his jacket and placed it over her chest to keep her warm. He could see her tears now and the pleading in her eyes when he crawled onto the bed. She shook her head, whispering, "No," but J.R. didn't understand.

"It's okay," he cooed in her ear. He kissed the side of her wet cheek all the way to her quivering lips. She didn't respond to his touch. Instead, she began to cry harder. This wasn't how it was supposed to be. He was J.R. Hudson. Any girl would want to be with him.

He looked down at her, confused. "It's okay, baby," he said softly as he began to unzip his pants. When he was free, he pressed himself against her, feeling the dampness between her legs. He moaned at the sensation, dying to dive in.

A slam on the door shook him as his head jerked back toward Caleb standing guard.

"Lila?" Ethan called out. "It's me, open the door."

A high-pitched scream broke from her mouth, startling J.R. enough to cover his ears.

"Lila!" Ethan yelled back, slamming his fists on the door. "Open the door!"

"Go away, Ethan," Caleb snarled, blocking the entrance with his body. The slams on the other side became frantic. And with every kick and thrust on the doorframe, Caleb's body jerked forward.

"Let me in!" Ethan screamed. "You sick fuck! Open the goddamn door."

Lila screamed for Ethan again.

"Shut her up!" Caleb growled at J.R.

J.R. sat back, dumbfounded. What was happening? She was wiggling beneath him to the point it knocked him over. He leaned down and tried to hold her. "Shh, it's okay, baby."

J.R. had the sense then that this was not what was supposed to be happening. Weren't they just having a good time? Why was she so upset? Why was Ethan yelling?

"Come on, man, it's all good," J.R. said to Caleb. "Open the door, it's just Ethan."

"Shut the fuck up, J.R.," Caleb snapped. "It's the drug talking, not you."

A thump brought their attention back to the bed. Lila had fallen onto the floor and was crawling toward the door. "Ethan!" she sobbed. "Help!"

Another kick and the door cracked on the hinges. Caleb fell forward enough for Ethan to push through. He took one wild look at Lila, then to J.R. with his pants down on the bed, and then finally to Caleb who stood back fuming and annoyed. Ethan turned on his friend and swung back and clocked him in the jaw with his fist.

"What the fuck!" Caleb cried out. J.R. was off the bed and between them before Caleb could retaliate. Ethan turned on him and shoved him hard toward the door. He fumbled on his feet and hit the ground. Ethan was on top of him, a fist in the air, the fury on his face unlike anything J.R. had ever seen. J.R. cradled his head to stop the blow, but it never came. When he looked up, Ethan was glaring down on him. "What the fuck is wrong with you?" Ethan yelled.

Caleb rubbed at his jaw. "Lighten up, Deadman. Nothing happened."

Ethan straightened up. He took one look at Caleb, and the greatest wave of disgust washed over him. He had always known there was something wrong with Caleb, that he was fucked in the head and wired differently than other human beings. He'd used to give him the benefit of the doubt, knowing about his upbringing and how he'd never had it as good as Ethan and J.R. did. But as he saw the way that Lila shivered in the corner, her body pressed as far into the wall as she could go, he knew it hadn't been nothing. That whatever had happened here tonight was his fault for leaving her alone when there were people like Caleb in the world.

"Get the fuck out," Ethan growled back at him.

J.R. stumbled to his feet. "Come on, Caleb."

Caleb stared hard at Ethan. It was a power play, and this time Ethan wouldn't back down. Slowly, Caleb stepped forward, keeping his eyes on Ethan as he pushed past him to the door. When he and J.R. were gone, Ethan ran to Lila and dropped to his knees in front of her. "Oh, Lila. I'm so sorry," he choked out.

"Don't touch me." She gasped, lifting a hand to defend herself from his embrace.

He threw his hands up in surrender. She was trembling, cradling her violated body into a tight ball.

"You left me." The words broke out of her shaky voice as her teeth chattered uncontrollably.

He sat back on his knees, afraid to touch her but wanting desperately to hold her. "I'm so sorry," he repeated over and over. "I wanted to get you help. But I couldn't find Olivia and Hannah, so I came back. I never should have left you."

She gripped J.R.'s coat around her torn dress. She felt filthy and disgusting and was grateful her friends couldn't be found. She didn't want anyone to see her this way. She could still feel Caleb dripping between her legs. When she closed her lids, she could still see the blackness of his vacant eyes. He was soulless, she realized, and Ethan was his friend.

Ethan leaned down gently. "Let me get you out of here," he said as his fingers caressed the side of her leg. "I can take you home." He wanted to pick her up and carry her far away from here.

She jerked when his hand made contact when her skin. "*Don't touch me!*"

He fell back on his seat. "Okay," he said with two hands up. "I'm sorry, Lila. I'm so sorry. I'm just trying to fix this."

She glared at him. "You can't fix what your *friends* did to me, Ethan."

The word *friends* sent bile down his throat. "Please, tell me what to do," he pleaded. He felt like crying for the first time in so long he couldn't remember. She looked broken. She *was* broken. And it was his fault.

"Go away." She stifled back a sob.

"No," he said with a violent shake of the head. "I'm not leaving you."

"Go away," she said again more fiercely. And when he didn't move, she sat up and screamed. "Go away, go away, go away!"

He slid back near the door. "Please, Lila," he begged. "Let me get help or take you home. I can't leave you like this."

She jumped to life, finding the first object she could find, a hardcover book on the nightstand. With all the strength she had left, she hurled it at him, hitting him in the head. "Go!"

He didn't say a word as he slithered out the door, defeated and despaired. He didn't want to be the one to add to her misery, so with a heavy heart, he did as she asked.

When she was alone, Lila fell apart, allowing every emotion to seep through her wounded soul. The anger, humiliation, and guilt ripped through her. How had she let this happen? Why had she gotten so drunk and let Ethan take her to the cabin? Why couldn't she have just stayed with her friends? She was a stupid girl who thought she could handle the older guys. Caleb was right, she had been playing with him, hadn't she? Had she been asking for this all along? She pounded her fist against her head as she cried. *Stupid, stupid, stupid.*

When she could manage to stand, she pushed her body against the wall and slid toward the door. She gripped the jacket tight around her chest and stumbled out, relieved to see that no one was around. She tripped and fell as her heel met the dirt path. She pulled herself up and kicked off her shoes, walking deeper into the forest and away from the party. She knew the road wasn't far from here, and if she could just get through the dark, she could find her path home. She pushed past overgrown brush, scratching her arms against fallen branches and sharp thorns. Her feet bled as she stepped on sharp rocks, but she couldn't feel the pain. Everything in her body hurt.

She was afraid she was going the wrong direction and went to turn around when she saw the faint glow of headlights pass by. She raced toward the sound of the engine and finally broke through the trees to see familiar concrete. She fell to the ground, exhaustion pouring out of her. She wanted to sleep right there. She closed her eyes and rested her cheek against the soft grass of the hillside beside the road. She curled into a ball and told herself, just one moment. Just one minute and then she would find her way home. But a minute came and went and she slept until she was jerked awake by the sound of her name and hands on her skin. She thrashed her body away from the prying fingers as memories flooded her mind.

"No!" she screamed.

Why hadn't she screamed, when Caleb had told her not to? Why hadn't she bitten his fingers when they were covering her mouth? Was she so afraid of him that she'd followed every instruction willingly, afraid of the consequence?

"Lila!" the familiar voice called out to her. She opened her eyes to see the recognizable police uniform crouching down beside her. And then the smell hit her. Old Spice cologne and spring breeze fabric softener. The scents of comfort, of home.

"Dad," she managed.

"Oh, my god, Lila. What happened to you?" She had never heard his voice like that before. Like he was about to crack. "We have to get you to a hospital."

"No!" she cried, lifting two hands to push him back. "I just want to go home, Dad, please." He leaned forward and she allowed him to scoop her up and carry her to the car.

"Lila, you're hurt, bad." He drew in a deep breath as he examined her body. "You've got blood running down your legs and on your arms."

She leaned back against the seat, feeling the warmth from the heater in the car. "I'm okay." She sighed, finally feeling safe. "I just want to go home."

She looked at him as he knelt down beside her, meeting her eye. "Who did this to you, Lila? Where were you? Where are Hannah and Olivia?"

"I don't know."

"Whose jacket is that?"

She remembered the coat she'd wrapped around her body. She was repulsed by it and wished she didn't need it to cover her torn dress. She rested her head back. "I don't know. I don't remember."

"Are you drunk?" he accused.

She nodded. Admitting that now seemed easier than any other question he could ask her.

"Jesus, Lila. Is that why you're out here in the middle of the night? How the hell—"

"Dad, please." She started to cry.

He sighed. She could feel the anger on him. "I'm just glad I found you and not someone else. Jesus, Lila, do you know what could have happened to you?"

She nodded.

"Are you sure you're alright?"

She nodded again.

He pushed off his knees and stood up. He walked to the driver's side and slid in beside her. "I am so disappointed in you, Lila. I thought I raised you better than to behave this way. Haven't I taught you the dangers of drinking?" He pulled the car into drive. "Consider yourself grounded."

She leaned her head back against the seat and closed her eyes. She was perfectly fine with that consequence. She had no desire to leave her house ever again.

CHAPTER 25

Seven days gone

Anna Hudson hated the smell of lilies.

She was eight when she first learned about death. Her grandpa Dean, her mother's father, had died suddenly of a heart attack, and Anna could still vividly remember sitting in the funeral home, the aroma strong of decay and Stargazer Lilies. They were the bitter fragrance of death, and now her home was filled with them. They came by the dozens. People sending their condolences from Timber Falls and from across the country. Family, friends, and business acquaintances. Everyone knew about the death of her son.

She hadn't left home in days. She didn't want to step into the world where her son no longer belonged. Here, she kept him near, his belongings surrounding her as though he were only out at practice and would be home any moment for dinner. Beyond her front door there were mourners, people who wanted to offer their condolences. She didn't want to see the look of pity in their eyes, or have to protect herself from an unwanted hug. She didn't want to hear the gossip that she knew was spreading about how her son had taken his own life by jumping off of Oracle Point. She knew the questions that were being asked, because she was asking them herself.

Why would he do such a thing?

Why didn't she see the signs?

Where did she go wrong as a mother?

How does she go on without him?

She envied those with strong faith, who could lean on God to get them through to the next day. But she never did. She could never believe in a Being who allowed such evil and ugliness in the world. She would not accept comfort from a religion that would condemn her son to the eternity of Hell for taking his own life.

She sat on the couch, her legs curled under her as her daughter lay sleeping in her lap. She brushed the hairs away from Emma's face, seeing so much of her eldest son in her complexion. Another tear fell from her eye; it happened so often she no longer bothered to brush it away.

"Mrs. Hudson?"

Anna looked up to see a solemn Grace standing in the entry of her living room, a large bouquet of pale pink roses in a vase. Anna smiled gratefully at the girl. "Grace, honey," she said. "Come in."

As Grace neared, Anna could see the anguish in her. Anna ached for the girl. She hadn't taken much thought into the devastation of J.R.'s death on anyone but her and Jameson and their family, but looking at Grace now she realized how hard it must be to lose the boy you loved. She had always adored Grace and assumed that someday down the road she would become a part of the Hudson family. The realization that that would never be brought more tears to Anna's eyes.

Grace sat the flowers down at the table nearest to Anna. She wiped a damp tear from her cheek as she said, "I wasn't sure if these were the right flowers to bring. My mom said that pink roses mean something like gratitude and appreciation, and she said I should stick to more of a classic white, but white just seemed so sad to me." She choked back a sob. "Sorry if they're the wrong color."

Anna reached out and grabbed ahold of her hand. "They are my favorite color."

188

Grace tried to smile. "Mine, too." She stood there awkwardly, not knowing her place in the Hudson home. How quickly it no longer belonged to her when the one person who'd wanted her there was gone.

Shouting came from behind Jameson's office door, the one-sided conversation muffled in sparring shouts. Anna closed her eyes as a crash of glass breaking slammed against the wall. When she looked up she could see Grace trembling.

"I'm sorry you have to hear that," she said to the girl.

Emma stirred in her sleep, a soft whimper escaping her lips. Anna hushed her gently, coaxing her back to her dreams. Sleep no longer came easily, but when it did, it was preferred to reality. As Anna moved her arm, a frame fell from the couch and onto the floor. Grace leaned down and picked it up, the image bringing her to her knees.

She gasped, looking at the picture of her and J.R. only a couple of weeks ago on their way to the Homecoming dance. "I haven't seen this." Everyone had gathered at the Hudson home for group photos, and usually it was J.R. who moaned his way through it, but here, looking back at her, he was beaming. It caught her breath to see the happiness on his face as he held her close to him.

"It was the last time I saw him smile," Anna admitted through tears. "After that night, he was different. I didn't know why and he never said."

Anna was right: everything changed after that night. Grace stared at the photo, wanting desperately to go back in time.

"We got in a fight that night, and I left," Grace told her.

Anna leaned her head forward. "What about?"

Grace shook her head, sniffling into her sweater sleeve. "It was stupid. Avery and Caleb got into a big fight and Avery wanted to leave so I took her home. But J.R. didn't want me to go and..." She left out the part about J.R. expecting sex that night. "I thought that when I called him the next day we would work it out. But he wouldn't even talk to me."

Anna ran the images in her mind of the day after Homecoming. J.R. had stayed in bed most of the morning and early afternoon. She remembered Grace calling. She recalled knocking on J.R.'s door to tell him Grace was on the phone and him muttering for her to leave him alone. Anna was embarrassed to admit she'd just assumed he was hungover at the time.

"Did you end up speaking at all that day?"

"No," Grace said. "I tried again in the evening, but Mr. Hudson said he was out. And he never called me back."

Anna pressed her lips together, trying to bring the day back into view. Caleb had called also, and J.R. had refused to speak to him as well. And then, had Nick said something about J.R. stopping by that evening? She closed her eyes as though the darkness would bring the answers to light. Yes, Nick had told her the next morning when they were together that J.R. had come by the house, but that Ethan wasn't feeling well and didn't want visitors. J.R. hadn't come down for dinner that evening either. Had she seen him the next morning before school? She couldn't recall. Her mind had been occupied with thoughts of her tryst with Nick. She felt shame and foolishness now, thinking back on how her sordid affair had clouded her intuition on her son.

"How was he on Monday?" Anna asked, absentmindedly running her fingers up and down Emma's arm. She needed the pieces of the puzzle to fit. Somehow, her son had found himself in a hole he couldn't get out of, and it had cost him his life. If he had just come to her, or to Jameson, they would have fixed it.

"He was strange," Grace started. "I tried to get his attention, but he seemed really distracted. He was asking if I'd seen Ethan and I hadn't. I don't even know if Ethan was at school that day. And when Caleb came up, J.R. got all panicky, like really weird. I'd never seen him like that before. I told him I wanted to talk about Saturday night and he just brushed it off like it was no big deal and that we were fine. I didn't see him for the rest of the day or after practice. And he didn't call me that night either." She stared at him in the photo. "I know he said we were fine, but it didn't feel like it, you know? But he also didn't seem mad at me like when we've gotten in fights before, so I didn't understand."

"Grace, why didn't you say any of this before?"

She shrugged. "I don't know. I guess I was just so focused on our problems that I had forgotten how weird everything else was. I was scared. I thought I was losing him." She choked out the last sentence.

Anna handed Grace the box of tissue she had forgotten about. Her own tears fell at every blink. Grace thanked her, taking a soft tissue to dab her eyes.

"So, J.R... He never said what was wrong?"

"No, he barely talked to me all week." Her voice cracked as she replayed their final days together. "No one was talking. Ethan was completely avoiding everyone when he actually did go to school, and Caleb was even more of a prick than usual. Avery and I had no idea what was going on. On Friday I was over it and found J.R. before the game. I told him I'd had enough and threatened to break up with him if he didn't change." Her glossy eyes widened. "I swear I wasn't trying to screw things up for the game. I was just upset."

Anna swallowed hard and nodded. How had she missed all of this? How had she not noticed that he wasn't speaking to Grace, and was avoiding his friends? She had chalked up his silence to nerves for the big football game. It had been all Jameson could talk about that week and Anna had warned him that he was putting too much pressure on J.R. He'd shrugged her off, and she'd turned away from him and given all of herself to Nick instead.

"Of course, Grace."

"That's the last time I talked to him," Grace said solemnly. "I don't know what happened on Saturday, or how they ended up on Oracle Point. I don't know why he would..." She couldn't bring herself to say the words. "I don't understand." She dropped her head into her hands as she sobbed.

Anna wanted to crawl into a hole and never come out. Would she ever have the answers she needed to feel at rest? Could she ever move on and find closure when there were so many misplaced pieces she couldn't grasp? Grace had been her missing link to moments she couldn't fit together. But instead of giving her peace, it left her with even more questions.

This couldn't have been the end. Her son's life would not finish on a cliffhanger. Somewhere, someone must have known something that would stop the incisive voices in her head. Otherwise, she worried she just might go mad.

CHAPTER 26

One week earlier

Coming down from X had been brutal for J.R. His body had gone plummeting from the highest high to the lowest of lows. He couldn't sleep, his mind kept trying to retrace the events on Saturday night, but he couldn't quite bring it into focus. When he did get blurry images, it would send him into a tailspin of nausea and self-hatred.

He couldn't look his mother in the eye. What kind of man was he? To stand back and allow his friend to violate another human that way, and then... He couldn't even fathom the words in his head. Every time he tried, a wave of emotion hit him stronger than anything he had ever felt in his whole life. It was as though he was being pulled underground, his body being sucked into the earth until was choking on dirt. He couldn't breathe, he couldn't concentrate, he was sweating even when his body wasn't moving.

He didn't want to feel this way. He needed the high, to keep him above the ground, so he couldn't feel the pain. He wanted nothing to do with Caleb, but Caleb was the only one he could score the drug from. And that was how he'd ended up on Caleb's doorstep Sunday night.

"Dude, you look like hell," Caleb said when he answered the door. He was in sweats and a Falcons tee with a slice of pizza in one hand and grease on his chin. He looked as though he'd just returned from a football game, without a care in the world.

J.R. pushed past him. "You should."

"What does that mean?" he huffed, shutting the door behind him.

J.R. spun on him. "It means we fucked up last night, Caleb, and you look like you don't give a shit."

Caleb took a bite of pizza before offering the box to J.R. who shoved it away. The sight of food still made him sick.

"You need to chill out," Caleb said. "Want a beer?"

J.R. shook his head. He scratched at his arm, nervous and agitated. "No, I want more X."

Caleb's head fell back as he laughed. "Of course you do, you little heathen. Greatest high in the world."

"Caleb, I'm not fucking around," J.R. snapped. "I feel like shit. Everything's just off. I don't want to think about what we did, but these thoughts just keep coming to my head." He tugged on his hair as though he could pull the images out of his brain.

"Damn," Caleb said, scrunching his face in disgust.

"What's wrong with me?"

Caleb sighed. "It's just the comedown. Usually, last a few hours or so, though I've seen it last up to a few days before."

"A few days? Caleb, I can't go to school like this, I can't play ball. I'm a fucking mess!" He leaned forward on the table between them. "Just get me some more, will you? I don't want to feel this."

"I don't have anymore."

J.R. swore under his breath. What was he going to do? He couldn't function this way. Quickly, his demeanor turned to rage. "Why did you even give it to me? Nothing would have happened if we hadn't taken it!"

Caleb snorted a laugh. "Don't blame me for something you did willingly."

J.R. didn't know if he meant the drug or the girl. He couldn't even say her name in his head. He rubbed his palm against his eye, trying to block out the picture of her crying beneath him. Her trembling lips, her sad eyes begging him to stop.

"Look, you just need to sleep," Caleb said. "I've got my hook-up in the morning and can get you stoned by first period. That will mellow you out."

J.R. thought about school. How could he ever face Grace after what he had done? How could he look her in the eye after that kind of betrayal? He had to get to Ethan before he said anything to her. The look of hatred in Ethan's eyes still was the clearest image that he had from last night.

"Ethan's never going to forgive us."

Caleb crossed his arms over his chest like he was getting bored with this conversation. "Ethan will get over it. We didn't bone his girl. He wasn't even there."

J.R. looked up at Caleb like he was seeing him for the first time. "What the hell's the matter with you?"

Caleb straightened up, puffing out his chest. "Chill, man. Get some sleep and find me in the morning before first."

J.R. stormed out with a slam of the door. He peeled out of Caleb's drive and headed toward Ethan's. He needed to make things right between them. He needed to make sure Ethan would keep his mouth shut so Grace never found out. But he didn't get the chance; he was turned away at the door. He swore under his breath and headed back home, where he was left with only his thoughts and his guilt.

He found Caleb before the first bell rang Monday morning. Without a word, he snatched the joint from Caleb's hands.

"You're welcome!" Caleb laughed as J.R. raced back to his car. He'd woken up that morning expecting to feel normal again, that this funk he was in would have just disappeared. But it hadn't. He needed something to get him through the day. He snuck into the driver seat of his BMW and waited till all the students had emptied out of the parking lot before lighting his joint. He took hit after hit, waiting for the wave of calm to take over. He smashed the last half of the joint out and popped it into his glove box. Fumbling out of the car with a fog of smoke surrounding him, he stumbled his way to English, falling into his desk in the back row. Mrs. Keanly was already at the front talking and gave him a stern glance for being late. He closed his eyes, finally feeling the peace he'd been waiting for. It wasn't X, but it was something. And at least for that moment, he didn't have to wallow in the self-loathing.

Mrs. Keanly instructed them to open their books and he slowly lifted his heavy lids. He reached down for his backpack at his feet when he caught sight of something in the corner of the room.

It was her.

He jerked back in his seat. What was she doing here? She wasn't in this class. His breath became shallow as he began to pant. Oh, my god, was she following him?

"You okay, J.R.?" a voice said behind him. He flinched from the sound, and when a hand landed on his shoulder, he shoved it away. He narrowed his eyes in her direction, but this time he couldn't see her. Where had she gone? She had just been right there, he could have sworn it. He jumped up from his seat.

"Mr. Hudson," Mrs. Keanly said alarmingly.

"I need..." He grabbed his backpack. "I gotta use the restroom."

A few girls giggled around him, and the sound made his head spin. Why were they laughing at him? Did they know what he'd done?

He needed to get the hell out of there. He ran back to his car and slid into the driver's seat. He needed to go home, to be away from her. Away from everyone who knew the horrible, awful thing he'd done. He put the key in the ignition and turned it on. And that's when he saw him.

Chief Tourney pulled his patrol car to a stop just in front of the office, only yards away from J.R. J.R. quickly turned his car off and scrunched down in the seat. He began to shake. The chief was here to arrest him. He knew it. She had told him what they'd done and he was here to get him. *Oh, god,* he thought as he slumped down in his seat, his eyes just barely over the steering wheel. *Could he escape now? Where could he go where no one would ever find him? Should he warn Caleb? No.* It was his fault they were in this mess. He thought maybe he could turn Caleb in, since what Caleb had done was worse than what he had done, and get a lesser sentence. They did that, right? He'd seen it on cop shows. He could be a snitch and get away with a slap on the wrist while Caleb got jail time. But then—then everyone would know what he'd done. He'd have to tell his mom, and dad, and Grace. And what about his football career? Could his dad buy him a place on the team?

Chief Tourney exited the building. J.R. held his breath as he watched him get back in his car and drive away. When the chief was no longer in sight, he let out a long, ragged breath.

He needed to get his shit together before something disastrous happened.

CHAPTER 27

Eight days gone

When Anna opened the door of the mayor's mansion, Nick let go of all of his willpower and pulled her to him for an embrace. He didn't care if they would be seen, or if Jameson walked by at that moment and all of their secrets were revealed. He just knew that he was tired of being strong.

She tensed when he grabbed ahold of her, her initial reaction to push him away. She didn't want to be touched. She'd spent the last few days being pawed at by anyone who could get ahold of her. At least she could count on Jameson to leave her alone.

But as Nick tightened his arms around her, she felt her own release as she slid her arms around his neck and pulled him closer to her. She could feel his damp cheeks on her skin, the sound of his ragged breath in her ear. She clung to him for survival, weeping against him for the loss of his son, the loss of her son, and the unimaginable new world they now had to suffer through.

A soft clearing of the throat brought their attention back to reality. Anna jerked back from Nick to see Sheriff Gibson standing in her doorway. She brushed her palm against her eyes, pressing the tears away.

"Come on in, Sheriff," Anna said, stepping aside, and then asked Nick, "Where's Nora?"

Nick turned his sorrowful gaze away from the sheriff, who walked past them. When they were alone again, he answered. "Home. She hasn't gotten out of bed in days."

Anna sighed, resting a hand on his arm. "Oh, Nick." She hadn't spoken to her best friend since the night Jameson and Nick had returned home with the unimaginable news that the boys' bodies had been found at Oracle Point. Grief was the most selfish emotion. She had been too wrapped up in her own to be strong for her friend.

"Anna," he whispered, resting his hand on top of hers. "I don't know how to be brave for her anymore." He entangled his fingers with her own. "I've been so worried about you."

Anna nodded tearfully. They both knew that nothing would ever be the same. That whatever was happening between them would never be. They both had to learn how to cope with their new normal, but to do it together would only destroy their families more. She didn't know if she loved Jameson anymore. Right now, her heart was only filled with sorrow. But she knew, no matter what she was feeling, that she would never be allowed to love Nick.

Instead of planning graduation parties together, they would now be planning funerals.

She squeezed his fingers and let her hand drop from his arm. He followed her into the parlor where just over a week ago they'd sat with the chief of police, discussing the whereabouts of their sons.

Jameson, who stood by the liquor cabinet, nodded at Nick when he walked into the room. It was only just past noon, but Jameson poured himself a drink anyway, his second of the day.

His head pounded, and his eyes burned from lack of sleep. He kept to himself in his office, afraid to be near Anna, to see her grief. He didn't know how to comfort her when he was filled with such rage.

Anna walked past her husband without a glance and wrapped her arm around Kate's shoulder. Anna may have never cared for Caleb, but that didn't keep her from mourning with his mother.

Kate managed an appreciative smile at her. Unlike Anna, Kate craved the physical touch she'd been denied since Caleb had gone missing. Kate envied Anna and Nora for having spouses and family to bear this burden with. Kate went home and cried alone.

She noticed the way the Jameson eyed her, sideways and with loud accusations. He told her without speaking that this was all her fault. It was always Caleb's doing, never Ethan and J.R.'s, and now Kate had to pay the ultimate price of guilt for the rest of her life.

"Thank you for opening your home, Mr. and Mrs. Hudson," the sheriff said, taking a seat on the velvet couch. "I had hoped for a more intimate setting outside of the station."

Anna guided Kate to a seat and pulled up an adjacent chair. Her eye caught Nick's as he sat on the couch facing the sheriff, while Jameson stood stiffly with his drink.

"My deepest condolences are with you," the sheriff continued. "I know you are looking for answers, for any reason why something this horrific could happen, and I want you to know that we are working with you."

"Thank you, Sheriff," Nick managed.

"With the results of the autopsy, we concluded that the cause of death was in fact due to the fall." A hush of breath was heard around the room as everyone let that sink in. The sheriff continued. "We saw no suspicious marks that could lead us to believe foul play was involved."

Jameson slammed his glass down, making everyone startle and look in his direction. "You're telling me I am to believe that my son drove up to Oracle Point and *willingly* jumped off a cliff?"

"I understand that is a hard concept to wrap your mind around, Mayor."

"No, Sheriff, that is not a hard concept. It's a downright *impossible* one. My son had a bright future in front of him. He had a family who loved and supported him." Jameson choked out the last words. "He had everything he could ever need. He would not throw that away."

Anna teared up listening to her husband.

"Of course, Mr. Hudson," the sheriff said carefully. "But we must look at the facts at hand. We have no indication that there was suspicious activity. Instead, we have three bodies that perished from a fall, and a suicide note."

Nick shrank at the reminder of Ethan's words.

"You have one suicide note," the mayor clarified sharply. "That says nothing about what my boy was doing face down in the lake!"

Anna shivered. The image of J.R. floating in the water haunted her sleep. She wondered if there would ever be a time when she closed her eyes and didn't see him lying there.

Silence hovered as Jameson glared at the sheriff. "You need to do your job and get out there and find out what happened. This is not a closed case, Sheriff."

"Mayor, I want you to understand this will never be a closed case for me. But I also want to make clear that none of you have given us anything to go off of, besides a poorly played football game. If you have any leads, anything at all that could indicate that this was somehow not self-induced, I will jump on it. In the meantime, we are waiting for toxicology reports to come back, that may help explain their state of mind at the time."

Jameson picked up his drink again and shot it back. He needed to stay numb. When he was sober, his mind wandered into places so dark he was afraid he'd never get out. He poured himself another drink, avoiding his wife's disapproving glare.

"Sheriff," a timid voice spoke up. Everyone turned to look at Kate. "I need to know," she started before sucking in a deep breath. Where was Rex when she needed him most? It should have been him here instead of the sheriff. This was his town, his boys, and his domain. She was furious when she learned that the mayor had fired him when he was vital to this case.

"Yes, Ms. Weston," the sheriff encouraged.

Anna placed a gentle hand on her forearm, willing her to speak her mind. Kate let out her breath and said, "Do you know... I mean, could the coroner tell if they suffered at all?"

She felt Anna's fingers grip tighter on her arm. The sheriff gave her an understanding nod. "In the circumstance regarding Ethan and J.R.," he said, looking between Nick and Anna. "The distance of the fall would have led to a zero chance survival rate. Though I have no way of actually knowing, we believe they died on impact." He turned his gaze to Kate. "Caleb's body was found at a shorter, but still fatal distance. The coroner noted that there was no dirt on his hands or fingernails indicating that he may have survived the initial fall and then tried to climb his way back up. So I believe that the answer is no. They did not suffer."

Kate let out a sob as she nodded her head. Anna closed her eyes, finding the only sense of comfort she had felt since her son had gone missing.

The sheriff stood from the couch. "I can be reached at any time, day or night, if you come across any information that could help us vindicate your sons." He looked up at Jameson, who was still scowling in the corner. "A word in private, please, Mayor?"

Jameson huffed as he followed the sheriff to the grand entryway. Alone, the sheriff treaded carefully as he said, "I don't mean to overstep, Mayor. And I respect that emotions are high at this time. But I'd like you to reconsider firing Chief Tourney."

Jameson's back stiffened as if he were being scolded by a teacher.

"He's a fine man and chief, and I know he cares deeply for this town." The sheriff waited for a response, and when one didn't come, he offered his condolences once again and saw himself out.

CHAPTER 28

Two days earlier

S he had been avoiding him, that much Ethan could tell. She hadn't come to school all week. He obsessively checked the halls, kept an eye on her friends, and waited near her locker in hopes that she would turn up. He got the odd eye from those who watched him hiding behind plants, waiting and ready to pounce the moment he saw her, but that time never came. Her friends smiled and waved to him in passing, and he knew in his gut she hadn't told them about Saturday night. If she had, they would be spitting in his face.

Several times at lunch he snuck away to the office to call her at home, but the phone just rang and rang, eventually going to voicemail. Once he even carelessly left a message saying that he hoped to talk to her. He wondered if she ever got the message.

He was in a tailspin, his world turning upside down as everything he'd ever known to be true no longer was.

His dad was having an affair with his best friend's mom.

His best friends had committed the most heinous crime, one that he could have prevented.

He hated his friends, hated his dad, and had never felt more alone in the world. And he had nothing to look forward to. The future he had planned with Caleb and J.R. now looked bleak. He wanted nothing to do with them.

They tried to talk to him at school, but he avoided them at all costs. J.R. looked crazed and paranoid every time he saw him, like he was afraid Ethan would call the cops on him and tell. Caleb was, well, Caleb. A total jackass, acting as though Ethan was the one with the problem. They'd ended up having a heated fight in the locker room after practice the night before that was the unraveling of a long friendship. Ethan didn't care that the Huskies coach was watching their game tonight; he would not be following J.R. and Caleb to The University of Washington.

Sitting in Econ, he couldn't concentrate. He ripped off a piece of paper and began to write.

Lila,

Please talk to me. I've been so worried about you. I feel sick about what happened and know it's all my fault. And you may never forgive me for leaving you there, but I have to try and beg for your forgiveness. I hate them for what they did to you. And I will do whatever it takes to get your trust back.

I'm so sorry. Please forgive me.

Ethan

When the bell rang, he jumped up from his seat and took his folded note in his hand and walked toward her locker. He would slip it through the slats and that way, when she came to school on Monday, she would see it. And then, maybe she would know how horrible he felt and how much he wanted to talk to her.

"Ethan!"

The familiar voice startled him as he stood in front of Lila's locker. He didn't bother turning around. "Fuck off, J.R.."

"Come on, man," he said, leaning up against the metal. He was agitated, scratching at his head like there were bugs in his hair. He looked like hell, which Ethan figured he deserved.

Ethan slipped the note into the back of his jeans and started to walk away.

"We just need to talk," J.R. was saying on his tail. "Come on, I know I screwed up, but you can't keep avoiding me." He grabbed his friend by the arm and turned him around. "Ethan, we have the game of our lives tonight, and I don't know if I can do it. I need you, man. I need to know we have each other's backs."

Ethan jerked his arm from J.R.'s grasp. A damn football game? That's what he was worked up about? J.R.'s ego disgusted Ethan. "I'll be at the game tonight. But only so I don't have to answer to everyone why I missed the big game with the Huskies coach." He glared at him. "But then I'm done. I won't step foot on a football field again with you, J.R. We are not friends, got that?"

J.R. flinched as Ethan brushed past him. J.R. was no longer in charge. Ethan would fulfill his obligation tonight, and then he was done. He didn't owe J.R. his future. He'd never even wanted football to be his path in life. And now, for the first time, he could really think about what he wanted, not what he, J.R., and Caleb wanted.

He pulled his hat down over his forehead and pushed open the door that led to the back parking lot where his car was parked. It was just after three, leaving him a couple of hours before he had to get ready for the game. His thoughts drifted back to Lila once again, as he cursed J.R. for getting in the way of him leaving a note for her. Maybe he had enough time to swing by her place. Would she answer the door for him?

"Ethan Young."

Jesus, what now, he thought. He turned toward the voice, taking a stumbled step back. He knew a look of surprise was on his face; he only hoped it also didn't show the fear.

"Chief Tourney," he said to the man in the patrol car that slid up beside him.

"Ready for the big game tonight?" the chief asked. But Ethan could hear the lack of genuineness in his voice. The chief didn't care about the football game. He looked agitated and tired, his normally smooth skin now covered in a short scruffy beard as though he'd neglected to shave.

Ethan swallowed hard before answering. "Yep."

Rex popped the car into park, leaning one arm out the window, looking up at the tall football player. "I heard your voice on my machine the other day."

Shit, Ethan thought. He knew he should have hung up.

"You sounded upset," the chief continued. "Everything alright?"

Ethan nodded hesitantly. He couldn't think of what to say. He could feel the weight in his legs like they were made of lead. What had Lila said to her dad? He was looking at him like he knew, like he didn't trust him.

"You were looking to talk to Lila," the chief said. "Sounded important."

"I, uh...hadn't seen her all week, and was just checking to see if she was alright."

"I didn't know you knew my daughter that well, Ethan," the chief said with a sideways glance.

His words hung in the air as Ethan stood silent, watching him. He didn't know how to respond. He was afraid if he tried to answer his voice would crack, giving him away.

"She's been sick this week." Rex stared at the boy long and hard, watching the way he squirmed under his scrutiny. He broke the stare long enough to reach for the item sitting in his passenger seat. He lifted the coat for Ethan to see. The one that he had found Lila in when she was passed out on the side of the street.

"This your jacket, Ethan?"

Ethan's face paled. "No, sir." It was the jacket Lila had been wearing that night. It was what she'd used to cover her body and her torn dress. The image of her cowering in the corner, using the jacket to protect herself, came rushing back to Ethan, along with the rise of bile to his throat. He was afraid he would be sick right there in the parking lot.

"Ahh, well, mind telling me whose jacket it is?" His voice was scary calm. Ethan knew that if he confessed that it was J.R.'s jacket, they were screwed. He saw it in the chief's eye. He was suspicious of him. What had Lila said? Had she told her dad everything that had happened, and he was just here testing Ethan to see if he would confess? Would he arrest him right now if he gave anything away? Ethan's palms began to sweat. He shoved them into his pockets to stop the tremors.

"I don't know, sir."

Rex turned his gaze forward. "Well, that's unfortunate," he said. "I was hoping to return it to its rightful owner."

Ethan was silent as he watched the chief sit there, waiting for Ethan to slip. Slowly, Rex lifted his eyes back to him. "There will be no more phone calls to my daughter, do I make myself clear?"

Ethan nodded again, afraid of his own voice. He stood there, trying to hide his trembling as the chief held his cool, hard gaze.

"Good luck at the game tonight, Ethan."

Ethan watched as the chief slowly drove away, his eyes on him in the rearview mirror. All he could think about was that he had to warn J.R. and Caleb. He turned back toward the school on the hunt for his teammates.

The fog drew in so thick it was hard to see the players on the field. But Rex had his eyes glued to the boys in blue. Kate stood beside him, cheering loudly to his silence. He couldn't tell her that something felt off, and he feared it had to do with her son.

The game was not in their favor. They were down by two points, something the Falcons scoreboard hadn't seen in years. J.R. held the ball like it was made of fire, dropping it like a hot potato. When he did get it in the air, it was often off mark or dropped by Ethan Young.

There were boos coming from the crowd, from both sides. Rex looked up at one point to see the mayor, his eyes in full fury, say something sharply to the man sitting next to him, who was decked out in purple Huskies attire. Kate groaned as Caleb once again was called out for another penalty, this time for pulling a player down to the ground by his helmet.

"What's going on with him tonight?" Kate shook her head in disappointment. "He's unusually hostile. He's going to get himself kicked off the field if he isn't careful." She took a drink of her soda and set it on the ground.

Caleb looked up to the stands, meeting the chief's eye and holding his stare. When Caleb eventually looked away, Rex said, "Maybe they're just nervous knowing the Huskies Coach is watching them."

"You're probably right," Kate agreed, standing back up. She missed the exchange between Rex and her son. "He needs this, Rex. He needs something good to come out of this week. You know he called his dad and told him about the coach coming and Dave promised he would be here for the game." She sighed. "But just like his asshole father always does, waits till the last minute and cancels. Leaving me to be the one to tell him. Caleb was so angry. It's like he had all of this pent-up aggression. Rex, he actually punched a hole in his bedroom wall."

Rex shifted his eyes to Kate. She looked shaken. "Really?"

She met his gaze. She could see the concern he had for her in his face. That was one of the things she loved about Rex. His soul was gentle. Even as a cop, he didn't understand brutality. He was the complete opposite of Dave. "I've never been afraid of Caleb. I know he can be a little intense, even rough at times. But when he did that, Rex, you should have seen the look on his face. I got a little scared."

Rex turned his attention back to the field. The opposing team got another touchdown. It was nearing the fourth quarter and we were down twenty-one points. It would take a miracle to win this game.

"Why didn't Lila come tonight?" Kate asked, breaking his thoughts. "Is she still not feeling well?"

He cleared his throat. He had already been asked the same question tonight from Hannah and Olivia, whom she hadn't spoken to all week. Her friends had expressed their concern when he'd told them she'd been sick.

"Yeah, still not good."

"Poor thing," Kate murmured. "Does she have much of an appetite? Maybe I can make her some chicken noodle soup."

He smiled softly at her. She was a good woman, and he felt lucky to have her. Though at times he knew he had keep her at arm's length, at least until Caleb was off to college. He had this feeling he couldn't shake about not wanting to merge Lila's life with Caleb's. Maybe once Caleb was gone, he would feel free to pursue Kate more.

"Thank you," he said.

Looking up at the clock, he felt an urgency to get back to Lila, whom he'd left lying in her bed, her headphones stuck to her ears. She may not have talked to him, but he needed her to know he was there. Her silence screamed at him. He only wished he knew what she was trying to say.

He said his goodbye to Kate and climbed the stadium steps down and out to his patrol car. He drove home, later learning he'd missed the moment Caleb lashed out on the field, tackling an opposing player and ripping his helmet from his head. From there, it would take a team of people to pull him off as he savagely punched the player over and over again, leaving his face bloody on the turf. Rex would also miss how Ethan would then toss his helmet on the ground, walking out of the stadium and away from his team. And how J.R., stoned and confused, would break down on the field crying, not knowing this was his very last football game.

CHAPTER 29

Fifteen days gone

The stands in the high school gym were packed with mourners. Everyone in town came to pay their respects to the three young men who had taken their lives. Everyone but Lila Tourney.

Reserved seating was placed on the basketball court for family members of the deceased. The mayor and his family sat center of the makeshift stage with the Youngs to his left and Kate and Dave Weston to his right. There would be individual funerals following, however, they all agreed a joint memorial would be what their sons would want.

On stage, Principal Harris spoke into the microphone about meeting the boys the first day of freshman year. "You could tell they were something special, and that was before I'd seen them on the football field." He smiled sadly at the memory. "They had a unique friendship about them," he continued. "I'd never met three young men with a stronger bond. They had each other's backs, lifting the other when one was down. I can remember the day I walked into the library during lunch, must have been their sophomore year. They were huddled around the table, much as you'd see them huddled around the field going over a play. But when I got closer, I saw that it wasn't field plays they were discussing, but geometry." He stifled a laugh that others echoed through the room. "When I asked them what they were doing, J.R. looked up all matter-of-fact and said they were studying. He told me that Caleb needed extra help on that week's test. If he failed then Coach said he couldn't play in Friday night's game, and Ethan and J.R. were going to make sure that didn't happen. Well, Caleb went on to pass that test, and many others, due to his and J.R. and Ethan's diligence." He paused a moment, letting the story sink in. "They had a respect for each other that couldn't be broken. They respected their school, their teammates, family, and community. They were leaders who set the standard high for others to follow."

He wiped at a tear in the corner of his eye. "They had their demons, as we all know. Demons that they kept among themselves. If we could learn anything from this devastation, it is to help one another. Lean on each other. If there is something you are suffering from, something you are afraid to talk about, please know that our doors are always open. We will welcome you without judgement, without criticism. I wish so much that J.R., Caleb, and Ethan had come to any of us and we could have shown them the optimism they needed. That whatever they were going through did not have to end in tragedy.

I, along with Mayor Hudson, are starting the J.R. Hudson Foundation to reach kids dealing with suicidal thoughts and tendencies. Together we will honor our boys and spread hope to those who need it most."

Nick sat stiffly, gripping his wife's hand. This was the first he had heard of the foundation in only J.R.'s name. It was a stab at his family and the Westons to not include their boys' names as well. Just another way that Jameson had to make it all about him. Even in death, J.R. was the star.

"And lastly," Principal Harris concluded, looking at the families. "Please let me extend my deepest remorse in the loss of your sons. Know that while their lives were short, they were exceptional. And they will be greatly missed."

Sobs echoed throughout the gym as students and faculty mourned with family and townsfolk who still couldn't believe what had happened. Even Sheriff Gibson came to pay his respects, even though he had never met the boys.

He found himself getting choked up at Principal Harris' words, wishing he had had the opportunity to get to know them in a different circumstance. This will be a case that will forever haunt him. He believed the cause of death was confirmed, that these boys willingly jumped off a cliff, meaning to end their lives. It's the why that kept him up at night.

Principal Harris stepped down from the stage, extending a hug to each family member. Rex watched from the stands as he went down the line, speaking quietly to each parent before moving on to the next, finishing with Dave Weston. Rex took a good, hard look at the man who greatly resembled Caleb. He thought of all of the times when he had let Kate down, and let his son down. Rex couldn't help but wonder if Caleb had been the way that he was because of a man like Dave.

Principal Harris took a seat behind the families, resting his arm on the back of Grace's chair. Coach Mitchell took the stage to share his favorite memories from the past four years and to speak of their commitment to the team both on the field and off. And then it was Grace's turn to take the mic and share her unwavering love and devotion to the boy she called her soul mate. She spoke of shared dreams and aspirations, of a future wedding and children that would never be. Principal Harris had to help her down from the stage, her tears making it hard to see.

As the mic was passed from person to person, it appeared that these boys had been more godlike than human. Death has a way of immortalizing a person's perfections to hide the ugly secret that they were actually flawed.

When the memorial was over, people lingered, embracing one another, not wanting to let go. Rex made his way down the steps, hoping to sneak out of the gym unnoticed. He was harder to pick out without his police uniform on, but that didn't stop Kate from finding him. She grabbed hold of him and held on tight. He saw the way Dave eyed him as his ex-wife leaned on him for support. Rex hugged her back, feeling how fragile she had become in the days since Caleb had gone.

"Are you coming to the funeral?" she asked when she pulled back.

Once they left this room, so did their bond. Each boy would be celebrated in their own way, with their own families. Even the Youngs and the Hudsons felt their ties begin to loosen.

"No," Rex said apologetically. "I need to get home to Lila."

Kate nodded in understanding. "I'm sorry she couldn't make it today."

"So is she," he added. He leaned down and kissed her lightly on the cheek.

She closed her eyes and then opened them to watch him walk away from her and out the metal doors.

She thanked Principal Harris and hugged Anna and Nora goodbye. As she walked out of the gym and into her car, she had a sickening feeling she couldn't quite place. And then it dawned on her. Unlike The Hudsons and Youngs, this would be her last time at Timber Falls High. She had no other children to watch grow older, enter high school, play football, and graduate with aspirations of their future ahead. Unlike Anna and Nora, Kate was no longer a mother.

"You okay?" Dave asked, stumped by her sobbing in the passenger seat. He pulled the car into drive and headed to the burial site.

Kate shook her head. He would never understand her grief. Dave hadn't been a father in years. To him, this may have come as a relief. She would no longer aim her disappointment at him.

She felt a hand on her shoulder from the back seat and felt comfort from Avery's touch. There in this young girl would be Kate's future. In her belly lay a piece of her son. She had the chance to do it all again. And this time, do it right. There was the selfish side of her that hoped that Avery would pass over her rights to her. That Kate would be able to raise this child as her own. But even if Avery decided to keep the baby, Kate knew she would be there every step of the way. Avery needed her, the baby needed her, and Caleb needed her. She would love this child like her own, like she loved Caleb. She would be at every birthday party, every milestone, no matter how small. She would be there when they learned to crawl, walk, speak. She wouldn't miss one recital, game, or graduation. Through this child, she could live again, and find a purpose.

Kate muffled a sigh. "Yes, Dave," she said with a shaky voice. "I'll be fine."

And she would be. But Dave would never know. She made Avery promise not to tell him about the baby. Dave didn't deserve the right to this precious life. He would not be responsible for damaging its soul the way that he had hurt their son. She would not allow it. So she would go to Caleb's funeral, united with the man who caused more damage than not in hers and her son's life, and then she would walk away from him. The only relief she felt was that she would never have to see her ex-husband again.

CHAPTER 30

The day before

J.R.'s father was waiting for him when he finally descended the stairs Saturday afternoon.

His head pounded with each step down. He didn't want to think about last night's game, or Grace's interrogation beforehand. All he could focus on were the words Ethan said about the chief finding his jacket. He was screwed. He knew they would be found out and it was the only way he could convince Ethan to meet with him and Caleb later that evening to discuss a plan.

"Look who decided to grace us with his presence today. The good ol' quarterback." Jameson scoffed as he eyed his son.

J.R. turned to see his father glaring at him from the parlor, and he rubbed at his head. He didn't need this shit today. Not from his dad, not from anyone. He didn't need to be reminded of his failures the night before. His dad had already laid into him once after the game.

"I don't want to talk about it," J.R. muttered as he passed the room and headed toward the kitchen.

"Oh, you're going to talk about it whether you want to or not," Jameson said, catching up to his son who was sitting on a stool at the island.

"Jameson, please." Anna sighed as she set a bowl of cereal in front of J.R. "Give him a break."

Jameson turned his wrath on his wife. "Give him a break? Do you realize the humiliation I endured last night? Do either of you realize the strings I had to pull to get the University of Washington's coach here to our little Timber Falls?"

"Yes." J.R. stirred the cereal around in his bowl, watching the drowning flakes. "And I already told you I was sorry."

"Sorry doesn't fix the damage you caused last night, J.R.!" Jameson yelled, slamming his fist onto the counter. "Sorry doesn't get you on the Huskies football team!"

Anna looked wide-eyed at her husband. "Maybe we should talk about this later, after you've calmed down."

"We will talk about this now!" Jameson bellowed. He knocked aside J.R.'s cereal bowl, causing it to crash and splatter on the ground.

"What the hell, Dad?"

Jameson was flabbergasted. "It's like it doesn't even bother you! You threw away your football career and you don't even care! I don't know who you are anymore, J.R. What the hell happened out there last night?"

"It was one game, Dad." J.R. knew he'd screwed up last night, but it couldn't be the end all. His dad had the connections. Surely he could pull some strings and make it happen. "Can't we just show him the other videos?"

"No, J.R. It was *the* game. It was your one shot. He's not going to waste his time with a kid who can't deliver. I would have killed to have the opportunity to play for a big college team. And you had it right in your hands. And you blew it away, for what?"

J.R. looked away, not wanting to meet his father's glare. It infuriated Jameson even more. He grabbed his son by the shirt and jerked him to his feet. "Look at me when I'm speaking to you."

Jameson ignored the sound of Anna's gasp behind him.

"Let go of me," J.R. sputtered.

Jameson tightened his hold, wrapping J.R.'s shirt around his fist, bringing him so close, J.R. could feel the heat of his breath.

"Not until you tell me what the hell is going on with you," Jameson said through clenched teeth. "What happened on that field last night?"

"Not everything is about football," J.R. spat.

"Football is everything, J.R. If you don't have football, you don't have anything. It's who you are."

"It's who *you* are, Dad," J.R. snapped. "Get your own life and stop trying to live through me."

Jameson moved so fast neither J.R. nor Anna had seen it coming. He shoved his son to the ground, J.R. slamming his back onto the cold tile floor. He could hear his mother scream through the ringing in his ear. When he looked up, his father was on top of him with a look of pure hatred.

"Don't you ever speak to me like that." He would not be disrespected, not by his son, and not in his own home. "I don't want you in this house if you can't be the man I raised you to be."

J.R. looked up at his father, truth spilling from his mouth as he replied, "Maybe I don't want to be in this house anymore."

"Go to hell, J.R."

"Jameson!" Anna cried out as he stormed from the room.

The sound of the front door slamming made J.R. flinch. He picked himself off the ground as his mother rushed to his side. He brushed her off, not wanting her pity. "I'm fine," he snapped.

He shuffled back upstairs, where he stayed locked in his room the rest of the afternoon. When it was time to pick up Ethan, he managed to make it out of the house without a glance toward his father.

Nick Young answered the door, not surprised to see J.R. on the other side of it. But what he didn't expect was his hostile tone and cold stare. It was the same way his son responded to him. Nick stepped aside, feeling a wave of sickness roll over him as he realized Ethan must have told J.R. about him and Anna.

When they returned down the steps moments later, Nick was still there. He wanted to divert any word that could cause Nora suspicion. He tried to play light and easy, hoping the boys would play along.

"Where you guys off to tonight?"

Ethan grabbed a coat from the hall closet and his Falcons baseball cap. But it was J.R. who answered. "Heading to grab Caleb."

Nick crossed his arms and rocked back on his feet. He smiled. "Is there a party tonight?" Nick knew better than to mention last night's game. But he remembered from experience that nothing fixed a hard loss like blowing off some steam.

"Yeah, I think so," J.R. answered. He followed Ethan out to the car who left the house without a word to his dad.

"That was cold," J.R. said as he started the car. "What's your deal with your dad?" Nick was not like Jameson. J.R. thought Ethan had it easy compared to him. Nick would never shove Ethan to the ground.

"Shut up," he answered. "You know the only reason I'm here is to save our asses."

J.R. sighed and put the car into reverse. The drive was silent to Caleb's house. J.R. wished he could tell his friend about the fight he'd had with his dad earlier, or how Grace had basically dumped him for acting weird. But Ethan made it clear that they were no longer friends.

J.R. pulled the car into the drive of the Weston's modest ranch-style house. He honked the horn as he always did and waited for Caleb to pop his head out.

"What the hell," Ethan muttered when Caleb appeared, a case of beer under his arm. "It's not a party," he said as Caleb crawled into the back seat.

J.R. was grateful for the booze. He wasn't sure how he would get through this night without it. He backed the car up and drove toward school.

"Do you have a plan?" Ethan asked.

"No," J.R. answered. He just knew he had to find a place where they could be alone to talk, and Ethan refused to step foot in Caleb's house. He drove the familiar road, letting his intuition take over. He parked the car in the back lot of the school that led to the football stadium.

He could still hear the boos of the crowd from the night before. And smell the scent of blood on Caleb's fist. But what stood out the most was the steely gaze the chief kept on him. He could feel the daggers through his pads. It messed with his head. He couldn't concentrate on the game.

"Come on," Caleb said, getting out of the car.

There was a chill in the November air. Frost covered the metal gate they passed through to climb to the top of the stadium seats. J.R. couldn't remember the last time he'd been in the stands rather than on the field.

He accepted a beer from Caleb and cracked it open. It was cold in his hands and even colder going down his throat, but he knew before long it would warm his blood.

Caleb threw a can in Ethan's direction, only to have it tossed back to him. "No, thanks," Ethan said dryly. He stood back against the railing, facing his one-time friends sitting on the bench two rows up.

"Come on, Deadman. Lighten up." Caleb popped the top of his beer and guzzled back a drink.

"Fuck off, Caleb."

Caleb lifted a brow. "So that's how it's gonna be. You're done with us now?"

"I should have been done with you a long time ago," Ethan smarted back. "I listened to J.R. instead of my own instinct."

Caleb huffed and took another drink, wiping the booze from his lip with the back of his hand.

"This isn't helping," J.R. said, assessing the situation. He needed his friends on the same page. They were a team. "We messed up, Ethan. Big time. Caleb had some X and—"

"I don't want to hear your excuses!" Ethan yelled, his voice echoing through the stands. "Jesus, J.R. When are you going to start thinking for yourself? When are you going to realize that Caleb is fucked in the head?"

Caleb threw Ethan a look of warning. "Watch it, Deadman."

"Stop calling me that," Ethan spat back. He leaned forward, one knee on the bench in front of them. "I'm not afraid of you, Caleb. You think you're big and tough, but let me tell you something: I think you're weak. Just sad and pathetic. Someone who likes to hurt other people to make themselves feel less small."

Caleb jumped to his feet, but J.R. grabbed ahold of him and held him back.

"What did she do to you, Caleb? Huh?" Ethan pushed. "Was it because she rejected you? You ruined her life, you sick fuck. And you act like you don't care. Probably wasn't even your first time."

Caleb growled loudly as he thrashed from J.R.'s hold. "I'll fucking kill you, Ethan!"

"Go ahead, asshole," Ethan taunted. "Beats going to jail. Which is exactly what's going to happen to us."

Caleb roared with laughter, startling J.R. "You are always so fucking scared! You have always been a pansy-ass, Ethan, following all the rules, making it so no one else can have fun." He threw his hands in the air. "No one is going to jail!"

"You don't know that, Caleb." J.R. shook his head, letting go of Caleb's shoulders and sitting back down on the bench.

"Don't let him get in your head," Caleb said with a roll of the eye. "You don't know if she said anything. Chief Puss was just trying to scare you into thinking he knew something. If he really did, he would have done something by now. You both need to chill the fuck out." He pulled out a plastic bag from his coat pocket. He lit the joint before handing it to J.R.

J.R. shook his head. "That shit's been making me paranoid all week."

"You gotta get out of your own head, quarterback. You keep acting up and people will get suspicious. That's when we're in trouble."

Ethan crossed his arms over his chest and leaned back against the railing. "What do you call taking a player down last night on the field?"

Caleb took a drag from his joint, looking down at Ethan. "He was mouthing off. Besides, people expect it from me, right, Ethan? I'm the fuck-up."

Ethan couldn't argue that point.

"Knock it off," J.R. reprimanded. "We need to come up with a plan. Chief knows that it was my jacket. Either she told him or he figured it out. We need to be on the same page so when he comes around asking questions again, we have the same story."

Ethan huffed as he kicked at a rock at his feet. "I'm not sticking up for you."

J.R. leaned forward, toward Ethan. "I know, but she will tell him that you were there."

Ethan felt the blood rush to his face. "I should have never left her alone."

"Listen," Caleb cut in. "Who gives a rat's ass what she says. It's her word against ours." Caleb slapped J.R. on the back. "It's not like your dad hasn't gotten us out of shit before." He smiled. "You're the golden boy."

"You're sick," Ethan snapped.

"You got a better idea?" Caleb asked, taking another drag.

J.R. cracked open a second beer. The last thing he wanted to do was tell his dad any of this. "I don't know, Caleb. My dad is pretty pissed at me right now."

"I'm not saying you tell him yet, just if it comes down to it." Caleb leaned forward in his seat, his elbows resting casually on his knees. "Look, here's what happened. She got sick. Ethan left to find us to help take her home."

"But we didn't take her home," J.R. said. "We don't know how she made it home."

Caleb thought for a moment. "We wanted to take her home, but she wanted to be with her friends, whatever their names are, so we left." Caleb gave a sloppy grin, his eyes heavy and glossed over. "It will work, I'm telling you."

J.R. took another drink. He could feel the alcohol running through his bloodstream. It calmed him. "Yeah, that could work." He cocked a smile while nodding his head. "Caleb, you're a genius."

Ethan's mouth dried up. How could these two be chummy right now, like they'd made a plan to ditch class, not get out of a rape charge? "I can't listen to this."

"Come on, Deadman," Caleb jabbed. "You came here tonight for a story. You need a way to clear your name, so don't act like you aren't happy about me providing you with an out."

"Fine," he said sharply. "We'll go with your story. But don't accuse me of being happy about it."

"So we're on the same page, then?" J.R. lifted a brow to each friend. Ethan gave a short nod as Caleb took another swig. J.R. let out a sigh of relief.

Caleb finished up his beer and then checked his watch. "It's only eleven. I bet Tommy Hoffman's party is just getting going."

"I can't show my face at that party," J.R. scoffed. "I'm the butt of the joke at school."

"Nah, bro. No one laughs at you." Caleb handed him one more beer. "You go there and show them you're still king. They will give you mad respect."

J.R. took a drink of beer, thinking about what Caleb said. He wondered if Grace had ended up at the party and he could have a moment alone with her to talk. He looked up at Ethan. "What'd ya say?"

Ethan glared at him. Did they really think he could be won over? How could they possibly talk about celebrating? "Take me home first."

J.R. looked hurt, but Caleb chuckled at him. "Alright, have it your way. But you'll come around again."

Ethan seriously doubted it. They may have collaborated on a story, but that didn't make them friends again. No words could ever be said for Ethan to forgive them for what they had done to Lila. He didn't even know how he was going to forgive himself for letting it happen.

They got back in the car, and this time Ethan took the back seat while Caleb sat shotgun. He was going on about who would be at the party, like nothing had ever happened. J.R., with the help of the booze, fell right into step with Caleb and it made Ethan sick. J.R. punched the gas and the car lunged forward. He spun out of the parking lot in a squeal of laughter, missing the stop sign and speeding through the red light. He wasn't heading to drop Ethan off, but out of town, toward Tommy Hoffman's house. Ethan yelled at him to stop, to pull over and let him out. And that's when flashing red and blue lights lit up behind them.

CHAPTER 31

The night of

Rex saw the car pass by him in a blur as J.R. ran the red light. He whipped around, heading back in the direction in which he had just come from and got behind the speeding BMW. J.R. swerved erratically on the empty road, and that's when Rex knew he must be intoxicated and threw on his lights. This would be the second time this year he would be pulling them over for drunk driving, and this time he wouldn't let the mayor talk him out of the consequences.

Instead of slowing down and coming to a stop, J.R. sped up, doing his best to outrun the chief. But Rex kept up, staying on his tail as J.R. passed the party and continued down the barren road.

What are you running from, Rex thought. He knew Ethan Young had not been truthful with him. He could see it in his eyes, the way he wouldn't look at him when Rex asked him why he was calling Lila, or when he asked whom the jacket belonged to. The same jacket Rex had found on his daughter while she lay on the side of the road in the middle of the night. Something had happened to her. Something awful that had caused her to shut down, to wither away in her room and refuse to eat or speak of her torment. He heard her cry behind closed doors. He heard her screams when she slept. It was agonizing to him to have to sit back and do nothing while his child suffered. She was in pain. And he had a sickening feeling that the boys in the car in front of him were to blame.

He was close enough that he could see the way Ethan looked at him through the rear window. His expression of terror as though he were helpless. But he wasn't helpless, was he, Rex thought. He had chosen to get in the car with Caleb and J.R., and even if he wasn't driving, he sure as hell wasn't doing anything to stop the driver.

Rex motioned for him to pull over. Ethan saw him and leaned forward to speak to J.R. But J.R. only jumped on the gas, and for a moment got a good lead on Rex. A deer stepped onto the pavement and Rex slammed on his brakes and swerved around, bypassing the animal by mere inches, allowing the boys a devastating lead. When he rounded the bend, miles from Timber Falls, he caught sight of red tail lights turning off the main road and up a gravel path. They were trying to hide from him, but they weren't slick enough. Rex jumped on the side road that took them to the top of Oracle Point. He slid his car into park at the top of the ledge and jumped out of his vehicle. The night was black, with only a shimmer of moonlight to see before him. It was silent besides the rustle of trees as they caught a gust of wind. He flicked on his flashlight and patted his gun on his hip. He circled around, looking for any sign of the car, and that's when he saw the tire tracks that led to the forest. He walked carefully, calling out to the boys as he stepped over branches and fallen debris until there, camouflaged inconspicuously under the tree, was J.R.'s black BMW. Lights off, engine cooling, as though it was trying to hide from him.

Rex crept up to the side. He could see the outline of the boys still in the car, trying their best to stay still as possible. When Rex finally tapped on the driver side window, J.R. jerked back so hard he hit his head on the seat.

"Get out of the car," Rex commanded.

J.R. shook his head, but a door did open. Ethan stepped out from the back.

"Stand right over there." Rex pointed to the side of him. He turned his attention back to a trembling J.R. Looking past him, he saw Caleb, sitting relaxed and unbothered, and it reminded Rex of the last time he'd picked the boys up and driven them to the Hudson home. Caleb had known that the mayor would make their problem just disappear. Well, not this time. Rex wouldn't be getting the mayor involved tonight.

Rex leaned forward until he was eye to eye with J.R. "You understand that running from a cop is a felony? You risk a permanent record as well as possible jail time."

J.R.'s eyes widened. Caleb leaned forward and whispered something to him. J.R. came back to the chief. "I want my dad here."

Rex shook his head. "Your dad isn't going to bail you out of this one, J.R. Now get out of the car."

J.R. sighed and then slowly opened the door. Rex grabbed him by the collar and pulled him out.

"Hey!" J.R. complained. "Watch it."

"Take your hands off him," Caleb warned as he came around the back of the car.

Rex was unfazed. "Keep your mouth shut, and get in line over there."

Caleb muttered something under his breath that the chief didn't understand, but did as he was told. They stood in a line together, and Rex debated handcuffing them right then and taking them to the station, but he wasn't ready to let them go just yet.

"Move it," he said, nodding in the direction of the cliff.

J.R. looked confused. "Why?"

"Take a seat, and stop asking questions," Rex huffed.

The boys shuffled to the edge, taking a seat on the concrete half-wall. Caleb and Ethan sat on the outside, with J.R. in the middle. Rex stood before them. He wanted to be able to look down on them, not the other way around. He wanted them to feel his power as they looked up to him. He crossed his arms over his chest and stared at them. He waited until their strength weakened and he had them in his control.

"You boys have caused a lot of trouble," Rex started. "And yet, time after time, your asses get bailed out because of who you are. You think the real world works like that? You think that once you leave Timber Falls you can screw up and Daddy will rush to fix it?"

J.R.'s face twisted in apprehension. Rex believed without a doubt that J.R. thought his dad could get him out of any tough situation.

"There are consequences for your actions," Rex continued. "You want to break the law, you want to push the limits, then you have to be willing to pay the price."

"I'm not going to jail," J.R. rebuffed. No way would his dad let that happen.

Caleb nodded in agreement. "You're in over your head, Tourney. Once the mayor hears about this, you're toast. You think you'll be able to keep your job if you throw us in jail?"

Rex glared down at the boy. He may have had a point, but that didn't stop Rex from wanting to do what was right.

"Shut up, Caleb," Ethan spat. He turned his attention back to Rex. "We're sorry, Chief. I swear, it won't happen again."

"You want to know what I'm going to do?" the chief said as he eyed each one of them. "I'm going to start by putting each of you in handcuffs. Then you will ride with me to the station where you will formally be charged with drunk driving, minor in possession, and evading arrest. From there, a judge will decide on jail time, financial obligations, and suspension of license. There goes your football careers." He watched as they withered in discomfort. Even Caleb was starting to believe him. "Unless..."

J.R.'s eyes widened. "Unless what?"

Rex stepped forward, meeting his gaze. "Unless you tell me exactly what happened to my daughter last Saturday night."

"Fuck this," Caleb sneered, standing up. But Rex was quick on the draw. His gun was in his hand and pointing in Caleb's direction. Caleb threw up his hands. "Whoa."

"Sit. Down."

Slowly, Caleb did as he was told, keeping his eye glued on the gun.

J.R. started to tremble. "We don't know anything, swear!"

Rex cocked a brow. He lowered his gun but kept it visible by his side. "That's not what she told me."

J.R. swallowed hard. The fear was sweating out of him, even in the cold November night. "What did she tell you?"

Caleb snapped his head toward his friend. What had happened to their story? "Shut up, J.R.!"

Ethan moaned, resting his head in his hands. "This is so messed up."

"It doesn't have to be," Rex encouraged. "Just tell me what happened, and I'll let you go. No one has to know we were up here. No jail time, no drunk driving record. Easy choice if you ask me."

Ethan lifted his hands from his face and looked at J.R., who returned the hesitant look.

"He's bluffing," Caleb said to them.

"Try me, Weston," Rex said, cocking a brow. "What do you have to lose, besides your future?"

"I was high," J.R. started. He was drunk, not thinking clearly. And if it ever got out what he was saying right then, he would just blame the alcohol.

Rex sucked in a deep breath. Finally, they were getting somewhere.

"Fuck," Ethan breathed.

"I swear to god, Hudson," Caleb growled. "Say one more word and I'll kill you."

J.R. looked at Caleb and then back at the chief, who nodded at him encouragingly. Rex could see the burden on J.R.'s face from keeping whatever secret he had in. Rex would remain patient, diligent, until he got the answers he wanted. Then he would decide what to do with them.

"Look at me, J.R.," the chief said, keeping his voice even and level. And when J.R. finally settled his gaze on him, Rex could see the tears in the boy's eyes.

"It was a mistake," J.R. cried. "I didn't know what was going on. I saw Caleb on her and then he told me it was my turn." He looked up at Rex, pleading with him to understand. "I didn't even do it. I swear."

"Because I stopped you!" Ethan yelled. If J.R. was going to tell the truth, Ethan was going to make damn sure he told the whole truth. "If I hadn't shown up, you would have done it, too!"

Rex stumbled back a step. He'd had his suspicions, but never wanted to bring the thought to light. He looked at Caleb, who sat there panting in anger.

"That's not true!" J.R. wiped the snot running from his nose with his jacket, as the tears fell. "I swear. I swear I wouldn't hurt her."

"You're a fucking coward, J.R.," Ethan sputtered.

"Shut up!" Rex bellowed. The boys went silent, looking up at him, except Caleb, who kept his eyes on the ground. "Is it true, Caleb?" he asked him, his voice shaking in rage. "Did you rape my daughter?"

"I want a lawyer," he muttered.

Rex's eyes glazed over, making everything a blur. He ran his arm over his face, muffling the cries in his throat.

"I'm so sorry I didn't save her." Ethan choked back the sob in his throat. "I tried, but I was too late. I should have never left her alone. She begged me not to leave her." He leaned forward. "Please, you have to tell her how sorry I am. I called every day and I even wrote her this note." He reached into his back pocket and pulled out the folded paper. He tried to pass it to the chief, but he wouldn't take it. The paper fell to the ground. Rex didn't want his apologies. He wanted answers. He wanted justice for his daughter.

He pushed the rage down his throat into the pit of his stomach, where he felt it burn. He stood up straight, and drew in a deep breath. He stared down at Caleb, daring him to meet his eye. He kept his voice deathly calm as he asked again, "Did you rape my daughter?"

Caleb slowly lifted his face to look at the chief. Rex saw his indignation as well as his disdain. He smiled just slightly as he told Rex in a cold voice, "Yeah, I fucked her. Just like you fuck my mom."

Rex jumped forward with a loud cry, pressing the gun against Caleb's forehead. His ears were ringing, but he could still hear the wailing as J.R. jumped toward Ethan, clinging to him. Rex held the gun steady against Caleb's forehead. He could see the sweat began to bead on his bald head.

"Shoot me, mother fucker," he taunted.

Rex cocked the gun back. Nothing would please him more than to watch Caleb Weston's brains splatter all over Oracle Point. But then he thought of Lila. What would become of her if he was sent to prison for murder? How would he be able to protect her behind a steel cage?

"You don't have the balls," Caleb scoffed.

Quicker than he could think, Rex lifted the barrel two inches above Caleb's head and pulled the trigger. The sound was deafening, echoing through the vast wilderness around them. It all happened so fast. In the seconds that Rex fired the shot, two things happened. He felt Caleb jerk back before gripping the side of the concrete wall and pulling himself forward. And out of the corner of his eye, he watched as J.R. threw himself on Ethan, the force of his body plunging him backward, pulling Ethan down over the cliff with him. Rex could hear the screams begin to fade the farther the boys fell.

And then Caleb was on his knees, his own scream matching theirs as he leaned over the wall and watched his friends fall to their death. Rex stumbled back. His gun dropped to the ground as he tried to comprehend what had just happened.

Caleb looked back at him, his mouth moving in fast, frantic motion, but Rex couldn't hear what he was saying. What he saw when he looked at the boy was what Caleb had been trying to hide. Fear.

Lila's face flashed before him. And when he looked at Caleb again, a rush came over him as he thought about his own daughter's fear caused by this boy who got off on her tears.

He lunged forward, taking Caleb by surprise as he gripped him by the shoulder. Caleb's balance was wavering as his knee dipped over the edge. Rex saw it again, the cowardice in his expression, and the cold horror of understanding that this was the end. It gave Rex the last burst of adrenaline he needed to push Caleb Weston over the cliff of Oracle Point.

Rex listened for when the screams ended in a thud. He was panting as he leaned over the edge, beaming his flashlight down, looking for any sign of life. But he knew there wouldn't be. Realization swept over him as he faltered back away from the edge. What had he done? He looked around him. The trees spun in his sight; he couldn't get a steady view. He knelt down, his palms resting on his knees. And that's when he saw the folded piece of paper sitting quietly next to his gun. He bent down and reached for it. With shaky fingers, he read the words meant for his daughter. But she would never see them. He tore the paper until the page read just as he wanted and then walked back to J.R.'s car and carefully placed the note on top of the dashboard, where it was meant to be found.

He grabbed his gun and fell into his car. His fingers trembled as he started the engine. He needed to get out of there before anyone saw him. Carefully, and as steadily as he could, he drove home. It took all of his concentration to keep his car between the lines.

His house was dark when he entered. He sat his holster on the chair in his bedroom, going through the motions as he peeled off his uniform and changed into sweats and a tee shirt. He sat on the edge of the bed, staring at nothing, nursing a bottle of whiskey.

Her scream jolted him into awareness. He had been warned to let her be, but tonight he refused to listen. He jumped off his bed and raced down the hall to the other side of the house, where his daughter fought off her attackers in her sleep. She was whimpering when he found her, sweat-drenched and trembling. Her eyes were still closed as she thrashed around the bed. His knees hit the ground beside her bed as he cradled her head in his arms. "Shhh," he hushed as she pushed against him. "You're safe, sweetheart." Slowly, her jerking stopped as she began to calm. He didn't know if she knew he was there, but he'd like to think that the sound of his voice brought her peace. He watched as a tear slipped from the corner of her closed lid. He brushed the sticky wet hair away from her face, seeing her again as he had when she was a child, but also as the young woman she was becoming. What those boys had done to her had damn well near broken her, but Rex wouldn't let that happen. And that's when he felt it, contentment for what he did. He would forever feel guilty for not saving his daughter from the pain, but he would never regret killing those who harmed her.

"Shh," he said again. Her quivering calmed as she fell back into a more peaceful slumber. "You're safe, Lila," he repeated in a whisper. "They will never hurt you again."

EPILOGUE

Six weeks gone

There was a light knock on the front door. Rex opened and gave a slight nod to the man he was expecting to see on the other side.

"Nick," he said as they shook hands. Nick looked gaunt, a shell of the man he used to be. His hair was thinner, his skin hung off him like a loose blanket. He'd lost so much weight his body no longer knew how to carry him.

"Chief," he replied and then caught himself. "Sorry, old habit."

"No apologies." Rex stepped back. "Come on in."

Nick walked through the door, doing a double take as he looked around the empty living room.

"I'd offer you a place to sit," Rex said. "But as you can see, I don't have one."

"Going somewhere, Rex?" Nick asked as he eyed the boxes lining the walls.

"I'll cut to the chase, Nick," Rex said, shoving his hands into his denim pockets. "I'd like to take you up on your offer to buy my property."

Nick's eyes widened. "What made you change your mind?" he asked. "James told me he offered you your job back but you turned him

233

down. You get a better offer?" Few words had been spoken between Nick and his best friend. Nick had lost more than just his son on that November night. But in passing one day, he'd stopped to speak to Jameson, who'd mentioned he'd reached out to Rex to no avail.

"Actually, I did," Rex said. "In Idaho."

"Wow." Nick nodded. "Congratulations." He scratched at his day-old beard. "Kate, now you. A lot of change in Timber Falls."

They let the rest land in the air between them. Rex didn't ask how he was doing dealing with the death of his son. Another man would have, but Rex couldn't bring himself to say the words.

Nick cleared his throat. "Have you talked to Kate since she left?"

Rex thought back to the day Kate had come to him in tears saying Avery had miscarried the baby. She had nothing left for her in Timber Falls, and like Rex, needed a new start. She was gone the next day.

"No," he answered honestly. "I just heard she moved out east with some friends from college. Sounded like one of them had some connections to a nursing job for her."

Rex stood back as Nick walked to the back of the house, looking out the window to the vast land before him.

"Well, Chief." Nick smiled back at him. "I'd be honored to take this off your hands. When are you leaving?"

"Today."

"Today?" Nick was taken aback.

Rex handed him a piece of paper. "Here's a forwarding address of where we'll be staying. I'll give you a call when we get settled in."

"Okay," Nick said, taking the paper from him. A chill went down his spine as he remembered the last time the chief handed him a folded note, with the words his son had written. He felt his throat tighten. "Thank you," he managed to say. "I'll have my guy draw up the paperwork."

Rex nodded. He'd never imagined there would come a time when he would willingly sell off his family's land. He'd always thought he would live out his days here and then pass it down to Lila. But now, he couldn't imagine staying in Timber Falls one more day. He walked Nick to the door and shook his hand again.

"Best of luck to you, Chief," Nick said sincerely.

Rex looked the man in the eye and held his stare. "Same to you, Nick."

Rex let out a deep breath as Nick's car pulled out of his drive. He heard footsteps behind him and turned to see Lila standing in the hallway, backpack on, pillow in hand, and headphones around her neck.

"I'm ready, Dad."

"Me too."

She walked up to him, close enough for him to put his arm around her. She looked up at him with her bright green eyes. The color was back in her cheeks, her face healthy and rounder, transforming back from its hollow form. She smiled slightly at him.

He leaned down and kissed the top of her head. A couple of weeks ago, she'd broken down and shared with him what had happened that night in the cabin. He held her while she cried, being the strength that she needed. He told her how proud he was of her for coming forward, and that she had nothing to feel shame for. It was the beginning of a very long journey to healing. But it was a start. He was in awe of her bravery. She was a hell of a lot stronger than he was.

He never told her what happened on Oracle Point that night, but sometimes he wondered if she knew.

"Thank you," she told him.

They loaded the last bag into the car, a used sedan that replaced his patrol car. The movers would be by in the morning to bring the rest of their belongings to Idaho. But he couldn't stay one more day in Timber Falls. He was ready to leave it all behind and start anew.

He didn't want Lila living in the shadow of the past, always being reminded of what had happened. She needed to be in a place that didn't haunt her at every corner—far away from Timber Falls, and those who lived there.

And maybe that was true for him as well.

Every time he closed his eyes, he heard the howls from the boys as they fell from Oracle Point. He saw the look of terror on Caleb's face when Rex lunged at him, his hands ending Caleb's life. He didn't regret what he'd done. But he wasn't without sin. He deserved for those images to follow him for the rest of his life, wherever he went.

He couldn't escape the guilt. It lived in his bones and pulsed in his blood. No amount of distance would help escape the screams for Rex. But he was going to try anyway. For Lila.

For more of Christa Weisman's novels, visit
christaweisman.com

https://www.facebook.com/C.E.Weisman/

https://www.instagram.com/christaweisman/

https://twitter.com/ChristaWeisman

Made in the
USA
Middletown, DE

74246622R00146